CRABBE
AND THE
KING'S GAMBIT

E. ATKINSON

652 Hogans Rd North Tumbulgum NSW 2490.
www.contempopublishing.com

A catalogue entry for this book is available from the National Library of Australia.

ISBN (Paperback): 978-0-6458077-8-3

Cover design and internal layout by www.bokprint.com.au

Printed and distributed internationally by Ingram Spark.

Dedication

For my Grand Pop, who was a naval man and a wonderful
gardener.

A special mention goes to the character of Trim who is based
on my beloved cat, Sonic.

Chapter 1

Crabbe stood on the burning deck. The sea seethed and boiled around him with the debris of burning ships and the detritus of the battle. He could still hear the muffled boom of the nine guns from the lead ship chasing away the Americans.

As the smoke cleared, he could make out Lieutenant Marshall on the quarter deck, blood running down his left cheek, shouting orders to the crew to trim the sails and heave to! Her several hundred crew duly brought around His Majesty's frigate *Donegal*. This manoeuvre exposed the *Donegal* to one of the enemy ships and it fired, but two shots fell short, the other two sailing over the top of her masts.

Midshipman Blake, not much older than Crabbe, did a jig upon the deck, hallo-ing and hollering for all he was worth, making crude gestures at the attacking ship.

Crabbe felt absolute relief at the departure of the enemy ships. Their first skirmish had resulted in a precipitous retreat by the enemy. He watched the retreating stern and went to assist with unloading the ship's cannon.

Thomas' first duties were assisting Gunner Leader. During the first few weeks on the *Donegal*, Thomas had witnessed a distressing incident that made him wary of firearms for the remainder of his life. While a few crew were stacking muskets in the storeroom, some of the powder stored there exploded, killing them outright. Thomas saw one of the men catapulted out of the hold and thrown against one of the bulkheads, leaving an imprint of himself upon it.

Thomas Crabbe, Able Seaman, had recently joined His Majesty's Navy at the ripe age of fifteen. His late father had been a soldier, having fought against Bonaparte, and had instilled a sense of duty in his only child. Having kissed his weeping mother goodbye, Thomas had spent a night and half a day bumping about in the Royal Mail coach from Ipswich to London and connected with another mail coach to Southampton. He had spent some weeks at a naval training base before embarking on a skiff joining his first Third Rate warship, which carried seventy-four guns manned by a crew of roughly six hundred and fifty men.

His first view of the warship was from the water, the ship's side rising like an enormous cliff above the small boat. Thomas boarded via a flimsy rope ladder tossed over the side. He felt like a monkey, climbing the side of the hull, clinging on for dear life, another lad called Frederick Marley pressing close behind him. Crabbe and Marley had been cadets together in Southampton. Both being the same age and minus their respective fathers, they had become fast friends. The duty officer greeted the new cadets and, after noting their names in the log, directed them where to go below decks to find their hammocks.

The ship seemed to be a heaving mass of humanity; sailors ran to and fro, making Thomas dizzy, although the large warship was a great deal steadier than the small boat they'd just left. An officer stood by a narrow companionway, which led down into the cavernous interior of the decks below, indicating to each boy where their separate sleeping quarters were.

'Quarters' was a generous description; each man had a hammock which measured less than six feet. During the day, the hammocks were put up, including the bedding, and stowed on the bulwarks allowing free movement below decks, but at night there were barely ten inches between each man suspended in their hammocks. Each seaman had to provide a mattress, pillow and blanket which belonged to him–the hammock belonged to the Royal Navy. The boys had to share a chest which contained all their possessions, not that they had many.

After they had settled in, Midshipman Blake collected them and showed them to the quartermaster's cabin. Both boys ducked their heads as they entered Quartermaster Jones' den. As they adjusted their eyes to the dimly lit cabin, Crabbe observed a large chart on a square table bolted to the floor. He also noticed a brass instrument lying on the chart– the likes he had only seen in the hands of an instructor in Southampton. Quartermaster Jones looked up as they entered and followed Crabbe's line of vision.

"Know how to use a sextant, boy? No, well, if you work hard and keep your nose clean, one of the officers might condescend to give you a lesson." With that, he opened his fob watch. "They will be ringing eight bells soon, gentlemen; that means you will be on the next watch from midday to four of the clock." He snapped the watch shut. "I suggest you both present yourselves on deck." He looked at both the boys who stood with eyes wide in wonder. "Come to think of it, do either of you have any experience with cooking? Food preparation of any kind?"

Thomas raised his hand and nodded briefly.

"Ah, Able Seaman Crabbe, good. Well, after you have completed your first watch, return here, and we will discuss the matter of assisting the officers' cook once you have learned the ropes."

With that, the quartermaster flicked his fingers at them. They were dismissed.

Marley went to the companionway stairs, which led to the upper deck, and Crabbe followed close behind.

The *Donegal*, as a Third-Rate warship, was tasked with tracking American hostiles. They were not expected to engage directly, however–if the opportunity presented itself, they would not turn to run from the action. It was less than thirty years since the end of the American Revolutionary War. The two leading causes of the latest conflict were the British Orders-in-Council, which limited American trade with Europe, and the Royal Navy's practice of taking seamen from American merchant vessels to fill out the crews of its own chronically undermanned warships.

The Donegal shucked her lines at exactly midday. The two recruits had soon learned the Donegal's commander, Captain Knox, was a stickler for punctuality. In fact, the captain was a stickler for many things and talking to other crew members during a hurried meal, Crabbe learned that although Knox was hard, he was fair.

"Ya darn't want to cross 'im!" This from Jimmy Weymouth, another able seaman who was talking from vast experience, being sixteen to Crabbe's fifteen. "He might look like he should be sitting in a lady's boudoir but make no mistake, he's a tough 'un, an' he'll flay the skin from your shoulders should ya step out of line."

Thomas digested this information; he felt it might be helpful in the future. Another bit of information divulged to him was that Captain Knox did not tolerate swearing; he had a man flogged for taking the Lord's name in vain. Thomas had been brought up by his mother to be clean in his language but had come in for some ridicule from the other cadets, who viewed his lack of profanity as unmanly. As a result, he finally was persuaded to begin swearing and to counterbalance his newfound habit, he prayed more earnestly at night, asking the Almighty for understanding and forgiveness.

After several discussions and a few weeks at sea, Quartermaster Jones ordered Thomas to the head galley to assist the officers' cook. After a wrong turn into the crewmen's galley, Thomas found the correct one and entered. All he could see was a lot of steam, accompanied by a grumbling monologue in a thick Scottish accent, with a cacophony of crashing pots and pans. He coughed politely, with no response. Crabbe coughed a bit louder.

"What?" roared the ship's cook, a face like a clenched oyster emerging from the steam. The clenched oyster wore a cloth beret in faded tartan and sported a thin ginger moustache perched above a mouth like a slash. "Who the feck are ye?" demanded the apparition.

"Ah, my name is Crabbe, sir, Thomas Crabbe; I be sent to assist you, the quartermaster said–"

"I nay care what the feckin' quartermaster said," snapped the cook. "Ya grab yon tongs an' help me get t'chook outta t'oven, ye ken?" He gestured impatiently to some metal tongs hanging on a hook from the galley wall. Thomas nodded like an automaton, reaching up and grabbing the tongs.

Then the world exploded.

"Ye feckin' arsewipes!" screamed the cook, "ya bluddy ruined ma fricassee!"

Part of Crabbe's brain, not immediately occupied with trying to stay alive, mentally applauded the cook's devotion to his work–clearly, he was passionate about food.

By now, Crabbe could tell that an American sloop-of-war had rapidly gained on the *Donegal*. While Crabbe was trying to work out how large the attacking ship was, the enemy drew broadside and fired another volley of shots; one blew a hole in the galley wall, sending shattered wood all over the captain's lunch and the two cowering cooks.

As the battle continued, Crabbe guessed the enemy ship's gunners were reloading, which gave the Donegal chance to keep firing at the smaller ship's topmast and mizzen. The ramming of the Donegal's weapons could be completed more quickly, given the number of gunners, giving her the advantage in resuming her fire. Crabbe could hear Gunner Leader screaming at the top of his lungs to the other gunners to reload and "Fire!" This they did with renewed vim and vigour.

After what seemed an eternity, the Americans decided the British wouldn't play nicely–so, shrugging their shoulders, they changed tack and sailed off, presumably to regroup and try another time.

As the guns stopped firing, Crabbe removed his hands from his ears where he'd been kneeling and looked over at the cook lying face down on the boards, praying to God and Sonny Jesus that they would be spared, so he could continue cleaning up the "bluddy mess yon colonials hev made o' ma' galley."

The *Donegal* had miraculously only suffered ten casualties. However, her starboard side had been badly damaged, causing Captain Knox to announce that they would head quickly to the Gulf of Honduras to make running repairs there.

As HMS *Donegal* limped along, Able Seaman Crabbe and William 'Billy' MacDonald cleared up the chaos left by the attacking ship after the American vessel's departure.

As Thomas knelt on the floor, sweeping up bits of splintered wood into a dustpan, he became aware of being under scrutiny. Slowly raising his head from his cleaning, he made out a pair of lime green eyes watching him from under one of the cabinets bolted to the wall. The unwavering green stare was set in a black face sporting a white muzzle along with truly prodigious white whiskers curved up at the ends, looking like they had been waxed just that morning. Thomas put the brush down and gently extended his knuckles to the large black and white cat, who condescended to sniff them before hissing soundlessly at him.

"Wha' the bluddy 'ell am I goin' feed yon officers, now?" Billy glared at Thomas as if expecting him to come up with a solution, but Thomas realised it was a rhetorical question. Billy followed Thomas' gaze, and a surprisingly gentle smile broke out on his crusty face. "Aye, so you've met Trim then?"

Thomas smiled at Billy in return and asked, "Is he your cat?"

"Nay, he's yon ship's cat; he keeps t' rats down and, in return, gets t'sleep in t'galley, the noo." It was incredible the cat was still on the ship, let alone in the galley and alive and well after the last foray.

The two men cobbled together some boiled corned beef, cheese, pickles, and fruit. Billy grumbled it was poor fare for seagoing men, yet until they got within sight of the shore and could trade with some of the local people, it was the best he could manage.

"We mun best talk to Jemmy Ducks an' see if he can get some more chickens whilst they repair yon ship."

It was a charming habit of the Royal Navy that the man in charge of poultry on board any ship was known as Jemmy Ducks, irrespective of his real name. However, the man had to be changed regularly to avoid getting too attached to his feathered charges. Crabbe had even heard a tale of one pig who was so popular amongst the crew that she died onboard of obesity, having been fed and petted regularly.

By mid-afternoon of the next day, they arrived at the inlet, as predicted. Some bumboats made their way out to the ship, with various local traders shouting and waving their wares to the ship's crew. While they dropped anchor, rope ladders were dropped over the side to allow the more brave or foolhardy to scramble up and begin haggling with the seamen. The ship's carpenters duly went to work dipping into the necessary stock of wooden boards, nails, glue, and other supplies that any self-respecting warship carried. The sound of hammering was accompanied by shouting, bleating, squawking, clucking, and the general mêlée of goods and money exchanging hands.

Just before sunset, with the repairs mostly concluded, Billy and Thomas were sufficiently victualled to cook a good meal for the officers. Having obtained some goats who were promptly slaughtered on board, the officers and crew dined on goat stew, complete with some yams and sweet potatoes. This repast was followed by caramelised oranges with a dollop of fresh cream whipped up by Crabbe using milk gleaned from the last remaining cow. A saucer was placed on the galley floor, and Trim deigned to creep out of his hidey hole to lap the whole lot up.

After Billy and Thomas had washed up the last of the plates and pots, Billy reached into a small nook to the left of the sink and withdrew a pipe and a tobacco pouch. He proceeded to fill this, packing the contents until satisfied. He lit a lighter from a pot next to the ship's oven then applied it to the pipe, puffing vigorously. After a few moments, he appeared satisfied with the result and sucked deeply once before removing the pipe from his mouth.

As the resultant tendrils of smoke drifted out of both nostrils, he took a sip of mulled wine from a pewter cup and settled himself more comfortably in his chair, looking meaningfully through the smoke that wreathed him like an irascible dragon. At this point, Trim decided to acquaint himself with the top of Crabbe's shoes and, after sniffing them industriously, proceeded to fling himself on top of them and lay there washing his face, much to Billy's amusement.

"Well, laddie, an' ye be helpin' me in t'galley the noo?"

Crabbe nodded, holding a small pewter cup containing beer.

"Ye may not be able to cook t'best food wi' what ye have, but it allus has to be hot, aye?"

Crabbe nodded again, hanging on Billy's every word.

"Ye may as well no' bother if ye dinna have it hot." Billy inclined his head sagely, dragging deeply on his pipe. "An' ye never, ever o'er cook t'meat. Nothin' sey bad as tough meat, like chewing an old bit o' leather."

Billy puckered his thin lips in thought before dropping another pearl of wisdom. "The captain likes 'is puddin', the sweeter t' better." He looked deeply into the stove bolted to the floor, manufactured by Lamb & Nicolson, his rough complexion highlighted in the firelight, sparking the hair in his thin moustache.

"Aye, yon captain has a sweet tooth," Billy smiled; "plum duff be 'is favourite, with a bucket o' runny custard."

Crabbe made a mental note, tucking it in the 'Cook's Law' file.

Billy reached back up into the nook and withdrew another pipe, smaller than his own, which he proceeded to pack with tobacco before handing it to Crabbe. Reaching into the stove to apply flames to the lighter, he lifted it towards Crabbe, indicating he should apply it to the bowl of the pipe. Crabbe did so and, sucking the smoke into his lungs, broke into a violent coughing fit.

Nay take such a deep drag, laddie, let the smoke tickle ya lungs, not drown 'em."

Crabbe nodded, not able to speak while turning a shade of purple.

Billy leaned forward and pounded him on the back, most unhelpfully, Crabbe thought.

"Ye'll get used to it, lad, ye mun get practice in."

Crabbe merely nodded, feeling slightly sick. Trim glanced up at him with a look of concern on his whiskered face, then, satisfying himself that Crabbe wasn't about to expire, went back to washing his ears.

Both men and cat spent the rest of the evening in companionable silence until the bells sounded for bed.

Chapter 2

Once repairs were completed, the *Donegal* left the Gulf of Honduras. It sailed northwest, making for a rendezvous with fellow British ships to attack a battery above Charleston Harbour in the state of South Carolina.

The harbour was a major port of entry for slave ships importing indentured people from West Africa. It was estimated that over forty percent of enslaved Africans came through the harbour into North America, making it one of the busiest ports in the whole country. En route to Charleston the *Donegal* had docked in the Cayman Islands, taking on board around one hundred slaves. The Cayman Islands were under the auspice of the United Kingdom and had supplied indentured people since the 1600's.

On arrival, the *Donegal* found the harbour completely blockaded. At Captain Knox's command, the British man of war dropped anchor before the battery and commenced cannonading with great vigour for upwards of an hour and a half. The *Donegal* blasted a few of the Americans' cannons resulting in their soldiers quitting the high ground.

Crabbe's job was to ferry cartridges to Gunner Leader, who manned the cannon with extreme zeal. His lips were drawn back in a feral grin, crouching over the long gun like a man possessed. During the intense exchange of cannon fire the ship received a twenty-four-pound ball, which lodged in the Donegal's side directly where Crabbe was standing. Luckily it bounced off the saltmarsh before striking the ship's hull or Crabbe would have been blown to smithereens. As it was, some of the resulting splinters of wood flew in various directions, one lodging in Crabbe's leg. Crabbe felt as if his leg had been taken clean off, but just before he collapsed, he shouted out to Midshipman Carter.

"Sir!"

"Yes Crabbe?"

"Sir, I think I may 'ave lost m'leg!" Crabbe tried to see through the thick smoke.

Carter glanced down as well. "By God Crabbe, I think you have!"

At which pronouncement, Crabbe promptly passed out.

Some hours later, Crabbe came around to see the ship's surgeon Superintendent Earnest looming over him, a relieved look on his round face.

"Ah, Crabbe, good–you are back with us." His blue eyes crinkled in a smile behind his horn-rimmed spectacles. "It was a close thing, but I've saved most of your lower leg. However, some of the muscle is damaged, which will, I'm afraid, leave you with a permanent limp."

Crabbe raised his head to try and see if his leg was indeed still there, but Earnest placed the palm of his hand on his chest, gently easing him back down onto the table.

"Trust me, man, it's still there, but it will take a few weeks for you to heal. For the time being you will be confined to sick quarters. Ah, Mr Bates, there you are. Would you be so kind as to help me lift Crabbe onto that bunk?"

Able Seaman Bates, who assisted Earnest in the sick bay, was already tall and broad-shouldered, although only twelve years old. Between him and the surgeon they managed to decant Crabbe onto a low, narrow bunk, where he promptly passed out again due to the jarring of his leg.

Some time later, he came to, at first not knowing where he was. Wooden boards greeted him, being a few inches in front of his nose. For a few seconds he panicked, thinking he might have been lying in his coffin, then common sense prevailed. There wouldn't be daylight in a coffin, nor would there be the murmur of mens' voices.

Turning his head to the right he dimly made out the stern but kind profile of Superintendent Earnest, deep in conversation with one of the crewmen, whose arm was encased in a sling. Being reminded of incapacitated limbs, he raised his head as far as he could without bashing it on the boards and noted his bandaged leg. Well, it was still there, and hadn't floated away during the night, nor been sawn off.

Aye, it was still there, but in what shape? How much of it was fit for purpose? He wouldn't be able to run around a ship now or shin up ropes to haul on sails. What would happen to him? He drifted off into a fitful sleep.

Crabbe spent a month in the sick bay, during which smallpox broke out on the ship. The disease swept through the vessel like a bushfire to carry off over fifty of its crew, one of whom was

Billy Macdonald.

One morning, whilst Crabbe was lying staring at the cracks in the warped boards above his head, he became aware of a slight commotion in the sick bay quarters and, turning his head on the pillow, saw Captain Knox talking intently to Earnest. The latter nodded and then turned, pointing to where Crabbe lay.

To Crabbe's astonishment, Captain Knox duck-walked over to where he lay, keeping his head low to avoid bashing it on the overhead beams. When he reached Crabbe he stood looking down at his prone form. Crabbe began struggling upright, but the captain made quelling gestures at him. Knox cleared his throat, cocking a dark eyebrow at Crabbe.

"Able Seaman Crabbe, is it not?"

Crabbe nodded, knuckling his forehead at the imposing figure of the ship's captain looming over him.

"I imagine the word has reached you of the demise of William MacDonald, officers' cook, hm?"

Crabbe nodded mutely.

"You were his assistant, were you not?"

Crabbe looked up at Captain Knox, who was looking intently at him.

"Aye, sir, I am, sir, I mean, I were, sir, I mean–"

"Enough! You are promoted." The captain waited for his response.

Crabbe stared stupidly at the older man bristling in his uniform. "Sir?"

"Cook, man, the cook. It is the rule of His Majesty's Navy

that any man permanently injured in service is made the ship's cook, and as you now have what Mr Earnest tells me to be a lasting limp, you are therefore transferred to the head galley permanently."

Crabbe's mouth fell open.

Captain Knox looked down at the young man before him, taking in his wispy auburn hair, piercing grey eyes under bushy eyebrows, mottled complexion and spare frame. Some men, he mused, looked middle-aged even when young–he would age well, therefore.

"So, Able Seaman Crabbe, you are now consigned to the pots and pans for the duration of our voyage." The captain turned away, then turned back as a thought occurred to him. "You may choose from one of the indentured seamen for your own assistant." He waved a long-fingered hand towards the part of the ship that housed the press-ganged crew. With that, he bowed as well as he could in the cramped quarters and duck-walked back to talk to Surgeon Earnest, leaving Crabbe gaping after him.

"Oh my Good Lord," Crabbe muttered to himself, "an' jest'ow the 'ell am I goin' to cook for all those officers, with jest me an' some other bugger?"

When he was deemed fit to return to duties and somewhat mobile thanks to a pair of crutches, he picked the 'other bugger' from one of the slaves captured in the Cayman Islands. He went by the name of Sam, but Crabbe would have bet a year's wages that was not the name his mother had given him.

Some weeks before, Thomas had been one of the contingent tasked with vitalling the slaves loaded onto the ship. Most warships allowed the indentured cargo to cook for themselves and Crabbe was impressed with one fellow. A tall, broad-shouldered man who was cooking over one of the small braziers the enslaved people were allowed below decks. He'd been making a soup in a billy can suspended over a frame he'd fashioned from some old hemp rope recycled from mending sails. At the time, Crabbe had inwardly applauded the man's enterprise, but now he realised he had culinary and possibly medicinal knowledge, which would come in handy.

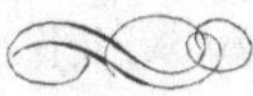

"Cap'n Knox allus likes 'is food hot." Crabbe and Sam were spending their first morning together in the galley. Sam nodded but didn't speak. He towered over Thomas, being six foot three to Thomas' five feet eight and a half, yet Thomas didn't feel threatened by the other man. He suspected that Sam could probably break his neck with one blow; he had a quiet power to him, but it was more a confidence that spoke of strength held in check. Rather than being frightened, Thomas felt oddly safe in Sam's presence.

The Cooking Lesson had begun early that morning. Now, it was approaching the dinner hour and Thomas had imparted all the knowledge he had gleaned from Billy Mac to his assistant. Sam was like a sponge. He soaked up whatever Thomas told him. Several times Thomas had asked him questions to check the transfer of knowledge to which Sam had answered softly and accurately. Added to that, Trim had been in and out of the galley several times, slaloming around first Thomas's ankles, then Sam's. Thomas didn't trust anyone who didn't like animals, but he *always* trusted an animal that didn't like a human. He had no qualms where the other man was concerned–Trim approved of him.

The inevitable time came when Crabbe had to deliver his first meal to the captain's quarters. Present were Captain Knox, Lieutenant Marshall, Sub-Lieutenant May, Master Pearson (the Captain of Marines), Mr Tween (the purser), Mr Earnest, and the chaplain, Reverend Wright.

As Sam held the door open, Crabbe shuffled backwards into the cabin bearing a vast tray which contained a large tureen of turtle soup, some freshly baked rolls and a decanter of the captain's favourite white wine. Absolute silence greeted him. He tried not to rattle the tray as he carefully placed it on the long table where all the commissioned officers were seated, looking expectant.

Crabbe ladled the fragrant soup into the warmed bowls, passing the first one to Captain Knox and then down the list of officers finishing with the chaplain. Meanwhile, Sam placed a warmed roll on each side plate. When the two men were done, they bowed to the assembly and quietly withdrew. As Crabbe shut the door behind him, he heard the captain say, "Eat up, gentlemen, and let us hope that we don't come down with a stomachache!" The men all laughed, and Crabbe felt his face grow hot.

"Serves 'im bluddy right if 'e do get the grippe," muttered Crabbe to Sam, who smiled in return, his white teeth showing in his handsome face in the dimly lit corridor as they returned to the galley.

Silence fell after their departure, punctuated only by the scraping of spoons in bowls and slurping.

The first man to finish was Lieutenant Marshall, a grizzled middle-aged man with wavy white hair who had seen and done it all. He was yet to gain the rank of captain, though his suspicion that he was too old now to achieve that position made him somewhat bitter. He sat back in his chair and, belching softly, declared, "That was an excellent turtle soup. What d'you suppose he flavoured it with, sherry?"

A murmur ran around the table, and after more slurping, Mr Earnest declared he thought it was indeed sherry.

Captain Knox nodded knowingly. "Crabbe has full access to my cellar on board the ship. As long as he doesn't run mad, I, for one, am quite content to have my food flavoured thus." All the men heartily agreed with their commanding officer.

The second course of beefsteak was delivered next. Crisp roast potatoes, orange carrots, and leafy greens accompanied the meat. Over this was a rich gravy, whose smell drifted enticingly up each officer's nose, hinting at a splash of port. Captain Knox declared it was a well-seared steak with a pink blush through the middle. The men unashamedly ate everything on their plates. Mr Earnest even ran a finger around the edge of his to clean up the last drop of gravy.

The detritus of the main course having been cleared away, Crabbe and Sam appeared again. Each man had a bowl placed in front of him. "Puddin'," Crabbe said, and there a dessert sat, steaming gently with a jug of golden custard to accompany each portion.

Sub-Lieutenant May, who wasn't much older than Crabbe,

took a childish delight in the nursery dessert, letting the sweetness of the plum duff soak into the membranes of his mouth, swirling around with the golden custard. Added to this was a small glass of what Crabbe termed a 'sticky', a glass of fortified wine. The officers sipped with pleasure whilst consuming the pudding.

After they cleared away the sweet course, a cheese platter appeared containing a fine English cheddar, a Welsh Caerphilly, and a soft creamy French Camembert. Flatbread, freshly baked, nestled amongst the cheeses, accompanied by some black grapes that a French bumboat had passed over trading with them off the coast the previous week.

At last, the meal was complete, and the officers sat around the table, waistcoat buttons straining. The captain summed up the general feeling in the room.

"Gentlemen, it may not have been the best meal I've ever eaten, but it's certainly not the worst!" All the officers laughed, nodding in agreement.

And so, Thomas Crabbe, at the ancient age of sixteen, was appointed cook to the officers' mess permanently, aided and abetted by his assistant, Sam.

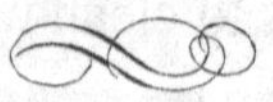

"Them's no good, Tom." Sam nodded at the vegetables lying limply on the galley worktop.

Crabbed pursed his lips, thinking quickly. "Aye, you be right thar Sam, we darn't want the 'ole damn ship goin' down with poisonin'."

"We still got them onions, Tom." Sam nodded towards a netted bag containing brown onions.

A frown appeared between Crabbe's auburn eyebrows.

"How much flour we got left, Sam?"

Sam turned to the storage hold. "Enough t'get t'end of da week, Tom."

Crabbe scratched his chin in an absent-minded fashion. "Roight, here's what we're gonna do. Sam, get thar flour an' grab yon eggs, and we still got enough milk from the goats, good—now, let's see—aye, we've got some hock left, an' those onions. I can make a savoury roly-poly."

Sam stared at the younger man. "Roly-poly?"

"Aye, it is a pastry made with flour, milk, and egg. I allus make sweet ones, but needs must, and we mun make do with a savoury one with the hock and onions." Crabbe wiped his sleeve under his nose, earning a tut of disapproval from Sam, which he ignored.

"We can eke out t'roly-poly with slices served with the rest of the bully beef." Crabbe nodded, mentally calculating how much pastry he would need to feed the officers and allow the other galley to feed the crew. He found multiplication easier than division, which was just as well under the circumstances.

The pastry was duly made and stuffed with hock and onions. Crabbe and Sam then placed two large trays containing several long roly-polys into the big Lamb & Nicolson stove.

Crabbe shut the large door and straightened up, wiping his dripping face. He turned to look at Sam, whose handsome black countenance was shiny with sweat. "That'll do for now, mate."

The two men collapsed onto their stools, which were bolted to the floorboards to keep them stationary during heavy weather and passed a canteen of water backwards and forwards between them.

After a few companionable gulps of water, Thomas plucked up the courage to ask Sam a question he'd wanted to ask for some time. "Sam, you darn't mind me askin' where you from?"

Sam did not answer for a few moments, and Thomas thought he'd overstepped the mark, but the older man heaved a deep sigh and said one word, "Africa."

Thomas regarded the older man. "How the hell did you get to the Cayman Islands, then?"

"I were captured off da coast, place called Quelimane, and took to da Cayman Islands by a man dat talk like you, Tom."

"An Englishman?"

Sam nodded sadly. "Dey want slaves there, so da white folk got dem from Africa an' took dem back."

That explained the colour of his skin and his accent, mused Crabbe.

"How old were you?"

Sam shook his head. "I don't know, only a small boy."

Thomas's jaw dropped. "You mean they took children?"

Sam raised his dark eyes to lock with Crabbe's. He never spoke but nodded slowly.

"Dear God, that's, that's..." He trailed off at a loss for

words.

"Yeah, man, they took da children."

A silence settled between the two men as the enormity of what Sam had just told Thomas sank in. Thomas was appalled. How could people do that to each other, especially taking children? Did Sam's mother even know where he was? Was she even alive? He hesitated to ask questions, but they kept ricocheting around his brain. He chewed his lip, turning the words over in his mind, groping for the right words.

"Where were you when they took you?"

Sam looked at the bare floorboards of the galley. Thomas could tell that he didn't see the planks and nails, but a distant scene in a far-off land. "We were gathering potatoes an' yams, me an' Mandinka." Sam saw Thomas's frown and mimed a woman rocking a baby in her arms.

"Oh, ya ma, right."

Sam nodded once. "Ya, my ma. We were out in da early morning; they are easy to pick. No heat then, ya? So, den, we are pickin' them an' Mandinka she sees a sail."

Sails were not commonplace yet, so Sam and his mother only gave it a curious look and then resumed their vegetable picking. The ship came closer and closer to the coast, eventually dropping anchor in the small bay near Sam's home.

By this time, they had finished their foraging and were returning to their village by way of the coastal path. As they rounded a bend in the path hidden by a rocky outcrop, they walked smack bang into a raiding party sent ashore. The half dozen sailors were accompanied by several indentured men, now under their command. One of the young slaves immediately seized Sam whilst another grabbed his mother, and both of them were gagged and bound. One of the white sailors threw her over his shoulder, scattering yams everywhere whilst the slave tucked Sam under his arm as if he were a sack of grain, and they returned to the bumboat and thence to the ship.

Chapter 3

Yacoumbe could smell himself, a mixture of fear, vomit, and sweat. The burlap sack under his cheek felt like a lump of stone rather than a makeshift pillow.

By his estimation, they had been at sea for three days. Yacoumbe believed his Mandinka was on the same ship, but the others he shared the hold with were children, like him. The youngest, he reckoned, was about five, the eldest maybe twelve.

His horizons had shrunk to this dark, dank space shot through with the occasional beam of sunlight. He kept himself occupied, counting the footsteps on the deck above. In time, he came to recognise individual footfalls. To keep himself amused and hold terror at bay, he gave the footsteps names, such as Oxen Tread, Lead Foot, Dancer, Prancer, Shuffler, etc.

The only break in the monotony was meal times. Gruel with some unidentified protein on good days, hard tack with another source of protein, weevils, on bad days.

After a day or so, the youngest began to sicken. First, griping in the belly, followed by vomiting with explosive diarrhoea. One by one, the children started to die. The crew members would unlock the door to the hold, come in, handkerchiefs wrapped around their faces, grab the deceased by the ankles and drag them out.

Yacoumbe later learned that the bodies were tossed overboard without ceremony or remorse. He counted over thirty companions when he and Mandinka joined this floating hell-hole. Eleven remained by the time they got to their destination, including himself.

After several weeks at sea, the ship docked in the Cayman Islands. He was hauled out of the pit, blinking like a mole, filthy, and covered in sores. Both mother and son went to an auction specialising in human flesh; his mother was sold to a white slave trader, while Sam worked on a plantation owned by an Englishman. He never saw his mother again. He couldn't discover what had happened to her despite enquiring where he could.

"Hey, boy! You come 'ere."

Yacoumbe straightened up cautiously. The young man who had grabbed him, named Kunto, stood before him, whip in hand, grinning from ear to ear.

"You hear me? You come here, *now*."

Yacoumbe dropped the shovel with which he'd been digging planter beds for the Big House. He walked reluctantly over to where Kunto was standing.

"How long you been diggin' those beds?"

"A few hours, sir."

"What? I can't hear you," Kunto said in a sing-song tone,

cupping his left hand behind his ear.

"I *said* a few hours, sir."

"You answerin' back, boy?" Kunto asked silkily.

"No, sir." Yacoumbe stood sullenly. He knew he shouldn't, but he couldn't help it.

"I think you answerin' back, boy."

"I'm not, I–"

"So, you *is* answerin' back, an' arguin' too now." Kunto grinned, showing a gold tooth in his upper jaw. "Time to whip your black ass to teach you a lesson, boy."

Kunto grabbed Yacoumbe's arm, making him yelp, which made him laugh. He dragged him into the barn, where the dry leaves of tobacco rustled at the inrush of air from outside. He pulled Yacoumbe over to a newel post at the bottom of a winding staircase that led to an upper floor. Grabbing a length of rope, he tied Yacoumbe to it, punching him in the kidney when he tried to escape.

Yacoumbe gritted his teeth. He knew what was coming. He'd gone through this pantomime several times since arriving at the plantation. His back had barely healed since the last whipping, but Kunto would have banked on that. The shirt was torn from his back, and at the feel of cool air between his shoulder blades, he braced his forehead against the post. The first lash stung, opening up the freshly healed skin. He bit down on his lower lip, tasting blood. The second lash bit deeper. By the sixth one, he could feel the blood running down his back, yet Kunto showed no signs of stopping.

Who knew where this would have ended, but the door of the barn banged open, and Yacoumbe heard a voice say in a guttural Dutch accent, "What the *hell* are you doing?"

Yacoumbe sighed with relief. Van Kruger, the overseer of the plantation. Due to his size and indolent nature, he delegated the responsibilities to the younger men of colour. Van Kruger was not personally cruel, thank God, sometimes looking the other way, but from the tone of his voice, he wasn't about to ignore what he saw.

"Just seein' to the boy, Boss. I caught this slackin'–"

"Enough!"
Kunto opened his mouth to argue, but Van Kruger cut in. "I said ENOUGH!"

Yacoumbe heard booted heels bang on the mud floor. Then, Van Kruger cut his bonds.

"Go into the kitchen up at the Big House and get those wounds seen to," Van Kruger breathed into his ear.

Yacoumbe stiffly pulled himself away from the post, using every ounce of willpower not to cry out–he wouldn't give Kunto the satisfaction.

Turning around slowly, his eyes met Kunto's. Pure hatred smouldered in the other man's face–that and frustration at having his entertainment thwarted.

After Yacoumbe's departure, Van Kruger rounded on Kunto.

"Don't *ever* let me see you doing that again–no!" He thrust his florid face into Kunto's. "I catch you again, and you go to the next auction, you understand me?"

Kunto nodded sulkily, shuffling his feet.

Days and weeks went by with no punishment. Yacoumbe learned to grow eyes in the back of his head, honing his hearing for a specific footfall.

After nearly two months, Kunto couldn't help himself and cornered Yacoumbe on the upper floor of the same barn. This time, Yacoumbe escaped by jumping out of the window, but he twisted his ankle in the process.

Van Kruger was not happy when he learned of the incident. Yacoumbe would be unable to work for some weeks due to the injury. That meant a pair of indentured hands idle.

Van Kruger summoned Kunto to his office at the Big House. "I warned you," pointing a chubby finger at Kunto.

"Hey Boss, I were on'y tryin'–"

"I know *exactly* what you were trying to do, you piece of shit!" Spittle flew from Van Kruger's full lips. Usually, he didn't pay much mind to the indentured servants, but this man made his flesh crawl. He was evil, taking pleasure in inflicting pain on others. His vendetta against young Yacoumbe was inexplicable as it was unnecessary. Van Kruger couldn't afford to ignore the situation any longer.

"There's a market next week–you'll be taken out on Wednesday."

"But, Boss–"

"No! I've had enough, an' so has the master. You go next week."

Kunto swore in his native tongue, his body language leaving Van Kruger with no doubt as to his meaning.

"Get out."

Kunto clenched his fists by his side. "I *said*, get out. Now."

For a split second, Van Kruger thought Kunto would attack him, but the other man saw sense, for once, turning on his heel and exiting the room, slamming the door after him.

Van Kruger breathed a sigh of relief. He would be gone in a few days.

Yacoumbe was summoned.

"Kunto will be leaving us next week."

Yacoumbe blinked in disbelief.

Van Kruger smiled at the young man's expression. "No doubt you will be relieved to hear this, hmm? Well, then, you may breathe easier now."

"Thank you, sir; I surely appreciate it."

"No problem. Keep your nose clean, work hard, stay out of trouble, eh?"

Yacoumbe nodded.

Van Kruger flicked his fingers in dismissal.

Many years later, when the abolition of slavery became a reality, Yacoumbe would remember the feel of the sun upon his face as he was dragged out of the ship's hold. He couldn't stand to see anyone or anything abused for the remainder of his life. The scars on his back were a daily reminder. Not that he needed one.

A silence fell after Sam's recounting of his capture. Crabbe became acutely aware of the silence in the galley; all extraneous noises had faded during the telling of Sam's story. Thankfully Trim came to his rescue, strolling through the galley door with a giant, dead rat in his mouth. Both men smiled at the sight and laughed when Trim dropped the dead rodent on Crabbe's shoes.

"He brings da gift to you, Tom." Sam nodded at the cat, who looked extremely pleased with himself.

"Aye, a rather wish 'e wouldn't, but he's doin' his job, so…" Thomas leaned over to the benchtop and picked up a small bowl of chopped hock he'd prepared earlier, which he deposited in front of Trim, who began industriously eating. Checking that Trim wasn't watching, Crabbe picked the rat up by its tail and flung the thing out, limping over to the open porthole. He didn't want to hurt Trim's feelings by rejecting his present.

Crabbe heard a soft laugh behind him and, turning, saw Sam grinning at him. "You be soft wi' dat cat."

Crabbe shrugged one shoulder; he wasn't going to deny it. Sometimes he felt terribly lonely in this floating city, just another cog in a giant wheel. His father had spoken rarely of his time in the army, so he had yet to learn what to expect. He might quietly go mad if he didn't have Sam and Trim. The pain in his leg kept him awake at night. Whilst he lay staring at the deck above his hammock, it gave him time to think, which he didn't want to do. He wondered why he'd enlisted in the Navy. What did the future hold for him? Would he be competent as the officer's cook? Would he ever see England again? Soon, he was about to find out…

Chapter 4

The *Donegal* was making her way to Bermuda, hoping to pick up more supplies. The morning had dawned humid but foggy, the sun rising in a blood-red sky, much to the dismay of the crewmen, being a superstitious bunch.

They tracked down the coast, encountering entire banks of fog, thick as pea soup, just as suddenly popping out into dazzling sunshine. As they emerged from one such fog bank, a sail appeared on the horizon.

The lad in the crow's nest shouted, "Sail ho!" rather unnecessarily, Crabbe thought as he sat on a three-legged stool, milking one of the cows. Even he could make out the sail around the brown rump of Hildegarde. As he gently squeezed and pulled her swollen teats, he idly watched the sail unfurl in the breeze, and then he heard a sibilant hiss behind him.

"Jaysus, it's a black flag."

Crabbe twisted his neck around and looked at the horrified expression on Midshipman Carter's face.

"Yew be alright, sir?" Crabbe enquired. No reply came, just the slow opening of Carter's mouth as his jaw dropped in realisation.

"Sir?" Crabbe repeated, pushing himself away from Hildegarde's side, moving the nearly full pail away from him.

"Sir?"

Carter didn't move; his eyes swivelled to meet Crabbe's.

"Ye best start praying, lad, tha's a black flag–which can only mean one thing. Privateers." The word dropped like a stone into a millpond.

It took a few seconds for Crabbe to grasp what Carter had said. His bowels, however, had registered the word before his brain had and gave an unwanted gurgle. Privateers. To use another word, pirates.

The constitution of the United States of America, Article 1, Section 8, Clause 11, states (and still says to this day);

"To declare War, grant Letters of Marque and Reprisal, and make Rules concerning Captures on Land and Water."

Effectively this meant that the Continental Navy could employ privateers, sanctioned by Congress, who could capture or destroy British ships with impunity. These ships usually sailed under a black flag that distinguished them from other American ships.

And one was heading their way.

Crabbe's bowels were not only exhibiting unwanted noises but some more urgent movement now. His first instinct was to gallop to the nearest bulkhead and relieve himself in one of the slop buckets, but he didn't want to appear cowardly in front of Carter.

The ship's bell rang urgently, and he whirled to see one of the crewmen moving the clapper backwards and forwards, sounding, "All hands on deck!" Complete hell broke loose. Where men had been standing and staring, they all began diving this way and that, Captain Knox bellowing orders at them. Panic started to transmit itself from one man to another as they all ran pell-mell around the decks. The phrase 'headless chicken' floated into Crabbe's confused mind as he watched the others darting hither and thither, tripping over each other, swearing and sweating. They wished to get as much canvas up as possible, hoping they could outrun the privateer ship, which seemed to be rapidly gaining on them.

To Crabbe's inexperienced eye, the pursuing vessel appeared to be a brigantine. He could see the fully square-rigged foremast and at least two sails on the main mast: yes, there they were, a square topsail and a gaff mainsail, all out to maximise the available wind. Whereas most of the American navy employed sloops, the brigantine was swifter and more easily maneuvered. Its design hinged upon increased speed and maneuverability, making it well-suited for both long voyages and combat operations. The brigantine was the top choice due to its speed, provided by an abundance of sail area spread over two masts which made it popular with privateers.

"You, there! Crabbe! Don't just bloody stand there gawping like a landed fish!" Crabbe spun around to see Captain Knox screaming at him, puce in the face. He swung about, tripping over the milk pail and spilling it all over the deck. He didn't even notice, so panicked and humiliated at being caught out by the captain. He immediately limped over to Carter and joined the line of men hauling on one of the ropes which led to one of the square topsails.

As Crabbe was at the back of the line of heaving men, he glanced over his right shoulder and, to his horror, saw that the privateer ship was almost upon them. How the *hell* had they managed that, he thought, mentally applauding the seamanship whilst feeling his bowels dissolve in terror.

As the *Donegal* tried manfully to haul to and change tack, the other vessel was now almost abreast of them. The enormous black flag streamed out behind the ship, and he could hear its captain screaming at his crew, much like their captain, who sounded demented as he bawled so loudly.

Unfortunately, Captain Knox's efforts were in vain, as Crabbe could see the grappling hooks swinging backwards and forwards by the enemy crew. *Shit*, they were getting up close and personal; that meant they were in deadly earnest. Crabbe could see one enormous black man grinning manically as he swung the grappling hook in a wide arc towards the *Donegal*'s starboard side. Some of the *Donegal*'s crew vainly attempted to unhook the irons, but they were embedded in the ship's rail.

As Crabbe watched, he saw more grappling hooks and ropes swing through the air to land on the ship's rail or deck. He felt the wooden boards under his feet begin to jar and shudder as the enemy vessel halted the ship's progress. He almost felt her confusion at being manhandled thus, trying vainly to escape her erstwhile captor like a skittish girl fondled by an unwanted suitor on her first date.

Suddenly it was all over, and the two ships were locked together in an embrace as close as two lovers. The enemy crew began walking across from their vessel to the *Donegal*. Crabbe heard their men's ribald shouts and hollering as they took possession of the *Donegal*. Each man brandished a sabre or cutlass of some description, easily overpowering the *Donegal*'s crew, nearly all of whom were unarmed, apart from the commissioned officers.

The giant man that Crabbe had spotted earlier jumped down onto the *Donegal*'s deck. Crabbe had never seen such a huge man. He must have been getting on for six feet five or six, bulging biceps, a huge neck and thighs like tree trunks. Crabbe could see the muscles outlined through his thin breeches, which ended just below the knees. His feet were bare, and he sported a chain holding charms around his right ankle. But it was his face that struck fear into Crabbe's heart. It was heavily tattooed, and his nose was pierced with a large ring, as were both his ear lobes. He sported a feral grin, thick lips peeled back from large, yellow, horse-like teeth. These he flashed at Crabbe, and suddenly the boy remembered hearing tales of men in the West Indies who ate human flesh. Some dim recess of his mind helpfully suggested that he might be asked to drag the large cauldron out of its usual home and, stoking up the fire in the galley, begin cooking the crew. He shook his head like a bull trying to dislodge an annoying fly. *For God's Sake, man, get a grip. The other men won't thank you for going to pieces.*

Another much smaller man climbed over the *Donegal*'s rail

and jumped neatly to the deck. He must be their captain, thought Crabbe, as the crew of the privateer ship began knuckling their foreheads.

Captain Knox looked murderous. He stood, hands clasped behind his back, feet planted wide apart on the dipping and yawing deck, flanked by the other officers with the remainder of the crew bunching up behind them.

The shorter man approached him, stopping a couple of feet before the captain. Crabbe was somewhat disappointed by the privateer's appearance. He'd half expected an eye patch, some colourful tattoos or at the very least a wooden leg, perhaps a hook in place of a hand, but this man sported a bald head, wispy sideburns, a frock coat with carved wooden buttons and a pair of horn-rimmed spectacles. These he pulled off and, removing a silk handkerchief from his coat pocket, proceeded to clean them. He appeared sound of body, missing no essential limbs, nor did he sport a parrot. If nothing else, he resembled an earnest shipping clerk.

In a soft colonial accent, he began. "Good mornin', captain, this sure be a fine ship ye have here. My name is Captain Wallace, an' these gentlemen be my crew." Crabbe thought 'gentlemen' was going a bit far, mainly where the grinning, tattooed Negro was concerned.

Wallace replaced his spectacles, carefully curling the wire arms around his small, neat ears. Returning the handkerchief, he coughed politely and continued, "Captain, I surely do apologise for this inconvenience to you and your crew here." He cast his myopic gaze around the deck, taking in the commissioned officers and seamen. "But I am assured that you grasp the seriousness of this 'ere situation." He smiled gently at the assembly, spreading his hands, palms upwards. "The government of the United States of America has furnished me with certain letters of marque." He coughed again and reaching into his right inside breast pocket, withdrew a letter which bore a large red seal. Peering over Captain Knox's shoulder, Crabbe made the first two sentences.

George Washington, President of the United States of America.

To all who shall see these presents, greeting.

Oh crap, thought Crabbe, we're in for it now.

Wallace handed the letter to Captain Knox, who accepted it gingerly between forefinger and thumb as if afraid it would spontaneously combust. He shook it open and began to read. The other officers leaned in to read as well.

Crabbe strained his thin neck to read over the captain's broad shoulder. He caught the odd word, including 'guns, appurtenance (*what the hell was that?*), goods, property, effects and valuables.' Glancing at the back of Knox's neck, he could see an ugly red stain washing up to the captain's neatly clubbed tail of hair. His eyes dropped back to the document, and he made out '*aggressive actions, except that of wilful murder.*' Well, that was something, they weren't all about to be lined up in front of the mast and shot.

He made the last bit of the letter quickly due to the slightly larger print.

Given under My Hand and the Seal of the United States of America, at Philadelphia, the Ninth day of February, in the year of our Lord, One Thousand Seven Hundred and Ninety-three and of the Independence of the said States, the Twenty-Seventh.

George Washington

Oh, bollocks, 'ere we go. Crabbe could see that the captain had also reached that conclusion by the way his shoulders had hunched, now nearly touching his ears. Crabbe was surprised steam wasn't coming out of them.

Captain Knox cleared his throat with a noise like tearing cloth. He raised his handsome profile to Wallace, who patiently awaited his reaction. Looking down his straight nose, he snapped, "Bloody pirates."

"I beg to differ, captain," replied Wallace. "We are… opportunists, and we have legal protection under that there document, see? Tis all legal and above board, I can assure you." He smiled apologetically again, wiping a forefinger under his nose. "Looky here, we have the right to seize this ship, her crew and all the contents, and there's not a mortal thing you can do, captain. I'm right sorry, but that's the rules."

Lieutenant Marshall sucked air between his teeth. "Now, just a minute, sir, I don't think you understand—"

"Oh, but I understand plenty, sir," responded Wallace with chagrin. "This 'ere ship, she is ours now, and we intend to impound her and all who sail in her. Good brave and honest men privateer nowadays, with the blessing of the United States of America, be you like it or not, captain." His eyes, somewhat magnified by his spectacles, swivelled from Marshall to Knox.

A silence descended upon the gathering. Captain Knox looked like he would like to punch Wallace in the nose, prompting Wallace to return the look, fully cognisant of the fact.

Knox ran his tongue over his lower lip, biting down upon it, thinking hard. Did he have a choice? Probably not, no, no, he didn't have a choice at all, dammit. But he wanted to save face in front of his men, who were looking at him as if he could pull a rabbit out of his arse by some alchemy.

Lieutenant Marshall waded into the debate. "So, Mr Wallace, am I given to understand that you seek to combine patriotism with, erm, well, profit, as opposed to pirates who are but, well, just plain thieves." He lowered his grey eyebrows at Wallace, inviting him to explain himself.

Wallace turned to Lieutenant Marshall, smiling pleasantly as if they were discussing the weather and whether they should take umbrellas with them if they chose to walk outside. "Well, yes, sir, that surely is the case; we seek to take vessels that will return a goodly profit. We are not barbarians, after all." He bowed slightly to the lieutenant as if acknowledging his superior grasp of the situation and his ability to gauge its fairness.

Sub-Lieutenant May, who had been wide-eyed as a deer up to this point, blurted out, "But it's still robbery, so where does that leave all of us? And the crew, what is to become of them?"

Captain Knox, who had privately been having the same thoughts, still believed it prudent to chastise the younger officer, if only to save face. He also wanted to clarify the ideas in his mind that had been flapping around like a panicked bird that had somehow found its way down the chimney and was now frantically looking for a way out. "May, these are the rules of engagement, man. Do you think we have a choice in the matter?"

May subsided instantly under the censure of not just Captain Knox but the other older, more experienced officers.

Wallace, however, took pity upon the younger man. "Well, sir, you have a point there. We do not seek to disenfranchise such men as are able-bodied and do have a use now. Although the ship is impounded, somebody will gainfully employ the crew, and as such, we hope they will see their way to sailing this 'ere ship to a destination of our choice." Wallace removed his spectacles and wiped them again to remove some mist that had started to form on them. Was he nervous or just hot? Crabbe noticed a film of sweat had developed over the bridge of his nose. Ah ha, so then, culley, not so calm after all.

Captain Knox squared his shoulders, seeking to drive home his younger officer's point. "Pray, sir, do you promise to keep the welfare of this crew uppermost and seek to provide a safe passage for them so that when they disembark at the port of your choice, they will be given discharge papers allowing them to seek gainful employment elsewhere?"

Wallace looked slightly shifty for the first time since he landed on the *Donegal*, avoiding Knox's blue, steely gaze. He continued to polish his glasses. This cove is tryin' to buy some time, thought Crabbe.

Eventually, Wallace stopped attacking his glasses with his

handkerchief, folding it neatly and laboriously into a perfect square before replacing it in his breast pocket. Crabbe wanted to scream with impatience. *Just get on wi' it, ya weary, willy of a man.*

"This 'ere crew, as I said, will be employed to sail this ship to the coast of Bermuda. There, certain members will be kept on board the ship, and others will be...released from their service." Wallace swallowed, making his Adam's apple bob, fixing Captain Knox with a direct stare.

Something passed between the two men. Crabbe felt a frisson of fear ripple up his forearms. *Released from service, what the 'ell did that mean?* His bowels began gurgling again as it drew up a list of possible scenarios, none savoury to its owner.

Knox snapped, "You mean press gangs. You will press my crew into unwilling service."

"Well, sir," replied Wallace, "ye do have some goodly crew here; I see a fine-lookin' lad from His Majesty's Navy over your shoulder." To the latter's horror, Wallace's magnified eyes looked over Knox's right shoulder and rested on Crabbe. Captain Knox and the other Donegal officers turned to look at the young cook.

"Well, Crabbe," Captain Knox said softly, "it would appear you are now a prisoner of war."

Crabbe felt his mouth open at the prospect of spending his days on an enemy's ship.

"Crabbe, you are obliged to do your duty to Captain Wallace." Knox imbued the word captain with a note of sarcasm in his voice, which was not lost on Crabbe.

It gave him the courage to answer his captain. "Aye, sir, but very much against my inclination, sir."

Knox, his face turned away from Wallace, gave the young lad the ghost of a wink, which gave Crabbe heart.

Captain Knox turned back. He squared his broad shoulders underneath his greatcoat. "Well, captain, it would appear that I have no say in the matter, so although it pains me, I shall submit the *Donegal* into your hands."

Wallace opened his mouth to respond, but Knox held up his hand. "I haven't finished, sir. If harm comes to any of my crew, I shall hold you personally responsible, and I shall be writing to the Royal Navy to tell them how you apprehended us and the treatment we received."

Wallace didn't appear very impressed with Knox's speech as he shrugged his left shoulder. "I don't make the rules, captain; governments make rules, and I will just be followin' orders."

And so, the business was concluded. Within a day or two, the ships arrived at the port of Hamilton Harbour, Bermuda. There, the goods of the *Donegal* were seized. The captain and officers incarcerated, the crew broken up, and Crabbe, Sam, and Trim (concealed in Crabbe's canvas bag) found themselves transferred and bound for Boston. The ship was named the *Patriot*, which Crabbe assumed was a reference to the recent war with the Americas. Less than thirty years ago they had gained their independence.

He watched the quayside of Hamilton Harbour disappear in the morning haze and glumly turned away to his new galley and duties.

Chapter 5

Life went on much the same as it had on the *Donegal*. Crabbe continued to serve as the officers' cook, assisted by the capable Sam. Trim continued to catch rats, the officers ate well, and the crew dined on plenty of fresh beef and poultry with a good supply of vegetables.

Glumly looking out of the galley porthole one morning whilst peeling potatoes, Thomas realised with a start that it was his sixteenth birthday. It had crept up on him whilst he wasn't looking. His current life was not what he had envisaged when he enlisted. With his permanent injury, escaping was not an option. He was resigned to his current fate. He had Sam and Trim, so it was bearable for now.

The *Patriot*'s captain was Captain Fox, who lived up to his name with a sly and cunning nature. He commanded the *Patriot* with an iron fist but was not popular with his crew, unlike Captain Knox. Men were flogged regularly, and one man, a Willis, so enraged the captain that he was keel-hauled so severely he drowned. The only upside of being under the heel of Fox was that when they captured ships, the crew got a share of the booty. The lowliest able seaman got a cut of any goods seized; his share calculated on a sliding scale dependent on the rank of each crew member. Thomas hid his money in a pocket he'd sewn into his hammock. The *Patriot* docked in Boston in just under a month. Thomas was amazed at the sheer size of Boston Harbour. During the last few years it had evolved from a bustling port town to a booming industrial city. What was once a town of not quite two square miles was now nearly forty square miles.

The crew were allowed a few hours ashore, so after weaving along the quayside for a few minutes trying to get his land legs, Thomas struck out down a cobbled street in search of some providores.

The wonderful scent of fresh hot pastry and spiced meat tickled his nostrils, and turning he saw a plump woman with a tray hung around her neck, the contents steaming in the cold morning air. He limped over to her waving a silver coin. She immediately trotted towards him, smiling.

"Morning darling! An' you'll be off one of the ships now?"

Thomas was vastly entertained by the woman's accent, particularly the way she flattened her vowels. 'Darling' came out as 'duhling.'

"Aye, I am at that."

"Well then, darling, you get one o' these into you!"

Thomas took his change and repaired to a nearby step to eat his hot pie.

Shortcrust pastry filled with meat, suet and onion accompanied by a rich gravy filled his mouth. He closed his eyes in sheer ecstasy. He hadn't eaten anything that good in months. What was it about someone else's cooking that tasted SO much better. He'd baked pies before on various ships, but they'd never tasted like *this*.

He heard a low chuckle, and opening his eyes saw that the pie seller was still there, openly grinning at him now.

"D'you want another one, darling?"

He really shouldn't, but of course he did, taking his change whilst cramming the second pie into his mouth.

After he'd brushed the crumbs from his shirt, wished the pie seller a good day, he headed up a narrow, cobbled lane that led into town. Halfway up the lane, a burly man with black curly hair, broad shoulders and hardly any neck, was unloading a chest of tea from a cart. He turned his head at the sound of footsteps and smiled at Thomas, who was reminded of an affable bull.

"Fine mornin', sir!" the bullish man said.

"Aye, it is that. What 'ave ye there?"

"Good quality tea, from China, no less."

"China?"

"Yep, came in this mornin' off the *Alonzo*."

"What sort o' tea?"

"Lapsang souchong."

Thomas had never heard of such tea. He raised his wispy eyebrows at the other man.

As if divining his thoughts, the other man said, "Would you

like to step in an' have a cup?"

Thomas replied he would, thinking it very kind that a complete stranger would invite him into his premises.

They entered a cool, dark room, wood panelling on the walls, but what Thomas noticed first were the prolific shelves. On each shelf was a tin container, on the front of which was a small, neatly written label. He stepped up to one and read *Jasmine, Fuzhou, China.* Each tea was labelled thus, all in a beautiful copperplate script.

"My wife does the writing; her 'and is better than mine."

Thomas turned back to him. "She possesses a fine 'and, an' no mistake."

"I'm William Talbot, tea merchant."

"Thomas Crabbe, Able Seaman, at your service, sir." The two men bowed to each other.

"Let me get you tha' cup o' tea."

William disappeared into the bowels of the back room, where Thomas could hear a kettle whistle, followed by rattling noises of cups being placed on saucers. He emerged after a few moments to place a tray on an oval table on one side of the room. Then a ceremony took place that involved the warming of a china teapot with hot water, ladling leaves into the pot, pouring on more water, replacing the lid and waiting for the beverage to draw.

"So, you're off one of the ships in port now?"

"Aye, tha's right, the *Patriot.* I'm serving as an indentured crew man."

"Ah, I heard your accent an' guessed something of the sort."

After about five minutes the tea, being judged just right, was poured into cups. No milk was added or offered. Thomas sniffed cautiously and was astonished at the smoky, dense aroma.

William laughed at his expression. "Not what you were expecting, eh?"

"No, indeed." He took a small sip, likening the peaty aftertaste to whisky. He took another sip, enjoying the lack of bitterness usually associated with black tea.

They sipped companionably. William placed his empty cup in its saucer. Wiping the back of his mouth he said, "So what d'you intend to do if you get back to England?"

Thomas thought for a minute or two. "Well, I 'ave some money put by, so t'would be nice to start a business of m'own."

William nodded, steepling his chubby fingers. "Importing tea, p'raps?"

Ah, canny man. He'd seen a business opportunity. "Maybe, ye never know." He smiled at his newfound friend.

"Well, if you ever make it back to Bonny Ol' England, write me, an' we can see what can be done."

Thomas finished his tea and stood up, thanking William for his hospitality.

"No problem, have some o' this 'ere tea; twill refresh you on board." William scooped some leaves into a small piece of paper, twisting the top, then handed them to Thomas.

"Many thanks, mate."

The two men parted cordially with promises to stay in touch when time and circumstances allowed.

After several months sailing in American waters, preying on unsuspecting ships, the *Patriot* was part of a large fleet heading homeward to Newfoundland. The fleet hit the Gulf Stream and the going was very heavy. Even Crabbe and Sam were violently sick, confined to the galley mostly and unable to get up on deck to gulp fresh air or glance at the horizon.

About seven o'clock of one particularly rough morning, Crabbe heard the man at the masthead shout, "Sail ho!" Crabbe heard running feet and guessed the signal was being made to the other cohort members. The *Patriot* was sailing as part of a flotilla of about one hundred and fifty ships, but she was in a smaller squadron towards the rear.

Another shout went up. "A sail on the starboard bow. Enemy ship!"

Crabbe rushed to the small porthole that afforded him a limited view of the outside world and could make out a large ship flying the colours of His Majesty's Navy. Crabbe's heart lifted to see the familiar standard, and he hoped something would develop.

During the next hour, the two ships pitched a running battle–one gaining the upper hand, now the other. The British vessel cleverly managed to separate the *Patriot* from the rest of her companions. The Americans fired several broadsides against the British ship, a three-decker with twenty-two guns. Crabbe and Sam clung on in the galley, valiantly trying to cook lunch for the ship's officers while tossed around like a couple of mops. The going got so rough at one point that Crabbe and Sam had to get out the galley slings. A man would pass these slings around his waist and clip on at either end to hooks screwed into the bench tops. Thus secured, they could still stand upright and cook on the gimbaled stoves whilst the ship tacked this way and that.

The *Patriot* kept dodging in and out of the rough waves, but the British vessel was larger with more canvas and pursued the American boat with grim determination. The British would have known the *Patriot* was loaded with cotton, coffee, sugar, and spices. After several exhausting hours it was getting on for dusk, but the British ship doggedly kept up with the *Patriot*. During a particularly tight tack, Crabbe chanced a quick look out of his small view of the world and saw the name of the enemy vessel as they shot across her bows–the *Providence*. Goosebumps formed on his forearms; was this a sign?

Anyone familiar with the banks of Newfoundland will know that during the summer months, whole banks of fog can form off the coast and then clear just as quickly so that everything is seen at once. The *Patriot* had been harried away from the rest of its flotilla and was now on its own, easy prey.

As the sun rose the following day, the *Patriot* suddenly burst out of the low foggy clouds, and smack bang in front of her were three more ships, come to keep the *Providence* company. Crabbe could hear Captain Fox screaming at the sailors on deck and thanked his lucky stars that he was down in the bowels of the galley and not having his back flayed because the sails weren't adjusted quickly enough to the captain's liking.

All four ships now turned, hot on the heels of the *Patriot*. They huddled together to give chase like a pack of wolves. As Thomas squinted in the bright sunshine, his heart leapt to make out all British colours. He couldn't believe it. He grabbed Sam's muscular arm. "Sam, look, they all be English. I reckon I'd never see thar' ships again, darn't it make a pretty sight?"

Sam forbore to comment on the attractiveness of the ships; he just merely nodded and smiled. Privately he thought that one ship was much like another, and he was still an indentured slave, no matter what colours the vessel flew or the accent the crew spoke with. "Yar, Tom, be good if them ships be English, ya might meet wid some friends."

Crabbe's heart sped up at the prospect that one of the ships might contain some old mates from the captured *Donegal*.

The larger ships began to gain on the lone Patriot, and Crabbe hoped the American ship would be overpowered and seized. But Captain Fox had other ideas and commenced firing at the enemy vessels. The British started their cannonading, and after several attempts which fell just short, a twenty-four-pound ball splintered the stern, landing right in the captain's cabin to add insult to injury. Crabbe grinned as he heard Fox screaming expletives at the crew, threatening dire consequences if they didn't "haul their salty codpieces to and trim the fuckin' sheets!"

The larger ships now pressed home their advantage, two coming up on the port side and the other two off the starboard bow. The now-limping *Patriot* was like a sitting duck, blown to bits by balls and shells from either side. Eventually, even the apoplectic Fox saw sense, and a flag of truce was raised. The British vessels surrounded what was left of the Patriot and herded her like sheepdogs rounding up a stray lamb.

Once one of the British ships came within earshot, negotiations began. The *Patriot* was ordered to sail for another few hours into the harbour's deep waters at Halifax, Nova Scotia. The port had served since 1749 as the headquarters of the British Royal Navy's North American station, so the *Patriot* was in hostile territory.

Just as Thomas and Sam were finishing dinner, the *Patriot* dropped anchor in the harbour flanked by the four British ships, like a skittish girl needing several chaperones to prevent her from fleeing the ball.

A bumboat launched from the *Providence*, and Crabbe wreathed in steam whilst basting several chickens, could make out one man standing proudly in the bow of the tender. So, this was the captain of the *Providence*. Captain Knox was more fine-looking, but this man had presence, noting the bulldog-like expression and outthrust chin. Ah well, there'd be a few more for dinner; turning to Sam, he instructed him to carve some more roast chicken.

Captain Anderson (he of the Providence) sat down to dine with Captain Fox, despite the gaping hole in the cabin wall.

Almost vibrating with excitement, Crabbe staggered under the weight of roast chicken aided by Sam, bearing the accompaniments. A stony silence fell as the two cooks entered. Crabbe studied Anderson through his eyelashes whilst laying out the pewter plates for each officer and their unwelcome guest. No-one spoke.

Captain Anderson cleared his throat. "You there, cook? What is your name?"

Crabbe looked up from ladling gravy over the roast chicken into two dark brown eyes fringed with surprisingly long lashes. Swallowing audibly, he replied, "Crabbe, sir, my name is Thomas Crabbe."

"An Englishman, as I live and breathe! Excellent! I look forward to tasting this delicious meal. What ship were you on before you were pressed into service?"

Crabbe felt Captain Fox go rigid at the word 'pressed' but stoically ignored him to answer the English captain's question. "I were on the Donegal, sir, serving under Captain Knox."

"Knox, you say? Well, I'll be damned, Knox and I were cadets together. You will be pleased to know that Captain Knox is doing well after his release from incarceration and is returning to England."

A grin broke out on Crabbe's face, making Fox turn puce. Crabbe continued to ignore the American. "I will be right glad to hear it, sir, and I hope he was hale when you saw him."

Captain Anderson returned Crabbe's grin and nodded slowly. "That he was, and I hope soon that you will follow–if you would like to return to Ol' Blighty?"

"Return, sir! I should like nothin' else!"

"Excellent! Well, Captain Fox and I will discuss the release of the crewmen on board this ship over dinner, and you can expect to receive orders."

Anderson nodded crisply to Crabbe, indicating that he should resume serving the dinner, which Crabbe did with a lighter heart.

Two days after the *Patriot* was captured, Thomas and Sam transferred to a vessel called the *Renown*. She was a sloop of war with eighteen guns – much smaller than what Crabbe had been used to, but he was simply happy to be back on a British ship. Plus, he didn't have so many men to cater for.

After four months on the *Renown* a mail ship intercepted them. The boat had been intending to meet with the *Donegal* but after learning the ship had been captured, the officers imprisoned, and the crew indentured elsewhere, it had taken some time for people to be located. The mailbag was duly emptied, letters distributed, and Crabbe was delighted to see his mother's handwriting on an envelope.

He inserted his thumb under the seal, breaking it with a snap. Eagerly he scanned the contents. She wrote how proud she was of him, delighting in his friendship with Sam and Trim. It gave him a pang to think that he was so far behind with this correspondence. He would pen a reply that very day.

Then he remembered that the *Renown* would sail to Portsmouth, and Crabbe was to disembark and report to the duty clerk at a designated office on arrival. The letter could wait. He would be home before then. Sam, on the other hand, would enter Captain Anderson's household.

In a private interview, Anderson stated that his wife, Wilhelmina, had a liking for Africans and that he wished to surprise her with a gift. Crabbe wisely held his tongue. Anything he said wouldn't make any difference to Sam's fate, but his wame curdled when he thought of his friend serving as a rich woman's plaything, dressed up in some fancy suit and wig, bowing and scraping to her empty- headed acquaintances. It was totally beneath the African's dignity, but the colour of his skin dictated his fate, and Crabbe comforted himself with the thought that it could be a lot worse for his friend.

Crabbe gritted his teeth, smiled, and nodded at Anderson, receiving his papers with good grace, and requested he be able to take the ship's cat with him.

The *Renown* set sail one balmy afternoon, making good headway with the wind and tide with her, commanded by Captain Walker, a stout, older man with broken veins around his nose that spoke of too much hard drinking.

Once on board, Crabbe found the crew to be a jovial company. Most of them, like him, had been indentured to colonial ships and with the British having defeated them, they were now homeward bound. The *Renown* had a full complement of officers (Crabbe was delighted to note that the young Sub Lieutenant May was one of them), the usual seamen and a good contingent of boys, some scarcely not a dozen years old. Crabbe felt vastly superior, being four years older than them. Still, he promised himself he would not be arrogant and overbearing, and a few of the lads warmed to him, even daring to ask his opinion on the ship, its ways and its crew.

On the seventh morning of their journey, the wind changed direction, and the ocean became wild and rough. Sub-Lieutenant May commented to Crabbe that the foremast was under stress, and the foresails were altered to suit the weather conditions accordingly.

The wind grew stronger that day, and the clouds began to lower, looking like bruises on the horizon as the ocean got steadily choppier. The *Renown* was heavily laden with rum, spices, coffee, and sugar; it could not afford to lose any cargo, so the crewmen were ordered to pull in canvas and tuck reefs into the sails. They did, but the going got heavier and heavier. The officers became fearful that the ship could not weather what appeared to be a full-blown squall bearing down on them at a rate of knots, so around noon of the eighth day, at Captain Walker's instruction, they reduced canvas even more. The storm gathered like a woman picking up her skirts, bunching them together, preparing for flight.

As Crabbe and Sam stood on deck lifting buckets of seawater to wash vegetables, Crabbe spotted a large bird with outstretched wings, hovering like two eyebrows, riding the thermals. With a sinking stomach, he recognised it as an albatross. More than any other, this bird struck fear and superstition into the hearts of stout seamen. To see one was considered ill luck and fear shot up his spine, making the hairs on the back of his neck stand up.

Looking over the starboard side, he noticed the increased swells in the ocean roiling towards the ship, looking green and glassy. He glanced up at the mainmast, which was straining even with what little canvas it had left up. The wind was not steady but blew in gusts, buffeting the ship and dumping copious amounts of seawater on the decks, making them slippery. The *Renown* lumbered along, labouring in such rough seas. The ship was not in sight of any land so after a quick consultation, the officers decided to drop the mainsail altogether, have only the foresail up, turn it onto a stern reach, and hope that they could surf the worst of the storm.

Crabbe and Sam stumbled below decks, groping their way to the galley where they found Trim cowering under one of the benches, whiskers drooping, pupils dilated from lack of light or fear; Crabbe couldn't tell.

"Aye, I know just how ya feel, lad." He reached to scratch between Trim's ears, earning a silent *merp* of recognition of their mutual fear. As if sensing this, the universe decided to take it as a challenge, and the wind started screaming around the masts like an old crone.

Crabbe staggered to his feet and, hauling himself to the porthole, looked out. The sky was purple now, and the green swells reminded him of the glass that the Americans bottled for what passed for beer in their country. He heard the shouts of Captain Walker up on deck, entreating the crewmen to hold fast and watch the foresail. Crabbe sent up a quick prayer to the Lord to deliver them from the ferocity of the wind and see them to a safe haven.

All through that night and into the dawn of the following day, the *Renown* battled the high seas, pitching and yawing. Sam and Crabbe spent a sleepless night sitting on the galley floor, tossed about with Trim plastered to Crabbe's chest, his small head wedged under Crabbe's left arm.

Around noon the ship discovered an island directly ahead and made for it with all haste, going around its tip and into the lee of a rough hill. There she dropped anchors fore and aft in a small inlet and hunkered down to sit out the rest of the storm. The afternoon seemed to crawl past, and after a second fitful night, the *Renown* woke to discover another ship had dropped anchor some yards from them. The other boat was smaller and less well maintained; its davits were dirty, there was a great gash in the port side, what sails Crabbe could see weren't furled well, and lines were dangling down. He squinted to make out the name on the stern–*Alexander*. Something about the ship gave Crabbe pause, but he was so relieved that the storm had passed over the top of them and that they were all still in one piece that after sending up a prayer to the Almighty, he and Sam commenced preparing the breakfast with vigour.

So engrossed were the two men that they, at first, didn't notice the commotion on deck. Whilst coddling eggs Crabbe belatedly became aware of running feet, grunts and thuds as objects hit the boards. Realisation dawned that the noises of impact were the bodies of the *Renown*'s crewmen being overpowered and hitting the deck above their heads.

Sam turned to Crabbe, his eyes wide with alarm. "Tom, that

don't sound so good, there be other men up there." He pointed a long finger at the ceiling above them.

Crabbe stopped what he was doing and listened. Sure enough, more sounds of struggle and shouts from the ship's officers were cut off as if by a hand over the mouth or a blow.

"What's to do, Sam?"

"It's not good; we mebbe go look, Tom." Sam made Crabbe's first name sound like a query.

Crabbe chewed his lower lip, thinking rapidly. Even if they lay low here, whoever had overtaken the ship would eventually find them. Best to grasp the nettle and meet whatever calamity had befallen the ship head-on.

Crabbe looked up at Sam. The two men's eyes met and held. "Yew be right, mate, we should look to see what's amiss."

The older man nodded and, leaning over, pulled one of the carving knives out of a wooden block bolted onto the bench top. He gestured with his chin to Crabbe, who grasped the handle of a meat cleaver and thus armed, the cooks ascended the stairs to the upper deck.

Chaos greeted them. Men lay groaning on the boards, some bleeding and various characters in shabby clothes stood over them, most holding weapons of some description. The erstwhile attackers had one thing in common; they were not white.

One such fellow, tall, with broad shoulders, sweat making his back glisten in the watery sunshine, turned as Crabbe and Sam arrived.

"Yacoumbe," he whispered, looking directly at Sam.

Thomas turned to Sam, surprised at his assistant cook being addressed thus.

"Yacoumbe." The newcomer said softly again.

Sam half turned his head, his handsome silhouette in profile. Crabbe went very still, looking at his friend's expression. My God, he thought, Sam knows this bugger!

Sam continued to stare at the larger man. He replied in a language that sounded like liquid chocolate poured over hot coals, all clicking vowels and rumbling consonants.

The taller man responded in the same dialect. He grinned from ear to ear, but it was not a pleasant smile. Something in that smile made every hair on Crabbe's forearms stand on end.

The two men then had a rapid verbal exchange. All Crabbe could do was observe Sam's body language. His friend stood erect, his fists clenched at his sides, and Crabbe was reminded of a dog defending his territory against rivals, hackles up, fur standing on end, teeth bared and snarling.

Thomas looked at the older, bigger fellow and saw that he was standing his ground, yet there was a flicker in the man's eyes. Shame? Embarrassment? Defensiveness? Crabbe couldn't put his finger on it, but somehow, he felt a shift in the paradigm between the two men.

Eventually their heated conversation ended, and the larger of the two men turned on his heel and strode off down the quarter-deck.

"What was tha' about?" Thomas asked.

"Dat man no good, he bad–he da one who took me with my ma."

"Who are they?"

"Dey marron."

"Marron?"

"Escaped slaves." A rasping croak sounded behind Crabbe, and he whirled to see Midshipman Carter lying on his back, a spectacular bruise beginning to form on his left cheekbone.

Crabbe limped the few feet to Carter and, kneeling, grasped the other man's hand. "Yew be alright, sir?"

Carter coughed, spat a tooth out and coughed again, wiping the back of his hand across his mouth. "Aye, I'll live. Those arsewipes are slaves escaped, an' they hijacked a ship. Now they're takin' this one and all its cargo. We are lucky if they let us live."

"Dey let us live, mun."

Crabbe looked over his shoulder and up at Sam. "How do ye know that, Sam? They won't want us to witness what happened 'ere today."

"I mek sure dey does not harm y'all. You let me speak to dem." Sam turned away and strode after the man he had had dialogue with earlier.

Kunto Bouassé turned at the sound of heavy footfalls behind him. Yacoumbe Kouame came to a halt before him. "You prick,"

Yacoumbe spat in their shared language. "What you say?"

"You heard what I said, you miserable piece of shit."

Kunto took steps towards Yacoumbe until they were practically nose to nose. "You wanna say that again? I beat your black hide once before, I can do it again.

"You reckon you're a man now, eh?"

"More than *you* know, arsewipe."

Kunto swung his right arm back, but not quickly enough for Yacoumbe.

One thing Yacoumbe had learned during his time as an indentured slave on board various ships was that balance was very important. That, and learning how to punch another man effectively.

Whilst he had served on one such ship, USS *Wasp*, an old American tar by the name of Bobby Jones, an ex-bare knuckle fighter from South Carolina, had kept himself amused teaching the young man to box properly.

"You see those dicks swingin' thar arms right back, tha's not the way it's done, boy, you hear me now? All you gotta do is bring you hand to you ribs an' then give the other guy a quick jab."

Yacoumbe had practised for hours with Bobby until he was lightning fast. Now he dodged the larger man's blow, drew his hand back six inches and delivered a short sharp jab to Kunto's nose. The other man's head snapped back and blood gushed down over his upper lip.

"That was for my ma, you bastard," he spat.

Kunto howled with pain, grabbing his nose which, although not broken was bleeding profusely.

"Now, you listen to me. You're gonna let these people go an' take me with you."

"Why the *hell* would we do that?" Yacoumbe barely made out Kunto's muffled voice.

"'Cos you don't know how to sail a ship, mun, I know more than you do, and it's the least you can do after what you did to me all those years ago."

Kunto wiped the back of his hand under his nose, looking dispassionately at the resultant blood. "Do I have a choice?"

"No, and I will watch you like a hawk every moment we're together on this ship."

After about half an hour Sam returned and, after saluting the officers being held at the end of several cutlasses, informed them that he had negotiated the *Renown*'s surviving crew in exchange for the ship and all its cargo. Captain Walker bristled at this, calling the marrons some choice words until one of them hit him in the face with the handle of his sabre.

Several tenders were lowered from the *Renown*, and whilst the officers organised this, Crabbe sidled away from the action and quietly limped down below to the galley. There he found his kit bag into which he packed his Bible, his set of knives (nestled in a cloth bag made for the purpose), his small pillow, some clothing and one black and white cat, who went in last so he could breathe.

Crabbe then quietly retraced his steps and emerged on deck

just as the last bumboat was lowered from its davits. He gently swung his kit bag over his shoulder, feeling Trim wriggle in protest at the confined space and movement.

Sam smiled as Crabbe corkscrewed towards him, his eyes cutting to the kit bag. He was probably the only man present who suspected what precious cargo Crabbe carried.

"You be goin' now, Tom." Sam fixed his dark eyes upon Crabbe. "No place for you now, mun."

Crabbe looked at his friend, noting his defiant stance. "Yew be staying with them, then?"

Sam nodded once.

Crabbe understood. He extended his right hand out to Sam. "Good luck, mate."

Sam reached out a hand and grabbed Crabbe's, pulling him in so that the two men stood, forearm to forearm. Sam looked at Crabbe intently, raised his left hand, and gently placed it on his forehead.

"You be livin' a long time, mun, a laaaannng time." Sam nodded slowly. He drew his hand down until it rested over Crabbe's eyes. "But you be seein' no more."

Crabbe felt a cold finger pass gently down his spine, from the nape of his neck to what would have been the tip of his tail had he had one. He stepped back out of Sam's reach and looked at his face.

"Wha's ya real name, culley?" he asked softly.

The whites of Sam's eyes were yellowed and bloodshot, but he looked at Crabbe with an unwavering stare.

"I be called Yacoumbe Kouame. I the fourth man in our line.

My Pa an' his Pa an' his Pa be medicine men' once we were respected. They are…lost to me." Crabbe saw Sam's adam's apple bob once as he swallowed hard. "They are…lost." Just one word, but in that word was a world of pain–separation, fear, worry, grief, mourning and, in the end, resignation.

"You go now," Yacoumbe repeated. "And you don't look back, mun, we are takin' da ship."

Crabbe nodded once. Yacoumbe and the marrons that had stormed the *Renown* would sail her, who knew where, but to safer shores and possibly to freedom. He wished them well.

"Go with God, mate," he said softly.

Yacoumbe smiled, showing his perfect white teeth. "I will no be seein' your God, but I hev mine wid me."

Crabbe smiled up at him. "Well, mate, whoever ya God is, I 'ope he knows what he's doin' lettin' *yew* lose on t'world."

The two men let go of each other's hands. Yacoumbe nodded briefly, then he stood back, saluted Crabbe, turned on his heel and disappeared back into the melée that was now the departing vessel containing the rebel crew of the *Renown*.

Crabbe barrelled quickly across the deck and, clinging one-handed to the rope ladder, dangled precariously down the massive side of the ship before dropping into the waiting longboat.

"Cast off!" Captain Walker shouted hoarsely to Sub-Lieutenant May, who responded with enthusiasm. The seamen began rowing for all they were worth to the *Alexander*, trying to put as much distance between them and the beleaguered mother ship.

Crabbe looked back at the Renown. The marrons were rushing to and fro, sloppily hoisting sails, making Captain Walker tut loudly, despite the swelling around his mouth.

After about twenty minutes, the bumboats reached the *Alexander*, and the men began climbing the rope ladders that had been left hanging over the sides. By the time all the boats had joined their new ship, the *Renown* had hauled anchors, turned about, and was departing the inlet. Crabbe watched her leave, willing Sam–Yacoumbe–the best of luck and a happier life. Gently holding the kit bag to his chest, he stumped across the deck to the companionway stairs to descend below decks and find the galley.

Chapter 6

The *Alexander* docked in Portsmouth a week later, having made good speed despite her smaller rig and reduced crew. On arrival, the usual rushing hither and thither accompanied a large ship's unpacking and disembarkation of her crew.

Able Seaman Crabbe, no longer the ship's cook, packed the kit bag with his few worldly goods, including his pillow and navy-issue blanket. Whilst he did this, Trim sat upon a wooden chest, regarding him gravely. Thomas avoided meeting his eye. He could tell by the droop of Trim's whiskers that the cat was not happy about the impending departure of Crabbe. Thomas kept telling himself that Trim was the ship's cat and, therefore, the property of His Majesty's Navy. However, with the demise of Billy, the capture of Captain Knox and the other commissioned officers of the *Donegal*, their stint on the *Patriot*, the seizure of the *Renown* and their narrow escape onto the *Alexander*, the lines as to Trim's ownership had become somewhat blurred.

After a short while, Crabbe finished packing and stood upright, checking that he had everything, which he knew very well he did, but he didn't want to face Trim and their impending separation. He fiddled with the drawstring of his kit bag for the umpteenth time, feeling waves of disappointment emanating from the cat. *Courage, man.* Finally, he looked Trim square in the eyes. Trim returned the look, Crabbe swearing that his whiskers had drooped even further, a look of dull resignation settling upon the animal's face.

Crabbe could still hear the feet of the crew running back and forth on the decks above, shouting and swearing, getting in each other's way as the controlled chaos of the ship's decommissioning continued. He hefted the kit bag more securely onto his thin shoulder, noting that the bag still had quite a bit of space left after he had stuffed his meagre possessions into it. Yes, a bit of room left, about the size of a medium cat. A glint showed in his grey eyes, and he swore an answering gleam was reflected in Trim's green ones.

Crabbe slid his bag onto the floor, opening the drawstring neck. He took two steps towards the cat, gently lifting him off the chest, gave him a hug, a scratch behind the ear eliciting a soft purr, and, turning, fed him into the top of the bag. He half expected Trim to hiss and jump out, but he promptly settled on top of Crabbe's clothes as he had when they'd transferred to other ships. Would Crabbe get on with it before somebody came by and raised a hue and cry? Crabbe gently pulled the drawstrings together, leaving a space to allow air to come in. He lifted the bag, more gently this time, and positioned it on his shoulder. Tucking his rolled-up mattress under his other arm, he left the below decks climbing the companionway stairs, feeling like a thief.

Once on deck, he strolled in what he hoped was a nonchalant fashion towards the gangplank, which now sat upon the stone quayside. No one stopped him, everyone was too busy with their duties and packing up their belongings. Sweating slightly despite the overcast, windy day, he ambled down the gangplank, feeling a slight movement in the bag over his shoulder–he panicked, *not now, not bloody now*. The movement stopped, presumably as Trim found a more comfortable position inside the bag, and Crabbe heaved a sigh of relief as his buckled shoes landed on stone. He slowly made his way down the crowded quayside, dodging barrels of salt tack, water, salted fish, crates of chickens, and other victuals whilst seagulls screamed overhead.

Crabbe continued slowly towards the row of houses squatting at the end of the quayside, taking in the signs swinging gently in the breeze above each doorway. The second from the last building sported a peeling painting depicting an almost cartoon-like portrait of Lord Nelson, complete with an eyepatch and missing arm accompanied by a totally inaccurate brig sailing behind him. This must be the boarding house that Billy had mentioned long ago on the *Donegal*; it didn't look like much from the outside, but Thomas suddenly smelt the unmistakable scent of roast beef and Yorkshire pudding wafting out of an open window. That settled it then; he'd chance it, still trying to figure out what he would do with the cat.

Thomas was not a particularly tall man, but he still had to duck his head beneath the lintel into the cool interior of the boarding house. He stood momentarily, waiting for his eyes to adjust to the gloom. Three faces turned to greet him with expressions ranging from suspicion to surprise. A middle-aged lady of ample bosom stood behind the bar, whose optics shone brightly in the light cast by several candles which hung in sconces from the walls. Two ruddy-faced sailors perched on wooden stools, both men of indeterminate age, one of whom was missing several essential teeth, sporting some spectacular tattoos upon his forearms.

An awkward silence descended upon the taproom. Just as Thomas began formulating some introduction in his head, the excellent landlady lifted the hatch that fitted into the countertop and came teetering towards him as if she might go careering across the room at any moment. Thankfully, she came to a halt before Thomas and smiled warmly at him, showing a dimple on her right cheek.

"Yew must be as one of them boys off the *Alexander*, now.

Thomas nodded.

"Well, tha's good now, yes, very good, now come this way, young sir, and this will be ya bag now? Please to meet yew, young sir; now if yew'll follow me down 'ere, an' up these 'ere stairs, yes, very good, mind those barrels thar young sir, don't want yew to dirty ya breeches, now."

The landlady continued her cheerful monologue up the stairs, leading the way, allowing Thomas to view her pumpkin-shaped backside as she huffed and puffed her way up to the next floor. She led the way down to the back of the building to a door painted in mission brown, which, once unlocked, revealed a small, furnished room consisting of a single iron-framed bed, a small bedside table, a chest of drawers with a basin and ewer accompanied by a chair.

"It's not much to look at, but it is clean and quiet, bein' at t'back." The landlady dimpled at Thomas again, and he returned the smile.

"Missus, compared to my bunk on board the *Alexander*, it is heaven."

The excellent landlady beamed at Thomas. "Well, I be leavin' yew now to settle in. Supper be around seven o'clock; it's roast beef and Yorkshire puddin' with vegetables."

Having confirmed his culinary guess, Thomas nodded enthusiastically. He paid the excellent lady a few coins, stating he would stay most of the week and would like a bit of supper.

Having pocketed the coins, she left, shutting the door behind her with a soft snick.

Thomas dumped his mattress upon the floor and, gently lowering the bag to join it, cautiously opened the top. Trim's face greeted him, whiskers quivering, making a silent *merp* of protest at being so rudely cooped up in this bag, and would he just let him out NOW, please? Thomas watched as Trim went straight to the window and hopped on the windowsill. Thomas was glad that the room was at the back and that the only people who might see Trim in the window would be the odd scullery maid out in the yard below, who would probably be too busy to glance up and see the cat, nose pressed to the mullioned glass.

"Well, lad, we are 'ere now, an' yon landlady won't be disturbin' us as long as we're allus quiet." Trim took no notice of Thomas, gazing out the window, his tail swishing to and fro. Shrugging his shoulders, Thomas picked up his bedroll, swapped the pillow on the bed for his own, and unpacked his few possessions, placing them on the chest of drawers. Thus settled in, he thought he would walk around the local market to try and source a bowl and some food for Trim.

Giving the cat a quick scratch on the top of his head, he tucked his now empty bag under his arm and left, carefully locking the door with the landlady's key. Down the stairs, through the taproom, nodding to the two sailors still propping up the bar and out the low door into the street. Turning left, he went to the awnings and stalls he had espied earlier when walking to the boarding house.

After about half an hour, his shopping consisted of a small tin bowl for Trim's water, some boiled corn beef wrapped in waxed paper, and some good quality oat biscuits that he could break into the corned beef. Trim loved corned beef; his diet had been supplemented with it on board the various ships, along with leftovers from whatever Thomas and Sam had cooked for the ship's officers.

Crabbe walked slowly back towards the boarding house, his leg paining him, and he heard the clock in the customs house crustily chime the half hour; half past six, then; time to return, give Trim his dinner, wash his face and hands and get his supper.

He unlocked the door to his room and found Trim where he'd left him, upon the windowsill, gazing down into the yard below. Crabbe unpacked his wares, and once Trim heard the ting of a metal fork upon tin, he leapt down and stalked across the room to inspect the contents of his dinner bowl. After sniffing it fastidiously for nearly a full minute, he condescended to nibble daintily upon some tiny morsels as if to say he was only doing it to please his master, not because he *liked* the fare thus presented.

After washing his hands and face, Crabbe rolled his eyes at this feline fussiness and descended to the taproom. There he consumed a genuinely prodigious plate of roast beef, Yorkshire pudding, bashed neeps, and collard greens, all swimming in a pool of gravy laced with what Crabbe suspected was port. It was good, honest fare, not something he wouldn't have served to Captain Knox, but decent enough.

Belching softly to himself, he thought about the following morning. He was supposed to present himself at the offices of R&W Paul. He had enquired at the market about the office's location and stood upon the quayside looking at the solid little building squatting by itself, looking smug in the early evening light. Now Crabbe found himself in a quandary. He was an enlisted member of His Majesty's Navy. However, how he had come ashore was unconventional. Captain Walker had drawn up a rudimentary muster roll which he would probably lodge with R&W Paul. Still, it had been hastily put together, and the captain hadn't managed to keep a daily log due to an infection in his wounded jaw after their hasty departure from the *Renown*.

Would anyone miss a seventeen-year-old cook? *Could he not just fade away down a side alley, never to be seen again? Who would come after him? Would anyone even bother?* The officers and crew of the *Alexander* would assume he had met with an accident in the vicinity of the wharf and was presumed lost.

Crabbe took another sip of his beer, thinking hard. He had been observed leaving the ship but had struck out on his own, and during the mêlée of the *Alexander* disembarking, had any person noted which way he had gone? He hadn't encountered any of the other crew members at the market. During the last part of their voyage, he had overheard a few of the others stating they would connect with a coaster heading north to try and visit their families before taking on another contract.

During his time on the *Patriot*, his cut of the privateering amounted to a tidy sum. Crabbe never thought he would have reason to bless Captain Fox, but he did so now. Crabbe was naturally parsimonious, not because he was hard-hearted but because he had been raised to be thrifty. Doing some quick mental sums, he deducted the cost of his board and provisions for the night and breakfast in the morning. With regret, he would tell the landlady that he had to leave earlier than intended and make his way into the centre of Portsmouth to locate a mail coach.

He did some more sums. Stagecoaches nowadays could reach a top speed of up to twelve miles an hour, so he could get to London in under two days if he managed to secure a seat. The only tricky part was Trim. How best to conceal a medium-sized cat in a kit bag for two days, being bumped and jolted in a confined space with probably two or three other people? Humans could take a toilet break on the road or at a public house but giving Trim a comfort stop made Crabbe's mind boggle.

He took another sip of his warm beer. He'd seen geese and chickens transported in crates relatively comfortably; why not a cat? He could line the crate with newspaper, so if Trim had to go, he had to go. The other passengers might object, however. Crabbe chewed his bottom lip. The only other choice was to part with the cat. Immediately he rejected the idea, out of the question.

He downed the last of his drink. First thing tomorrow, he would return to the market and purchase a wooden crate, then a broadsheet from one of the lads dotting the quayside plying their newspapers. After that, he would inform the landlady, pack his belongings and disappear into the town centre. With a plan in mind, Crabbe rose, thanked the landlady for his dinner and climbed the stairs to his room to share his plans with Trim.

By noon the next day, Thomas Crabbe had purchased a ticket on a mail coach destined for London. He stood outside the public house watching whilst the four horses were brought out of the stables, snorting and stamping, their breath dissipating on the morning air, the anticipation of the journey proving infectious. A decent-sized wooden crate containing Trim and a blanket sat on the ground between his feet. Trim was not happy about being confined thus, but Crabbe told him it was either that or he would be left to fend for himself in the alleyways of Portsmouth. Suitably chastened, Trim settled down with a resigned expression on his whiskered face.

As the horses were harnessed, a light footstep sounded behind Crabbe, and a piping voice exclaimed, "Oh, Mamma, do look at the cat!"

Crabbe turned his head, then looked down about four inches to see a young girl–no, a woman, he amended, noting the swell of bosom. Her gloved hands were clasped together under her chin in a gesture of delight.

The mother in question was slightly taller than her daughter, her severe parting showing under one of the ugliest bonnets Crabbe had ever seen. Her mouth was drawn up in a moue of distaste as she looked down at Trim. "Come away, dear; it might be diseased."

Both Crabbe and Trim bristled at this statement. The young lady completely ignored her mother, much to Crabbe's amusement, and instead squatted down in a puff of skirts to draw off her glove and extend her right index finger through the crate's bars.

Trim decided to come down off his indignant high horse to sniff the proffered digit gently.

"Oh, Mamma, his nose is so soft; come and look!" she exclaimed.

"As I *said*, do come away and leave the creature alone."

The 'creature' hissed soundlessly at the older woman eliciting a soft giggle from her daughter. Straightening up, she smiled sweetly at Crabbe from beneath thick black lashes.

"Dear sir, I perceive you are the owner of this darling cat. Are you to board the mail coach?"

Crabbe looked into the soft, dove grey eyes fringed with long lashes and felt his stomach flip over. Clearing his throat, he croaked, "Aye, Miss, we be headed for London."

"Wonderful! We shall all be travellers together, and you can tell us your story whilst we jog along together, can we not, Mamma?" She appealed to her dyspeptic-looking parent, who looked even more disapproving than before.

"I, ah, that is…" Crabbe looked helplessly at the girl's mother, down at Trim, up at the horses, then gave up the fight and fell hopelessly under the young woman's spell.

As they boarded the mail coach, Amelia Cope, having introduced herself and her miserable mother, continued chatting away like a little bird, filling Crabbe in on their recent history. This amounted to the death of her uncle (her late papa's brother). Until his untimely demise he had been her sole benefactor, but the shuffling off of his mortal coil had (being childless) left her his whole estate, the upshot of which was that Amelia was now a Woman of Substance.

The Woman of Substance fixed Crabbe, now ensconced within the carriage, Trim between his ankles, with a glint in her eye, weighing him up for a prospective mate. Crabbe glanced at Amelia's mother, who regarded him with a gimlet stare. At this point Crabbe felt some kinship with the matriarch, as he did not want to be sucked into a situation he knew nothing about. Clearing his throat, Crabbe filled them in on his recent adventures on the high seas and, commending his soul to God, lied through his teeth, stating that his aged and infirm mother was at death's door and that he had to make all haste to her bedside. He could not afford to dally as time was of the essence, so it was with regret that he must focus all his attention on his ailing mother.

Amelia's mother actually smiled at the telling of this tale and, turning to her daughter, said, "Now, dear, you see how it is, this young man is bent on an errand of mercy, and we must respect that. He must be with his dying mother, and we shall not interfere. No!" Here she raised a bony index finger in remonstration. "We *shall not* interfere with that."

Amelia subsided with a sulky countenance. She could see her chances of marriage and motherhood reducing by the minute.

At that precise moment, Trim, who had sensed nervous anxiety emanating from his owner and his own stress, decided to fart. It was silent but deadly, the smell wafting up the noses of the human occupants causing them to look at one another in alarm and distaste until the source of the unspeakable smell was ascertained. Amelia fell into a fit of giggles, making her mother even crosser than she was already.

Trim, in response, looked at them as if to say, well, if you will take me against my will, shut me up in a crate and put me in a moving vehicle where I get joggled about with no food and just some water, what do you expect?

Crabbe, who had tried to look stern and remonstrate with Trim, found Amelia's giggling contagious and began snorting, earning a severe look from her Mamma, who moved Crabbe further down the social ladder. He was not unhappy with that, as he felt that Amelia might try and pull him into their domestic drama.

"Can't that thing go on the back of the coach with the mailbags?" The matriarch cut into his mirth.

"Oh, Mamma, how can you suggest such a thing? He would catch a cold for sure. He is but an animal and animals do not have the manners we people do, so we must forgive them their transgressions."

At that moment, Crabbe thought he might fling all caution to the wind and kiss Amelia's hand, but one glance at her mother's face dissuaded him immediately.

She subsided, her mouth drawn up like a button, casting evil glances in Trim's direction now and again. Still, she satisfied herself after a while by watching the passing countryside out of the grimy sash window.

Truth be told, Crabbe, who was quite used to cramped quarters that had a habit of bobbing up and down, found the mail coach not uncomfortable. It had a pleasant swaying motion similar to a ship, and after a couple of hours, he nodded off.

When he awoke, the countryside had changed from city buildings to open fields lined with hedgerows, cows and sheep grazing in verdant pastures. When they had departed Portsmouth, the morning had been misty and cold, but the cloud had burned off, and the sun shone brightly. He smelled the fresh grass, animal dung and flowers in the hedgerows. Used as he was to salt spray, unwashed men and hemp, it made a pleasant change to his olfactory senses.

Crabbe glanced at his travelling companions, who were both asleep, so he took the opportunity to reach down and, unlatching the door to the crate, eased Trim out. The cat stood, getting his balance, whilst Crabbe unhooked his hip flask containing water and poured a small amount into a tin bowl. Trim immediately began lapping the water, his delicate pink tongue moving in and out. Crabbe smiled to see him drink heartily and, removing a few strips of dried bully beef from his jacket pocket, broke them into small pieces and fed them to Trim. All this was done without Amelia or her mother's knowledge, so when the cat had finished, he gently coaxed him back into his crate and settled to watch the countryside slide past the window.

They made two stops on the first day before spending the night in a country inn. They were all up at dawn the following day to board the coach and resume their journey. By the evening of the second day, the broad country road began to narrow and looking out of the besmeared window, Crabbe espied the Thames, curving gently as it led them into the heart of the great city of London.

Chapter 7

The stallholders' cries filled the air as they descended from the carriage at Charing Cross terminus. One woman screeched, "Fresh veg!" Another yelled, "Pretty flowers, come and see!"

Wherever Crabbe turned, he saw action and industry. His senses were assailed by colour and noise. And underlying it all was a smell; the smell of London. Later he would analyse it as a mixture of ordure, salt, and human misery. But, for now, he was fascinated by this incredible city's colours, smells, tastes, and feel. Sitting in the carriage, his leg had become quite stiff, so it was a relief to stretch it out and restore some of the circulation.

Amelia's eyes were round as saucers, her head moving from side to side, trying to take it all in. Crabbe smiled to see her face, then turned and looked at her mother, and the smile disappeared rapidly. The severe matriarch clutched her skirts about her as if she thought they might be contaminated by touching another human being. Crabbe sighed inwardly; the glass was always half empty for some people. Speaking for himself, he couldn't wait for his next adventure to begin.

A young woman leaning against a nearby wall gave him a knowing smile. She pushed herself away from the wall, walking slowly towards Crabbe. Crabbe accurately deduced what she was about, having seen similar ladies in various ports so, placing the basket containing Trim at his feet, he doffed his hat to both Amelia and her mother. "I be leaving yew now; I needs find the connecting coach to Ipswich so's I can go home."

"Oh, your poor mother, yes of course." Amelia pouted prettily up at him. "We wish you godspeed on your journey north."

Crabbe bowed to her, made a quicker obeisance to her mother, and limped off, picking up the basket before either Amelia or her parent could call him back. The harlot pouted prettily after him, returning to her previous station.

He made his way through the crowds of people, noting the swirl of colour, the different sounds of humans and animals, stepped aside to watch a flock of geese waddle past, their webbed feet tarred to withstand the long journey to London on foot, neatly dodged a couple of draymen unloading barrels of ale into a hatch set into the pavement, and gave a quarter farthing to a ragtag child spinning a wooden top, all the while asking for directions to Cheapside. It was from this place that the Royal Mail coach was due to depart the following day.

After much asking of passers-by, Crabbe got decent directions, and it took him roughly half an hour to reach the terminus, where he immediately recognised the black and red colours of the coaches. He located the office where he paid his fare, then adjourned to the nearby Swan with Two Necks to have an early lunch and find a room for the night.

Crabbe settled into a high-backed booth seat in a quiet nook and opened the door, placing Trim gently on the floor. The cat didn't budge at first, his whiskers twitching as he sensed the air, but after a few minutes, he judged it safe to creep out of the basket and gratefully lapped water from his usual tin bowl. Both Crabbe and Trim dined on steak-and-kidney pie with fresh vegetables–extra gravy for Trim–both relieving themselves in the yard to the rear of the pub before retiring to a tiny but adequate room on the ground floor near the stables.

At half-past seven the following day, Crabbe, Trim, and three other passengers stood waiting for the horses to be harnessed and secured. They embarked on the coach, waiting for the off. At two minutes to eight, the driver leapt up onto the box and, with a 'hep, hep!' cracked the whip, and the coach lurched forward into the early morning.

Crabbe looked out of the coach window and watched the sights of London recede as they made their way to the high road leading to the east coast and East Anglia. All had an uncomfortable day, being thrown about in the interior of the mail coach doing a top speed of nine miles per hour. They made two stops to change horses before the open fields began to narrow, the hedgerows shorten, and the open road began to dwindle into not much more than a dirt track.

As the coach slowed to pass a farmer driving some sheep, Crabbe quickly looked out the window. Yes, there it was, the church spire of St Nicholas. He would have recognised it anywhere and felt his heart lift as he noted familiar buildings and scenery. They passed over the river Gipping and into the heart of the large market town.

Founded in the early 1300's, Ipswich had always been prosperous. Its primary industries were farming, agriculture and maritime. It had served as a port since Anglo-Saxon times and, with its proximity to the continent, had been a bustling gateway ever since. It even had royal connections, being the birthplace of Cardinal Thomas Wolsey, servant to Henry the Eighth.

The coach bumped into the heart of the busy town, eventually coming to a halt outside the Corn Exchange, where all the occupants descended, collected their luggage and went their separate ways.

Crabbe was left with the crate at his feet and his kit bag slung over one thin shoulder. Now all he had to do was find a vehicle going in the direction of Bramford, where his ma lived. It took nearly half an hour to find a farmer who was returning to his farm. Crabbe paid him a few coins and settled in the back of his wagon, he and Trim sharing it with two sheep and a small piglet, who took great interest in Trim. The farmer had exchanged the sheep and piglet for sacks of corn and was in a cheerful mood, regaling Crabbe with stories of some of the deals that had just taken place in the Corn Exchange.

Crabbe only half listened to the cheerful monologue, his excitement growing at the thought of seeing his mother. It had been nearly two years since he'd journeyed to the coast and boarded the Donegal. Was he much changed? He thought he'd grown a bit more and gained a permanent limp and some crow's feet around his eyes. And a cat; he glanced down at Trim, who was looking disdainfully at the piglet, snorfing at the door of his crate. Crabbe smiled. He'd owned his first cat when, as a young boy, he'd found a kitten curled up in their barn, fast asleep on a hay bale. It had been the middle of winter, and he and his ma had gone in to collect hay for hard feeding the cows. The poor little mite had hissed and spat at them both until Thomas, who wasn't much taller than a hay bale then, had walked over, picked it up and thrust it into the inside of his worn jacket. A small purr started immediately, and Thomas felt the tiny claws needling his thin chest through the cotton shirt. They'd named the cat Jude, after the patron saint of lost things. Jude had grown from a skinny, malnourished kitten to a sleek, strong cat, supplementing his diet of mice and rats with kitchen leftovers. Ultimately, he had died of old age; they'd found his cold body curled up underneath a hedge at the front of the cottage. He'd died in his sleep after a good breakfast, warming his old bones in the sun. If only we could all go that way, mused Thomas as they jolted over a particularly bad rut in the road.

The outskirts of the town fell away, and they were now on the Norwich Road. After another half an hour, Thomas could make out the sign of the Bramford Cock and Bull, with its garishly painted depiction of a rooster and a constipated-looking bull swinging in the stiff breeze. Here the ruddy-faced farmer let him down, wishing him good luck and godspeed. Thomas knew he could walk the remaining few miles after a feed at the public house. After he and Trim had dined on chicken pie, washed down with a couple of pints of the local Pale Ale, Thomas popped Trim back in his crate, shouldered his kit bag once more and trudged up the dusty road in the direction of his mother's cottage. The walk was hot; he had to remove his jacket, stuffing it into his kit bag.

The warm, muggy afternoon eased into a sultry evening, whining insects emerging to feast on his warm flesh. He looked forward to a cool drink and his old bed, feeling familiar surroundings settle around him. He raised his eyes from the dust at his feet, anticipating the first glimpse of the white paling fence enclosing his ma's herb garden, the scent of lavender and rosemary warm upon the summer's night, smelling in his memory her warm scent, redolent with being out in the garden all day, the smell of baking clinging to the creases of her skirts.

The cottage appeared as he rounded the last oak tree adjacent to the road. He stopped dead. No white picket fence, no herb garden, no smoke issuing from the chimney, just a hollowed-out shell of a house, the two windows on either side of the front door appearing as two eye sockets in a bleached skull. The front door hung off its hinges, leaning drunkenly against the door jamb.

Thomas broke into an uneven run. Trim protested loudly as he bumped along in his crate but Thomas paid him no heed. He dumped him unceremoniously in what had been once a well-tended garden and tore open what was left of the door.

"Ma! Ma! It's me, Thomas! Ma–!" Calling out his mother's name. His voice echoed in the space inside. Not a stick of furniture was left; the hearth was void of all firewood, and no shining copper pots hung from the ceiling. The usual bunches of dried herbs were not in their customary places on the mantelpiece above the fireplace. No smell of baking, cooking, bottling, or drying greeted him. He felt like he would be sick on the spot. Where was his ma? What had happened here? He thought rapidly to the last letter he had received from her, whilst on board the *Renown*.

As he stood, surveying the bare walls, he heard the faint

clop of hooves and, turning to the door, emerged into the dying light in time to see Abel Bedford, the farmer who worked the land adjacent to his ma's, pulled in his trap by his trusty pony, Robin. At the sight of a man outside the cottage, he pulled the reins sharply, stopping Robin in his tracks.

"Hullo there, bor–if yew be wantin' Mrs Crabbe, she ain't thar no more." Abel waved a large hand towards Thomas, not recognising him at that distance.

Thomas covered the ground between them quickly, despite his limp, and as he got closer to Abel, he saw the older man's ruddy complexion pale as he realised who the visitor was.

"As I live an' breathe–Thomas." Abel's weatherbeaten face creased in grief as he looked down into Thomas's upturned one.

"Where is she, Abel?" Thomas asked without preamble.

Abel removed his shabby slouch hat, holding it to his chest whilst searching for the right words. The gesture was enough for Thomas. No words were necessary. He knew what had happened. He clutched the top of the wheel nearest him for support.

"When?"

"'Bout twa months ago. There were a fire; me an' the missus tried to save 'er, but..." Abel's rheumy eyes filled with tears. "She be buried over thar." He gestured with his hat towards the village church, its small, grey spire silhouetted against the setting sun.

"Yew be wantin' to see' er tonight?"

Thomas shook his head mutely. Time enough for him to find her grave tomorrow. A heavy fatigue stole over him, and he knew he couldn't put another foot forward, even if his life depended on it. A sudden wave of dizziness made him put out a hand to steady himself on the pony, making Robin snort.

"Yew look done in, lad. Come awa' with me now, the missus will 'ave a pot o' stew on. Yew bide with us the night, then yew can mek plans in t'mornin'."

Crabbe lifted his head. "Are yew sure, Abel? It's not just me, I 'ave a cat with me." He pointed at the crate lying on the ground, a rustling sound coming from the inside as if Trim was getting more comfortable.

"A cat, yew say? The missus will like 'im; set 'im to work on our mice." Abel smiled kindly at the younger man.

"Go an' get yon cat, an' ya bag, an' we'll find yew a bed for the night."

Thomas did as he was bid, collecting a restless Trim, passing him up to the waiting Abel, then mounting the cart, squashing in next to the farmer. He found the solid feel of the other man beside him very comforting, and the gentle swaying of the cart reminded him of lying in his hammock onboard the ship. By the time they got to Abel's farm cottage, Thomas was nearly asleep, the long journey and the shock of his mother's death taking their toll. He rubbed his tired eyes, trying to clear them long enough to collect Trim and his bag, walking up the path to the farmhouse where Mrs Bedford stood in the open doorway, backlit by cheerful lamps. He began to explain, but she shushed him, ushering him in, sitting him down and plonking a bowl of steaming stew accompanied by a hunk of freshly baked bread in his cold hands.

The next hour or so passed in a blur of tiredness. He briefly filled the Bedfords in on his adventures, his indenture, release, adoption of Trim (who had disappeared into the cow byre next door after a plate of corned beef in gravy and a massive drink of water), and his return to England in the hope of finding his mother. Mrs Bedford, noting that Thomas was nodding into his empty bowl, gestured to her husband to take him upstairs to the small attic room where a bed was always made up in case their son visited from Ipswich, where he was completing an apprenticeship.

After a cursory wash of hands and face in the bowl of water provided, Thomas managed to stagger up the narrow stairs and reeled to bed, utterly exhausted. As he teetered on the verge of sleep, his last thought was that if Trim decided to escape, he didn't have the energy to look for him.

Chapter 8

It had been a tiring day, picking herbs from the hedgerows, berries from the side of the lanes and foraging for anything else Alinor Crabbe could find. Her back felt like to snap, but her baskets were full, and she had enough to bottle, pickle, dry, and distil to see her through what promised to be a harsh winter.

As she returned to the cottage, her thoughts turned to Thomas. Her son, her one and only, his father having perished from the morbid sore throat five years past.

She paused, setting her baskets down, easing her back, and feeling the vertebrae crackle with the day's effort. Where was he now? His last letter had been hastily written, the ink sprawling across the parchment like a drunken spider. He had been indentured onto a colonial ship crewed by privateers, and her wame curdled to think he was amongst the enemy, friendless and alone. No, not friendless, she corrected herself, he had mentioned a negro sailor named Sam. And the ship's cat. She smiled at that last detail, remembering Jude and how Thomas had protected him from the beginning.

Dusk was coming on fast; she best stir herself and make for home. Picking up her bounty, she trudged on through the gathering gloom, only pausing to watch the silent flight of a barn owl, its pale colour the only thing announcing its passing.

She felt immeasurably relieved at reaching the front door. After unlocking it, setting the baskets down, and unwinding the shawl from her head and shoulders, she stoked the embers in the fireplace, coaxing them to life and feeding them fresh firewood.

She had left a small pot of stew upon the table, covered with muslin and leftovers from last night's supper, and she attached a butcher's hook to the pot's handles, ready to suspend it over the open fire.

As she leaned in to hang the pot from the ring set into the top of the fireplace, a wave of dizziness overtook her, and the flames swam before her eyes. She reached out to steady herself on the hearth but, in her confusion, missed the stones and instead put the palm of her hand on the metal hook. A searing pain shot through her hand and she staggered, clutching it to her chest. So preoccupied was she in her agony that she didn't feel the heat engulfing her skirts until it was too late. She looked down and screamed at the flames igniting her skirt and petticoats, turning her into a pillar of fire. Frantically she beat at the material, not heeding her blistering skin, the smoke wreathing her in a cloud. The heat intensified as she desperately attempted to rip the clothing from her body, but the cheap homespun of her gown went up like a Roman candle. She ran to the door, thinking that she stood a chance if she could get to the water trough outside. Despite her best efforts, it took less than five minutes for her to be wholly consumed with fire.

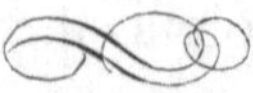

Thomas stood looking down at his mother's grave. The Bedfords had told him the whole story that morning. They had heard the screams from their cottage and, in horror, saw a figure ablaze outside the cottage. Abel had sprinted towards the garden, throwing Alinor to the ground, but despite tearing his great coat off and beating at her clothing, he was too late to save Alinor; the damage was done, and she was so severely burned that they hardly recognised her.

Alinor's charred body was buried in the local cemetery, the Bedfords cleared out her belongings, and the landlord took possession of the cottage, trying to let it again. Still, no one wanted to live there after the tragedy, and it had fallen into disrepair. None had known how to contact Thomas. He felt cold, so cold. The only person he had loved in the world was gone, and he felt like a ship adrift without an anchor.

Abel Bedford stood some way apart from Thomas. He waited until the young lad had laid a posy of flowers on his mother's grave, watching the droop of his thin shoulders. He wasn't yet eighteen; what would he do; where would he go? Thomas turned away from the grave, limping slowly back to join Abel.

"What will yew do, lad?"

Thomas heaved a sigh. "I'll ask the landlord if he'll let the cottage to me, an' I'll move in with Trim."

"What, on ya own?"

"Well, I'll have you both for neighbours." Thomas smiled sadly.

"But what will you do for money?"

"I have a fair bit from bein' in the navy, an' I'll ask round 'ere for work." Thomas chewed his lip thinking about how to go about seeking employment.

"What did they train yew for in the navy?"

"I were officers' cook."

"A cook, yew say! Well, I've got good news for yew, Thomas; the local pub just lost their cook due to 'im movin' to Colchester to be near 'is daughter. He were getting' on in years, an' to be honest, the food weren't much cop. So, I reckon if yew walk down thar an' have a word, they might take yew on."

Thomas couldn't believe his ears. Here was a God-given opportunity in the local village, a walk from the cottage where he'd lived with his ma. He could stay in the area, he and Trim would have a home–and the Bedfords would be close by should he get into strife. He smiled for the first time in twenty-four hours.

"Reckon I'll walk down there this arternoon and 'ave a chat with the publican."

"Yew do that, Thomas," Abel nodded encouragingly, "it can't hurt."

So, that afternoon saw Thomas walking slowly to the Cock and Bull to order a pint and ask for a chat with the publican.

Three faces turned to greet him as he entered. A young, fresh-faced girl of curvy proportions stood behind the bar, polishing a glass tankard. The other two occupants were ruddy-faced farmers, both men of indeterminate age, one with an enormous mutant strawberry nose.

He greeted Thomas with, "Awright bor, yew jest in toime for a drink!"

Thomas smiled and nodded to both men and, approaching the bar asked the barmaid if she would furnish him with a pint of the Pale Ale on tap.

Flashing a broad smile which made a dimple wink in her right cheek, she duly lifted a pint glass from the shelf and placed it beneath the tap.

"Yew new around here, then?" she asked, arching a shapely eyebrow at him.

Thomas thought for a second. How much to reveal on the first visit? Honesty was always the best policy, but he could be economical with some of the truth, such as his monetary situation. "Ah, not exactly, no. I were born 'ere, but I've been at sea the last three years or so."

The young woman looked impressed at this statement. She opened her mouth to comment but was beaten to it by one of the locals leaning his elbows on the bar, who had been watching Thomas closely, eyes like dark currants in a face mottled by broken veins.

"As I live an' breathe, yew be Allie's son!"

Thomas felt a pang at the mention of his mother's name and buried his discomfort in the foamy ale, taking a couple of gulps to steady himself.

"Allie?" the young barmaid asked.

"Aye, Alinor Crabbe; she were known as a wise woman in these 'ere parts, knew 'erbs an' such." The farmer nodded sagely, his small eyes cutting to Crabbe.

Thomas had recovered himself sufficiently to raise his head and smile wanly. "Yew said 'were' so yew'll know she's dead?"

He saw the older man's expression. "I did, bor, I'm right, sorry for it, she were a lovely gel…" The farmer trailed off, not sure how to continue.

Thomas took pity on him; it wasn't his fault his mother had met with an accident and died. "The Bedfords told me. I stayed with them last night, an' they told me to come down 'ere in the hopes of findin' some work." He looked appealingly at the attractive young woman.

She dimpled at him. "Yew be right. Ol' Arthur upped an' left us, so's it's jest me tryin' to keep the place runnin' for Ned. He's out the back. Shall I tell 'im yew'd like a chat?"

Thomas nodded, smiling shyly at her. She flashed him a pert smile and bustled into the back.

Thomas continued to sip the cool ale, enjoying the feel of it sliding down his dusty throat. The walk had taken longer than expected, but he still found that his leg tired quickly, even after all this time. He hoped it would improve as he got older; only time would tell.

The young barmaid came bustling back, a smile upon her heart-shaped face. "Ned'll see yew now. He's out back peeling spuds; he'd be glad of a break."

Thomas downed the last of his ale, wiped the back of his

hand across his mouth, and, nodding to the bar's occupants, followed the young lady through the bar, noting her narrow waist and well-rounded hips.

She led him down a short corridor and into a small yard at the rear of the pub. "I'm Daisy, by the way," she threw over her shoulder.

The publican sat on a low stool, a bucket between his knees, a pile of potatoes next to him, wielding a paring knife. He turned and spat as Thomas walked into the yard and nodded to Daisy that she could go, as he would be alright to talk to the young visitor.

"Yew be Allie Crabbe's boy?" he said, more as a statement than a question.

"Aye, that be right, sir, I've taken o'er her cottage, so I be stayin' in the area a while."

Ned Stokes nodded, pondering the information. "An' yew can cook, 'pparently."

"Aye, tha's right, I were a ship's cook for nigh on three years in the navy; I were used to feedin' a goodly number o' men, an' can make somethin' outta nothin'." Crabbe stopped talking, chewing his bottom lip. He didn't know why, but suddenly it seemed very important that he secure this position.

Ned looked at Thomas Crabbe long and hard. He noted the medium height, narrow shoulders, thinning hair, thick eyebrows above sharp, intelligent grey eyes. The lad might be young, but his eyes looked older than his smooth, hairless face. He felt the young man's spirit, a wisdom beyond his years, and was content with what he saw. He would do very nicely.

"Well, I reckon we'll try yew for a week an' see 'ow yew go. If the locals darn't die of food poisonin', you're hired, alright?" Ned smiled broadly and spat into the palm of his right hand, extending it to Thomas.

Thomas spat into his own palm and shook Ned's heartily. Ned looked at the pile of potatoes.

"Now, how about yew be 'elpin us with this 'ere pile of spuds?"

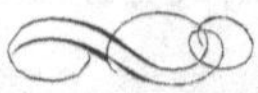

Thomas became the new cook at the Cock and Bull, Ned gladly took a back seat, and Daisy continued to work front of the house. Thomas would check with Ned as to the week's menu, keeping the cost down by choosing what was in season, supplemented by a poacher friend of Ned's who wasn't opposed to bringing in a brace of pheasant or a few rabbits obtained by the light of a good moon.

Word spread. The Cock and Bull soon became known for its good, hearty food served with a smile by the curvaceous, cheeky Daisy.

The only issue was that Thomas was becoming very fond of the vivacious barmaid and was uncomfortable with how some clientele treated her. Daisy, however, managed the local populace with panache, not allowing their familiarity to bother her unduly. Thomas, on the other hand, was a different matter. One evening, a young farmer with a face like a rosy apple and hands like dinner plates grabbed Daisy whilst she was placing tankards of beer on the table in front of him and his friend, drawing her onto his lap. She gently pushed him in the chest, trying to get off his lap, but he held her tightly, making her squirm. The farmer's friend laughed, braying like a donkey at Daisy's discomfiture. One of the older locals, Bert, saw the horseplay and quietly walked through the serving hatch into the kitchen at the back.

"Thomas! Yew'd best get yaself out o' the kitchen an' into front o' house, some yokel's tryin' to stick his hand down Daisy's bodice, she darn't like–" He stopped talking abruptly as Thomas blazed past him, leg notwithstanding, clutching a large kitchen knife.

A ruckus broke out in the front bar. By the time Bert had made his way back, the young farmer and his friend had been thrown out of the pub at knifepoint by an irate Thomas. Jeers and shouts followed them out into the street; Daisy was popular with the locals, and none liked her being taken advantage of.

Thomas slammed the door and turned, breathing like a carthorse, finding Daisy standing behind him, hands on hips, head tilted to one side, looking like she'd never seen him before.

"Thomas Crabbe, what yew think you're doin'? I 'ad it under control, 'e were only–"

"I darn't care what 'e were only doin', I weren't prepared to let 'im do anymore of it!" Thomas shouted, brushing past her, and stumped back to the kitchen.

Daisy stared after him open-mouthed.

Bert winked at her in an avuncular fashion. "Best yew go

arter 'im, eh?"

Daisy sniffed, pretending to be cross when secretly she was pleased and flattered that Thomas had leapt to her defence. Thomas might not be the most handsome man in the world, but he had a noble quality about him and he was kind, patient, and a hard worker. She knew a few men who were fair of face but black in soul, a bit like the lad who'd just been ejected. Handsome men, in her experience, were self-centred and selfish. She smoothed her skirts, patted her hair, and walked in a dignified manner through the bar and into the kitchen, feeling the remaining drinkers grinning into their beers at the developments about to take place amongst the pots and pans.

Said pots and pans were being crashed about vigorously by the angry cook. Daisy stood watching Thomas for a moment, letting him get whatever it was out of his system. She waited patiently for the metal cacophony to finish. Eventually, the cook ran out of steam, slamming his meat cleaver down on the worn bench top.

"Yew finished, 'ave yew?" she inquired, arching a well-plucked eyebrow.

"Aye," snapped Thomas, glaring balefully at her.

"No need to be so prickly, I darn't want to fight with yew. I jest wanted to say thank you for what yew did out there." She jerked her head at the bar.

Thomas blew his cheeks out, trying to get a grip on his emotions. He was in turmoil, angry at the lout who had assaulted Daisy, jealous because she hadn't seemed unduly bothered by the attention, attracted to her dimples and womanly curves, ashamed of his outburst, and frustrated because she had only treated him as a friend up to this point. He picked at a torn fingernail on his left hand, not looking at her.

Out of the corner of his eye, he saw Daisy move closer until she stood beside him. She nudged him with her elbow, forcing him to look at her.

Thomas swallowed, his adam's apple bobbing nervously. His grey eyes had gone perfectly round and he could feel sweat beginning to bead his hairline. He felt like a rabbit in front of a cobra, terrified but unable to look away.

The cobra, dimples winking, drew nearer.

Up close, Thomas had very attractive eyes, Daisy thought. A pale grey, with a faint blue ring around the iris. These clear eyes now looked into hers as she leaned in to kiss him gently upon his wide, mobile mouth. She felt his start of astonishment and a slight hesitation before a smile formed underneath her kiss, and he returned the gesture with enthusiasm, snaking an arm around her waist.

Thomas was not a passionate man. His outburst a few minutes ago was most out of character. He was considered, measured even. A deep thinker who looked at things from various angles, weighed up the pros and cons, looked left, looked right, looked both ways again (just to be sure) and then, and only then, did he leap, or instead put a firm foot forward. But where Daisy was concerned, deep thought flew out of the window, leaving a vacuum behind which her sights, tastes, and sounds filled. Common sense dictated that he should take it slow, calm down, court her properly, but a more visceral part of his brain, one hitherto untapped, blotted out all reason and revelled in the sheer delight of animal sensation. He tasted her mouth, smelled lavender water on her skin, felt the softness of her ample bosom against his chest.

Where this canoodling would have ended was anyone's guess, but at that moment, Ned entered the kitchen via the back door, a sack of turnips slung over his shoulder.

"If yew two 'ave finished, yew can at least help me with these 'ere vegetables," Ned wheezed grumpily.

"Stow it, ye ol' numpty," Daisy said, dimples flashing as she shot forward to relieve Ned of some of his wares.

Thomas took the sack onto his shoulder, letting it slide to the floor, shoving it under the worn worktop.

Ned straightened, fixing them both with a minatory eye. "Do I be hearin' weddin' bells?"

Daisy snorted, and Crabbe's mouth dropped open. "Now, jest a minute–"

"I'm only funnin' yew." Ned flapped a lined hand at him. "Although if yew are goin' to start fornicatin' in the kitchen, jest mek sure the door to the bar is shut, hm?" And with that, he turned on his heel and made one of the best exits that Thomas had ever witnessed.

Daisy turned slowly back to face Thomas, who by this time was the same colour as the bowl of tomatoes sitting on the benchtop. "Take no notice of what 'e jest said. I darn't expect anythin' from yew, Thomas."

Thomas swallowed audibly, feeling perspiration forming at the back of his knees, which had gone quite weak with the last kiss. He desperately cast about in his mind for a suitable reply.

He did not want to lose this girl, but he didn't want to rush pell-mell into anything.

"Can I court yew, then?" he blurted, heart hammering in his thin chest.

Daisy pretended to inspect her fingernails, appearing to consider his request when she'd already made up her mind that she'd be mad to let this young man slip through her grasp. She had a feeling that Thomas was going places–where, she didn't know. All she *did* know was that she wanted to be alongside him.

"We can step out, yes," she replied, fluttering her eyelashes at him. "But darn't yew be goin' an' g'tting' ideas, I'm not a flossy."

"I darn't think yew were, I jest–"

"I know what yew jest thought." She interrupted him crisply.

"Like I said, I darn't put it about, I on'y pretend to flirt with the punters. Most of 'em are scallywags an' not fit to kiss, let alone step out with." Daisy plonked her hands on her hips, glaring at the hapless Thomas, who wisely remained silent.

"Now, afore we step out, there's one thing I need to check." "An' what's that?" Thomas asked nervously.

"Trim." She dimpled at him. "When can I meet 'im?"

Chapter 9

They approached Thomas's cottage one evening, the sun sinking in the sky and crickets chirping in the hedgerows. Walking up the garden path, Thomas could see Trim sitting in the rusty wheelbarrow, waiting patiently for his master to return and give him his dinner. Thomas had put a blanket inside the wheelbarrow, and Trim had adopted it as his general lookout post, border security and welcome home spot.

The cat stretched lazily, his eyes never leaving the stranger's face, wondering who this young lady was his master had brought visiting.

"He'll want to sniff yew first," advised Thomas, "then he'll most likely want 'is dinner. Then he'll come over an' lay on ya feet."

Daisy smiled at him. "I *love* cats," she informed him for probably the tenth time. Thomas smiled to himself; that was one of the several reasons he loved Daisy. Anyone who loved cats he automatically liked, and anyone who loved Trim went straight to the top of the Favourite People list.

Trim jumped down from his sentry duty and strolled

towards them both, looking from one to the other.

"Alright, alright, I know I'm a bit late, but 'ere we are, come on then, give over tha'." He gently chastised Trim, who had begun slaloming around his ankles. "Yew'll trip us both up carryin' on." Trim took no notice and continued to weave in and out of Thomas's ankles as he inserted the key into the front door. He shoved it open, and Trim walked in ahead of them both.

"Oi, it should be ladies first!" Thomas protested. Daisy laughed. "He's a cat, o' course 'e goes first."

Trim flung himself down on the flagstone floor and looked over his stomach at Thomas as if to say, well, get on with it then, I'm *starving*!

Daisy took the proffered chair and whilst Thomas prepared Trim's dinner, she looked around the cottage. It was neat, almost to the point of being monastic, and she noted with satisfaction that it was also clean. She guessed that Thomas's time in the navy had taught him discipline regarding personal effects and surroundings. He had told her about his time in the navy, working with Sam and the latter's escape with the marrons.

"You're neat, I'll give yew that, Thomas." She smiled approvingly.

Thomas laughed quietly. "Not much room onboard a ship makes yew tidy, whether yew like it or not," he replied, confirming her guess. He placed a tin bowl on the floor underneath the wooden table. Trim got up, walked over, and to begin eating. Thomas rolled his eyes at Daisy, sniffed the contents for nearly half a minute before he condescended eliciting a grin.

"Now, can I be getting' yew a drink o' something?"

"Watcha got?"

"Ah, some red wine, a bit o' ale, an' some 'ome-made cider, although 'as a bit young…needs more time." Thomas nodded critically at the pantry, where a large earthenware jar could be seen.

"Yew make the ale an' all?"

"Bless yew, no, Abel makes it, 'as not bad, but I think yew prefer wine, no?" At her nod, he went into the small room where the jug lived and, rummaging around under a low shelf, emerged with a respectable bottle of French claret.

"Where'd yew get tha', then?" Daisy's eyes widened at the sight of the label.

"Ask me no questions an' I'll tell yew no lies," Thomas replied succinctly.

"Do I dare ask 'ow much it cost yew?"

"Yew can ask, but I won't tell yew." Thomas drew the cork with a meaty pop and, reaching for two glasses from the shelf, placed them on the table and poured them each a healthy measure.

"So, what we celebratin'?"

Thomas took a restorative gulp of his wine closing his eyes, letting the ruby liquid soak into the membranes of his mouth. Very, very nice. He essayed another sip, this one for Dutch courage.

"Yew carry on like tha' an' yew'll be under the table in no

time," Daisy said.

Thomas opened his eyes, plunked his glass on the table in a decisive manner, stood up, hitched his breeches, and got stiffly down on one knee.

"Daisy Lawrence," he coughed, wiping a finger under his nose. "Daisy Lawrence," he repeated.

"The answer's yes. Get up, ya numpty."

Thomas's mouth fell open. "I 'aven't finished!" he protested. "Lemme finish!"

Daisy made a rude noise and, leaning forward, placed her hands on either side of his face and kissed him heartily. "As I said, the answer's yes. Now get up off that 'ard floor."

Thomas slowly got up off his knee and slid back into his chair, his eyes never leaving her face.

Daisy sipped her wine. "Reckon we should get married afore the autumn sets in." She nodded sagely. "I'll 'ave a word with the vicar, see' ow he's placed. O' course the bans'll 'ave to be read pretty soon. I'll write me Ma, let 'er know, give 'er as much notice as I can so's she can plan 'er trip."

Thomas looked at Daisy like he'd never seen her before. She was all bustle and business now that she'd accepted his proposal, not that he'd had chance to make it properly.

By this time, Trim had finished most of his dinner and had wandered over to Daisy's shoes. Whilst she continued her happy monologue, he lay down on them and washed his face. Without skipping a beat, she leaned forward and scratched between his ears. He narrowed his eyes and stopped washing, a deep rumble starting in his throat. Thomas smiled. The two things he loved most in the world, in the same room, getting along well.

Daisy continued her happy chatter, so Thomas leaned back in his chair and sipped his wine, letting the warmth percolate down his gullet and into his stomach, blooming like a late summer rose. He felt very content, peaceful even, contemplating an upcoming wedding, married life, and later a family. For now, though, he must satisfy himself with the four-legged child lying on the floor, whose eyes had been reduced to green slits under the ministrations of his wife-to-be.

By now, Daisy had drawn up a verbal list of wedding guests, appointed a cake maker, chosen a spot for a short honeymoon, and was now onto the design of her dress. Thomas snapped back to the present as the fiscal part of his brain nudged him to start paying attention. He cleared his throat meaningfully. Trim's eyes popped open, but Daisy remained oblivious, weighing up the pros and cons of a train for the dress.

Trim looked over his shoulder at Thomas. Thomas looked down at him. They both thought the same thing. She had to be reined back. Thomas cleared his throat again, more loudly this time.

Daisy became aware of the change in the room's atmosphere and ceased her monologue. "What?"

"I think we'd better start addin' all this lot up, darn't yew?"

"I've got some coin put by. I darn't expect yew to pay for everything, Thomas Crabbe." She cocked an eyebrow at him.

He returned the look, plus a cocked eyebrow of his own.

"An' jest where were yew thinkin' of having the weddin' reception?"

"At the pub, where else?"

"Oh aye, an' do I 'ave to make the savouries for all these folk yew be invitin'?"

Daisy stuck her tongue out at him and made another rude noise. "Course not, yew ninny. We'll get one o' the hotels in Ipswich to cater."

Thomas's eyes widened at the prospect of how much that would cost. "I'd rather mek the food meself, if it's all the same."

"What's wrong wi' caterers?"

"I jest trust me own food, tha's all."

Now it was time for an eye-roll of her own. She'd learned a long time ago that Thomas was very fussy about food, almost to the point of mania, but she was concerned he'd be run ragged trying to do everything himself. "I'll help yew, an' so will Ned. Come to think on it, Bert will probably lend a hand an' all."

"Aye, reckon he will at that. If we do things in small stages, it'll spread the work, an' if we do smoked meat an' fish, they'll keep well." Now that they were on familiar ground, Thomas waxed lyrical on the menu's contents.

When the sun had set entirely in a blood orange sky, mackerel clouds tinted pink with the last rays, Thomas walked Daisy back to her rooms at the Cock and Bull. They kissed gently but thoroughly at the back door and parted with promises to continue wedding plans the following evening.

Chapter 10

Some weeks later, as Daisy worked behind the bar, the taproom fell silent as a tall shape darkened the doorway. Daisy looked up from where she'd been pouring a tankard of porter for Bert, and her mouth fell open to see her brother standing there, dressed in a double-breasted frock coat and sporting a battered tricorn hat.

"Joe!" She plunked the tankard on the bar, lifted the hatch and went careering across the taproom to tackle her brother around the midriff.

He grunted with the impact of the sisterly assault, kissing the top of her head, which rested just under his chin.

"Now, now, gel–darn't tek on so–"

"But it's been weeks!" Daisy protested. "I was beginnin' to think sommat had 'appened to you–"

Her brother held up a finger to silence her. "Why darn't we go an' finish this chat somewhere private, hm?"

Daisy caught the gleam in her elder brother's eye and promptly clammed up. She jerked her head towards the kitchen. "Come an' meet Thomas."

"Thomas?"

"My beau." She grinned up at him. "Can 'e be trusted?"

"You'll see once yew meet 'im."

She led the way through the serving hatch, down the short corridor to the back of the pub where Crabbe was rolling shortcrust pastry for the steak and kidney pies he'd made earlier.

Daisy heard her brother's stomach rumble and giggled, making Thomas glance up. He started when he saw the older, taller man standing behind Daisy, hat under his arm, his black hair gleaming in the light streaming in from the back door.

"You're, you're–" spluttered Crabbe.

"Tha's right, Daisy's brother," the tall man cut in. "I thought I'd call in an' see how she were doin'."

Crabbe nodded mechanically, his eyes cutting from Daisy back to the man who he recognised from the local broadsheet as the infamous Joseph Lawrence–highwayman, bandit, and the terror of East Anglia.

The two men were silent, sizing each other up like a couple of male dogs. Next thing they'd be sniffing each other's backsides, Daisy thought, smiling. Joseph caught the smile and returned it. It had always been thus with them, ever since they were little. Joe and Daisy could conduct a whole conversation without the need for words. Sometimes the arch of an eyebrow, a smirk or a widening of the eyes was enough to communicate.

Thomas watched the facial gyrations of brother and sister. Side by side, they weren't physically alike at all. Joseph was a full head taller than Daisy, broad-shouldered and long-limbed with hair like a raven's wing. Daisy, by comparison, had lighter-coloured hair and a more open countenance with rounder features. But something about the tilt of the head, the way they both stood, looked similar, even though Daisy's face was lighter than her taciturn sibling's.

The taciturn sibling turned back to Crabbe, looking him up and down as if he were a broodmare. After a few seconds of scrutiny, Thomas passed some test as Joseph stepped forward and extended his right hand.

Thomas wiped his flour-covered one on his apron and shook Joseph's firmly.

The older man let go. "Never trust a man with a weak handshake or a sweaty palm," he added, smiling to take the sting out of his words.

Thomas saw Daisy's eyes widen and her mouth open, ready to remonstrate with him, but Joseph flapped a hand at her and said, "I'm glad to report 'e has neither."

"Well, tha's a relief," Thomas grinned at Joseph.

"Yew can cook then?" Joseph gestured at the pies with his unshaven chin.

"Aye, nearly three years in the navy; I learned from a Scotsman, Billy Mac. 'e taught me well."

"Well, at least I know m' sister won't starve. She's very dear to me, an' seein' as our Pa died when we were little, I like to look out for her." Joseph turned back to Daisy, who was looking with fondness at both of them.

"Thomas'll stick 'em in the oven, so yew can 'ave one for your dinner."

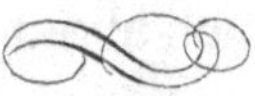

Daisy and Joseph spent a late supper catching up on their respective news. Once the last drinker had departed, she locked up, and the three of them regarded each other over the worn tabletop whilst finishing off a bottle of fine claret that Thomas had squirrelled away.

Daisy looked questioningly at Joseph. "So, yew'll be tryin' your luck on the high road to London?"

"Aye, it's been slim pickings lately. I 'ave to go where there's more traffic."

Daisy chewed her lower lip on hearing this. She didn't like the thought of Joe nearer to London–there was more chance of him being caught. But he was adamant, saying he'd be extra careful and return in the morning before the Cock and Bull opened to clients.

"Yew be good now, lass," Joseph said, gently pinching Daisy's cheek as she stood holding the door open. "I'll be back tomorrow." With that, he clapped the tricorn hat upon his head and, touching his forefinger in an ironic salute, exited the tap room leaving a whiff of danger in his wake.

Daisy shut the door and bolted it, turning slowly to face Crabbe. "Darn't yew be judgin' 'im now, 'e only robs those as 'ave plenty–"

"Oh, aye?" interrupted Crabbe, "an' 'ow do 'e know that? Does 'e question 'em first afore 'e puts a stick in their faces?"

Daisy started as if stung. "Darn't yew be such a hypocrite,

Thomas! Yew been guilty o' stealin' from those who can part wi' it, yew told me some such about those American folks as kept slaves an' were cruel to 'em, no? Yew thought it proper to take from 'em an' not feel guilty!" Her bosom heaved with passion as she glared at Crabbe. "So wha's the difference atween tha' an' Joe? What 'e takes 'e mostly give away, an' only keeps a small bit for 'imself an' me."

Crabbe made quelling motions with his hands; he couldn't bear to see his girl distressed, even if he disagreed with her brother's activities. "Now, now, lass, darn't get upset; I know yew believe in what 'e's doin', right? Tha's good enough for me, so why darn't we go an' clean up?"

Lawrence returned in the early morning after a night of little takings on the high road. He sat at the kitchen table, yawning and blinking like an owl in the pale morning light shining through the back window, glumly contemplating the tankard of ale and hunk of bread and cheese which comprised his breakfast.

"I'll 'ave to go further afield," he announced, gulping the cool ale.

Just then, Thomas arrived through the back door, nodding to Joseph as he shucked his coat off and hung it on one of the worn hooks fixed to a wooden board on the wall.

Thomas regarded Joseph, noting the dark smudges underneath his eyes, then glanced at Daisy, who was chewing thoughtfully on a thumbnail.

"Such as where?" she asked.

"Dunno, mebbe nearer to London, catch the coaches goin' south."

"More risky though, yew'll be on strange turf," offered Thomas as he bent to put more wood into the oven.

"Aye, but it's a risk I'll take if it means more coin." Joseph crammed the rest of the bread into his mouth and washed it down with the remainder of his ale.

Daisy glanced out of the window, watching the first rays of sun gild the roof of the privy next door. "Reckon yew might be temptin' fate, though."

Daisy saw Joseph's mouth purse as if he wasn't sure to be pleased or affronted by his sister's attitude. She narrowed her eyes at her brother, eliciting a snort in response.

"Alright, I'll be careful!"

Daisy nodded slowly, her eyes never leaving Joseph's face.

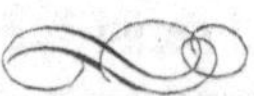

Daisy and Thomas were married in the early autumn, the trees all russet, gold, red and orange like nature's fireworks.

Trim was allowed to attend. Only one awkward moment occurred during the ceremony. When the priest asked, "If any of you can show just cause why they may not lawfully be married, speak now; or else forever hold your peace," Trim chose that exact moment to meow. The sound echoed in the small country church followed by even louder laughter.

Joseph gave Daisy away, and their ma carried her train. They walked from the church back to the tavern, kicking up leaves like a couple of children. A merry afternoon was had by all, the general topics of conversation being the tastiness and plentitude of the food, along with the beauty of the bride.

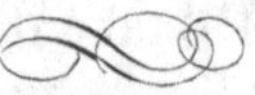

After a short honeymoon in the Norfolk Broads, Daisy and Thomas settled back into working life. One morning, Daisy was polishing the windows at the front of the Cock and Bull and heard the clop of hooves in the distance. She turned towards the sound and smiled at the pony and cart coming into view. Isaiah Goldburger was a wine merchant. He travelled all over East Anglia in his open wagon, pulled by Abraham, his trusty but bad-tempered piebald pony. He was instantly recognisable by the Star of David the local authorities insisted he embroider on his lapel. Most dismissed him, but those who knew him well came to learn of his sharp brain, even sharper wit, and sensitive nose, which he applied regularly to the wares he sold. He hadn't visited for some months, so Daisy was delighted to see him again.

Isaiah pulled Abraham to a halt outside the Cock and Bull descended from the trap, unbolted the tailgate, and removed two casks from the back, one of claret and the other a fortified, sweet wine. As he was fastening the tailgate Daisy went bustling towards him, a smile on her face, ready to welcome Isaiah, bring him into the tavern and introduce him to Thomas. However, the smile faded from her face when Isaiah shoved both his hands into his capacious sleeves and bowed to her. He never did that–he was always courteous, but not this formal. Something must be wrong.

Daisy hovered expectantly, waiting for Goldburger to

speak.

"How are you, mistress?" Isaiah always addressed her thus, he believed her first name was too familiar, and she felt ridiculous if he used her surname.

Despite his soft voice, Daisy felt a cold chill as if he had hissed her name. Her lips felt frozen as she replied, "Well, I thank yew, and yourself?"

Isaiah nodded a couple of times, the ringlets on either side of his face swinging in time with the motion. "Well, I thank you." He began gnawing his bottom lip, clearly deciding how to proceed. Daisy wanted to scream with impatience whilst not wanting to hear what he had to say. He didn't meet her eyes, seeming to scan the dust at his feet as if it held the world's secrets. She suppressed the urge to slap him, all in good time, but she felt like a thousand ants were crawling under her skin.

Apparently, Isaiah reached a decision. He cleared his throat with a noise like a creaky door. He cleared his throat again. Daisy closed her eyes and ground her teeth, willing him with every fibre of her being to get the hell on with it.

"Joseph."

One word, but her heart clenched like a fist to hear it said in his soft tone. "Yes?"

Goldburger shuffled his feet, stirring up more dust to coat his disreputable shoes.

Daisy thought that if he didn't spit it out, she was about to throttle him with her bare hands, friendship be damned.

Isaiah finally lifted his dark brown eyes to meet hers. She

felt a frisson of fear shoot down her spine, from nape to tailbone.

"Joseph?"

"Yes, erm, well, he is…in Newgate Gaol." The words shimmered in the morning air.

"Newgate?" Daisy croaked.

"Ah, yes, mistress, that is…correct."

Newgate, that den of inequity, a quagmire of misery, the cessation of all hope, the end of the line. And her brother was incarcerated there.

"How? Why?"

Isaiah swallowed audibly. "He, that is, erm, I believe he was seized upon the London road in the act of–well. The act of…highway robbery." Isaiah spread his long-fingered hands in mute apology as if he was to blame for her brother's arrest and imprisonment.

Daisy closed her eyes, feeling a chill settle in her bones. She felt cold, so cold, to the marrow of her being. What was to be done? She slowly opened her eyes to see Isaiah looking at her, an expression of extreme distress on his long face. She took pity on him. Don't shoot the messenger; he was not to blame.

"Thomas."

"Thomas?"

"He'll know what to do."

"He will?"

"Aye, he allus does," Daisy said more firmly than she felt. She nodded to underline her statement. "Follow me." She spun on her heel, skirts swishing, making for the kitchen, not looking back, trusting that Isaiah was behind her.

She burst into the kitchen, surprising Thomas, who was deboning and butterflying a chicken.

"Allo lass, what yew been doin; now? I fort–" Thomas almost swallowed what he had been about to say seeing the apparition behind Daisy. His gaze swept from the top of Isaiah's skull-capped head to his dusty, oversized shoes. His first instinct was one of astonishment which he manfully suppressed, hearing his ma's voice admonishing him, "darn't yew judge a book by its cover, boy!"

He put his cleaver down and, turning to face the visitor, bowed formally to him, eliciting a start of surprise in the other man.

"I'm Thomas, Thomas Crabbe, an' yew are?"

"Isaiah Goldburger, wine merchant, at your service." Goldburger bowed in return to Thomas.

Daisy appreciated Thomas being polite to the young wine merchant. She felt her heart swell in love for him.

"Thomas, Isaiah has news of Joe."

"Oh, ah?"

Daisy felt her heart skip a beat. "He's in Newgate Gaol."

Thomas's eyes cut to Goldburger.

"Newgate?"

Isaiah nodded sorrowfully. "I am afraid so. I heard from a publican on the outskirts of Chelmsford. Apparently, Joseph was apprehended a few miles from there, holding up a stagecoach on the road to London. According to eyewitnesses, he was ambushed by the local constabulary who had received a…how do you say? A tip-off."

He nodded once more.

"Someone betrayed 'im?" spat Daisy.

"It would appear so, mistress."

At that moment, Daisy felt as if she could commit murder.

Thomas watched her expression harden. He wasn't surprised but wasn't about to share his thoughts with her; it wouldn't help.

"'e be in Newgate awaiting trial?"

Goldburger chewed his lip again. Daisy could see that he was choosing his words with care, and the chill came back, plus interest.

"Ah, no, no, there will not be a trial. He will hang next week." His voice trailed off.

Absolute silence followed this pronouncement.

Daisy felt as if she would be sick on the spot. Her face felt clammy, and sounds started to become distorted. Dots swam before her eyes.

She came to lying on the kitchen floor, her head in Thomas's lap, Isaiah applying smelling salts to her nostrils. She coughed, waved him away, coughed again and looked up into Thomas's upside-down face hanging over her, a frown of concern between his auburn eyebrows. "Yew alright, lass? Yew fainted clean away."

Daisy nodded, although she didn't feel well. Her head felt

like it was floating a few inches above her body; everything had a slightly unreal quality.

"We 'ave to rescue 'im, Thomas." She whispered the words, but Thomas flinched as if she had shouted.

"Now then, just a minute."

"He's my brother, an' he's goin' to hang!"

"I know, lass, but 'ow do you propose we break into Newgate? An' then break out again with ya brother in tow?"

"Ned'll help." Daisy nodded despite her head resting in Thomas' lap.

Two evenings after their discussion saw Daisy and Thomas mounted atop an old stagecoach drawn by four horses. Ned knew William Shephard, the owner of the Greene King brewery, who had an unusual passion for collecting old coaches. Ned had persuaded William to lend them the decommissioned stagecoach, citing some family emergency.

Daisy had two muskets under the seat, care of Abel Bedford. Thomas had baulked at carrying firearms. His time in the navy had instilled a dislike of all guns and cannons, so he contented himself with a long kitchen knife concealed in the inside breast pocket of his jacket. Ned had tutted at Thomas' reticence where weapons were concerned, but Thomas was quietly stubborn.

"Darn't know 'ow you're gonna break into a gaol with nobbut a knife an' bad attitude." Ned shook his head at Thomas.

What Ned didn't know was that Abel had a brother who was a locksmith in Charing Cross. Abel's brother, Adam, not only made locks, but he could pick any lock you cared to mention and some that you didn't care to mention.

Abel had sent a letter via first-class post to Adam at his workshop, explaining that Daisy and Thomas had a friend who had wrongfully been imprisoned and had to be freed. He failed to mention where said friend needed to be released from–he felt it would be better coming from Daisy directly, and he was wary about putting too much in writing.

Thomas had gained some knowledge of horses from living next door to the Bedfords, enough to allow him to drive the coach and four. They set out very early in the morning, hoping to get through Ipswich before most folk were up and about–the fewer people who saw them, the better.

They got to Colchester within several hours, resting at a public house with stables. The horses were unharnessed, rubbed down, fed, and watered for a few coins. They barely had enough energy to feed and water themselves before retiring to a cramped room with a lumpy double bed before falling deeply asleep.

During a hurried breakfast of bread, cheese, and ale, Thomas watched Daisy closely. She was pale, with dark circles under her eyes. Although they'd both fallen asleep quickly, she had woken in the small hours, fretting for her brother, and dozed on and off for the remainder of the night.

Thomas urged the horses on to London, Daisy now sitting next to him, straining to see the road ahead as if by sheer will she could make them go faster. Her impatience was palpable and several times Thomas saw her biting her thumbnail.

After a brief stop at Chelmsford to relieve themselves and

secure a fresh set of horses they pressed on, Thomas slapping the reins regularly, trying to coax as much speed from the borrowed animals. Thomas fell into an almost hypnotic trance, lulled by the churning horses, his heartbeat in time with their cantering gate. The movement of the coach and laboured breathing of the animals formed a sort of mantra in his mind. *We'll be too late, we'll be too late, we'll be too late …*

After another three hours, Thomas espied the Thames making its lugubrious way into the city's heart. They had spent so much time being the only coach travelling towards the metropolis that it was a comfort to be joined by other large and small vehicles, making their respective ways into the city.

"Nice to 'ave other people around," Daisy commented, echoing Thomas's thoughts.

"Aye, although we best keep to ourselves so no one recalls us later," he warned her.

She nodded her agreement, wrapping her shawl tighter around her shoulders, whether because of the cold or nerves, Thomas couldn't tell.

Another hour and a half passed before they reached the locksmith's premises. Adam had been waiting for them, for he opened the door as the coach pulled up outside. A young lad, presumably one of his apprentices, came forward quickly to take the reins from Thomas, who was so stiff he could barely clamber down from the driver's seat. The horses couldn't have gone much further, he concluded, so it was with an inexpressible sense of relief that he relinquished the horses into the boy's care.

Thomas ducked his head beneath the lintel as he entered the dim interior of Adam's workshop. The smell of oil and iron filings filled his nostrils, and Daisy pulled her skirts close to avoid soiling them on the tools lying about.

"Aye, come in, come in, mind ya skirts there now, that's right, come away into the back, it's quite a bit warmer than out 'ere!"

They followed Adam down a short corridor into a back room, which stretched the width of the whole house. A worn wooden table with knife marks from the preparation of hundreds of meals sat in the centre, accompanied by four wooden chairs. Adam gestured to these whilst he grabbed a cloth and, leaning over the open fire, lifted a black cast-iron pot off the hook. He ladled a hearty chicken and vegetable soup into wooden bowls, and Daisy and Thomas tucked into it and the freshly baked loaf that accompanied it.

Adam did not join them in eating but packed a pipe with tobacco and, taking a lighter wick from the pot next to the fire, dipped it into the flames and applied the lit end. Tendrils of smoke wreathed him, filling the room with the fragrant scent of cherry tobacco.

Daisy thought she was so tired she could fold her arms on the table, rest her head on them and fall sound asleep where she sat. She adjusted her bottom on the chair, hoping that she could remain awake by fidgeting. Thomas caught the agitated shufflings and laid his hand on her arm.

"Lass, why darn't yew go to bed now?"

Daisy looked gratefully at him, not just because he'd given her a chance to withdraw, but because she knew he must be just as tired as she was, yet he was excusing her. She smiled at Thomas and, heaving herself to her feet, wished them goodnight and climbed the wooden hill to the small room that Adam had put aside for them both. She reeled to bed, utterly exhausted, lulled to sleep by the rumble of men's voices drifting up through the floorboards.

Chapter 11

The sun rose in a blood-red dawn, making Thomas feel uneasy. He automatically crossed himself hearing Billy Mac's voice, "red sky in the morning, sailor, take warning." Thomas was not as superstitious as most seafaring men, but a ripple of premonition raised the hairs on his forearms. He chastised himself for being a fool. It stood to reason that he would feel uneasy this day–today, they would set out to break Joseph out of one of the most notorious gaols in the kingdom.

Over several tankards of ale the previous evening, Thomas and Adam had hatched a plan. The three of them would travel to the gaol first thing. Even condemned men were allowed visits from family members, and Daisy could provide proof that she was his sister. Not wanting her to enter Newgate on her own, Adam would pose as Daisy's husband, carrying a bag containing a flask of rum (all those set to hang were allowed a tot of rum before walking to the execution platform outside Debtor's Door).

Accompanying the rum would be some bread and a hunk of cheese, concealed in which would be a skeleton key to unlock Joseph's cell door.

Daisy would be slightly more curvaceous than usual, for she would be wearing two cloaks, two blouses, two bodices and two overskirts. A frilled cap would be in her pocket, and thus disguised, Joseph could leave the prison dressed as a woman. Hopefully, no sharp-eyed guard would spot the lack of petticoats under Joseph's skirt or count the number of visitors leaving the prison that morning. There were at least ten people on death row, so there would be a fair few comings and goings, and as they would let themselves out of the cell without the aid of the resident turnkey, by the time the visiting hour was finished, they would be clear of the prison and halfway across London. Thomas would be waiting with the coach a couple of streets away, ready to crack the whip at the horses as soon as Daisy and Joseph were safely aboard. Adam would melt into the alleyways and make a circumlocutious walk home.

They arrived in good time, or so they thought. A huge crowd had gathered, so Adam bade Daisy and Thomas to stay put whilst he skirted the edges of the gathering. He espied an elderly gentleman at the back of the crowd and asked him who was about to be executed. The reply came, "Joseph Lawrence."

He ran back to the coach where Daisy had disembarked, ready to follow Adam inside to visit her brother.

"I'm now coming!" she exclaimed breathlessly, hampered by all the extra clothes she was wearing.

"We're too late, lass." Adam stood looking down at her. Her upturned face went pale.

"What?" she whispered through frozen lips.

"The crowd's already gathered an' they're bringin' 'im out shortly. One of the bystanders confirmed it be 'im. We're too late," he repeated.

Daisy stood like a pillar of salt. Her ears absorbed what Adam said, but her brain refused to believe it.

"Arter all that, comin' all this way, an' he's still goin' to hang?"

"Aye, I'm that sorry, Daisy, but they're set to start soon." Adam shuffled his feet, wringing his felt cap between his large, workworn hands.

Thomas knotted the reins and jumped down from the driver's box. Taking Daisy's hands in his, he chafed them to get some warmth back into them.

"What do yew want to do, lass?" he asked her softly. Daisy felt numb.

"Daisy?"

"He's my brother."

"I know 'e is, lass; what do yew want to do?"

"I 'ave to be there."

"Where?"

"To see 'im. I can't stay away."

Thomas glanced at Adam, whose eyes had gone wide. "I darn't think–"

"Yew darn't want to–"

Both men spoke simultaneously, but she shook her head vehemently.

"No!" Just one word, but the men saw she was adamant.

Thomas thought he would try one more time. "Do yew really want to watch?"

"I owe 'im that much, Thomas, to let 'im know that we're here an' he's not alone."

No one paid any attention to the three latecomers at the back of the crowd. Thomas had found a low wall on which Daisy could stand, so she got a better view. She hoped desperately that her brother would scan the gathering and see her. She'd removed her white-frilled cap and loosened her hair so that he should recognise her better.

The Debtor's Door opened, and three men emerged into the watery sunshine. Joseph, hands bound; the ordinary, reciting a prayer for the condemned in a bored manner; and 'Jemmy' James Botting, Newgate's zealous overseer and hangman.

As Joseph stepped up to the platform, a roar went up from the crowd. They loved a good hanging, particularly of

notorious people, and Joseph was infamous. Botting placed the noose around Joseph's head, and the crowd quietened down. Thomas could almost hear people licking their lips in anticipation–he felt slightly sick. He put his arm around Daisy's legs, who grabbed his shoulder and gripped it tightly. Thomas looked up at her, but she didn't return his look, her eyes never leaving her brother's face.

The priest had finished intoning the last rights, and Joseph stepped onto the platform at a prod from Botting. This platform was released by moving a pin acting on a drawbar that would drop him several feet to his death. He scanned the crowd, his head moving slowly due to the noose. Finally, he spotted his sister. He turned his face full towards her and, smiling, mouthed, "such is life."

The hangman pulled the pin, Joseph disappeared from view, and a roar went up from the spectators.

Daisy's last thought before she fainted was that Jemmy Botting had done an excellent job…that rope would never break.

Chapter 12

Thomas was urging the horses on in the pale dawn light, trying to make for the next public house before dawn broke and people could ask questions. The horses were winded, he could hear them puffing from where he sat. He just hoped they had enough energy to reach their destination.

As they emerged from a tunnel of trees, Thomas could see a lamp glowing in the distance, and as they drew nearer, he could make out a coach, the horses whinnying in confusion as the vehicle was canted over at an awkward angle.

Thomas thumped on the side of the carriage, and Daisy pushed the sash window down, leaning out to see what was amiss.

"Another carriage up ahead," Thomas informed her curtly. He heard her intake of breath. "We'll tell 'em that we've been visiting ya brother who's sick, and we're makin' our way back home, alright?"

He sensed her nod and heard the window close with a snick. Daisy had spoken less than half a dozen words since they'd departed London. Thomas slowed the horses to a walk as they drew level with the other coach.

A lad, not much younger than Thomas, ran towards them, his lamp swinging in time with his gait. "Good sir, can you help us? Our coach has broken an axle, and we must make haste to London."

Thomas's eyebrows went up as he took in the young lad's livery and then shot up further as he saw the crest on the side of the vehicle. At the sound of his driver's shout, a grey wigged head appeared at one of the sash windows, hastily withdrawing it, then opening the door and descending from the carriage.

By this time Thomas had drawn rein and, with his free hand, groped for the musket under his seat, just as a precaution, hoping sincerely he wouldn't have to use it.

"I am sorry to inconvenience you, sir, but I must ask you to assist us, you and your companion," the older man said as Daisy poked her head out of the other window, taking in the scene. "We are travelling to our house in Kew, we have come from Lincolnshire with great haste, too great as you see, as our carriage is now broken..."

"I appreciate that, sir, but we are headin' home–"

"Let me handle this, Willis." This was from the other occupant, who had walked around the coach's side, where he had been taking stock of the damage. He was tall, with a crooked nose hinting at pugilism, and a nasal twang to his voice.

Thomas opened his mouth to say something else when the second man continued.

"This is Doctor Francis Willis, and my name is Richard Neale. I am equerry to His Majesty King George, and you have just saved the day, my friend." The man fixed him with a steely look from under finely shaped eyebrows. "I beg you to assist us so we can continue on our way." He bowed slightly.

As Thomas had been listening to Neale, Daisy had been watching the first man closely. He was considerably older than she had initially thought, with a lined but kind face and slightly mournful eyes. Those eyes now moved to her, and an unspoken appeal communicated itself.

Neale was still talking to Thomas, so Daisy coughed politely to get his attention.

"What?" Demanded Thomas.

"I think we best help these good folk."

"An' how do yew suggest we do that?"

"Thomas, this man is a physician, an' he's goin' to London to see the King."

Thomas glanced at her, then back to the wigged man, who waited patiently for them to decide.

Neale interrupted before Thomas could say anything else.

"Our coach is beyond repair, and even if it wasn't, we cannot dally; we must make all haste to London."

"Well, yew can't leave us 'ere!" Daisy protested.

Neale narrowed his eyes at her, but she pressed home her point before he could object. "There's only me an' my husband, an' our horses are spent as it is. They need rest. We'll exchange animals an' hook 'em to our carriage; then we can all be on our way."

Neale started with the use of 'our'. "What do you mean by that, Madam?"

Daisy opened the door and stepped down, walking up to him. "I *mean* that we be comin' with yew."

"Now, just a minute–" Thomas interposed as Neale said precisely the same thing.

"She's right." Dr Willis spoke softly but with a note of command in his voice that made everyone go quiet. "Besides, more hands make light work; isn't that right, m'dear?" He looked kindly at Daisy, his mournful eyes showing a slight twinkle in their depths.

Daisy warmed to him immediately. She couldn't explain why but felt oddly comforted, and she needed comfort after the last twenty-four hours.

The next twenty minutes saw the driver, Jack, Neale, Dr Willis, and Thomas unhook all the horses, hobbling their animals under a copse of trees nearby, where they began munching contentedly. The other four horses were harnessed to their carriage, and once the baggage was transferred, the small party boarded the coach–Thomas up top with Jack, having retrieved their muskets, whilst Daisy joined Neale and the excellent doctor inside.

"Will the horses be safe?" Dr Willis enquired.

"As safe as anywhere else, I reckon," replied Daisy. "If anyone wants to pinch them, luck to them, but I can't see any folk wantin' to be abroad at this time of day in the middle of nowhere."

Dr Willis smiled at her confidence. Neale did not share her

view.

"If anyone chances upon them, I fear they may take them. To whom do they belong?"

"The Fox and Hounds at Colchester, sir."

"A public house?" Neale arched a dark eyebrow at her.

"That's right." Daisy shut her mouth with a snap. Best to keep it simple. The more she divulged, the more she might get them into trouble.

Conversation was becoming increasingly more difficult as Jack whipped the horses onto London, making it very uncomfortable for the three occupants due to the roughness of the road and the speed. This relieved Daisy, who felt that Neale would have interrogated her further if he had had the opportunity.

After a couple of hours they stopped for a change of horses in Chelmsford and a well-needed comfort stop for the humans.

"My bladder's like to bust!" was all Daisy said as she shot past Thomas, making for the privy to the side of the inn. He smiled at her retreating back, skirts bunched in both fists. Luckily, being a man, he found the nearest tree and emptied his bladder, sighing with relief at the easing of the internal pressure. Evidently, the doctor thought that a suitable tree would serve the purpose and joined him.

"Thank you for your help," Willis said quietly whilst buttoning up his flies.

Thomas affected to examine a non-existent bit of fluff on the cuff of his coat. "Tha's alright, sir, we mun help yew on your errand."

"I am very grateful, and so is Neale, although he hides it well." Dr Willis smiled wryly. "And, of course, her Majesty, Queen Charlotte will be *very* grateful."

At the mention of the Queen Consort, Thomas started. What with Joseph's execution at Newgate, their hasty departure from London, the meeting on the road and the logistics of changing horses with the doctor and his companions, he hadn't absorbed the fact that royalty was involved with this quest. Now the enormity of what they were doing began to sink in.

"Sir, what will 'appen when we reach Kew?"

"His Majesty King George is–how do you say–resting there. Queen Charlotte sent Neale to fetch me immediately as His Majesty has deteriorated somewhat in the past few weeks. I had some success treating him before, and I hope to do so again." The older man smiled gently at Thomas.

Thomas heard the rustle of skirts and, turning, saw Daisy approaching them, smiling now that she was comfortable.

"Bumping around in tha' thing, I reckon I'll be black an' blue by the time we get to London." She dimpled at Dr Willis to take the sting out of her words.

"I truly regret the punishing pace we must keep, but time is of the essence. I was explaining to your husband about the King's health." Willis waved a pudgy hand at Thomas. "We must make all haste to get to him so I may begin treatment."

"Of course, sir, we know tha', don't we, Thomas?" She dug Thomas in the ribs, making him jump. "Whatever we can do to 'elp, we will." She dimpled again, making Dr Willis turn slightly pink. He coughed to cover his discomfort. Thomas mentally rolled his eyes.

"Well, then, I, ah, oh there you are, Neale." Willis looked relieved to see the equerry.

"We are ready–let us embark again," Neale said curtly, jerking his head towards the coach.

Another two hours, another coaching inn. They made one more stop before the carriage rumbled into view of the palace at Kew.

Thomas was somewhat disappointed by the first glimpse of the palace. He had expected something far more grand than the red brick edifice with three gables. He counted only twenty-four windows now reflecting the setting sun. As they bumped down the uneven driveway, he noted the avenue of trees on either side and as they neared the palace, he made out a small knot garden at the front surrounded by a cobbled courtyard. After some moments, Jack drew the steaming horses up at the front door, where a footman was already waiting, stiff in livery and powdered wig.

Neale leapt from the carriage while still moving, barely landing on the cobbles safely before sprinting into the palace. The footman came forward to pull the step down from the carriage, allowing Dr Willis and Daisy to disembark in a more dignified fashion.

Willis nodded at the footman. "Cope, how nice to see you again."

"And it is a pleasure to see you, sir," replied Cope, bowing to the doctor and then to Daisy.

Thomas jumped down off the driver's box. Once the baggage was removed, Jack coaxed the steaming horses around the side of the house into the waiting care of the grooms.

Dr Willis gestured to Daisy and Thomas. "These goodly folk assisted us on the high road, exchanging their carriage for ours, and have accompanied us without further misadventure. Please ensure that they are taken care of."

Cope bowed again to Dr Willis, opening his mouth to reply when a shout rang out from the front entrance. "Willis, come *on*! Bring them in, Cope–we must go to the King!" Neale beckoned Willis frantically, making the older man break into a trot clutching his worn, leather medicine bag.

Cope watched the retreating back of the physician, then turned back to Daisy and Thomas. "Sir, Madam, please accompany me into the house?"

Thomas and Daisy looked at each other. There wasn't much else to do except stand in the cobbled courtyard like a couple of lemons, so with an approximation of a bow from Thomas and a bobbed curtsy from Daisy by way of reply, they linked arms and sallied forth into Kew Palace.

A long gallery greeted them, wood panelling lining the walls on either side. Portraits of various royal family members adorned them, and they heard their footsteps echoing in the resultant void. The footman went ahead of them, his Moroccan heels tapping on the parquet floor, back straight as a ramrod, not a hair out of place on his powdered wig.

As they made their way down the interminably long gallery, raised voices could be heard. Thomas and Daisy exchanged glances but kept up with the servant, who had quickened his pace.

They rounded a ninety-degree corner and were presented with a tableau neither thought they should ever see. An argument was raging between the Prince Regent, the equerry Neale, and Dr Willis.

The Prince Regent spat at Neale. "What the fuck is that quack doing here?"

"Your Highness, he has come to attend your father–"

"I know what he fucking is! He's a jumped-up snake oil merchant who should know his *bloody* place!"

Dr Willis stiffened. "Your Highness, I have been summoned by your mother; she is most concerned–"

"The fuck she is!" The Prince Regent pulled himself upright, making his substantial paunch more prominent. Even the whalebone corset couldn't hide the full state of his corpulence. "She just bloody well doesn't want to see me on the throne, the cow."

Thomas started on hearing such a term coming out of another person's mouth, let alone the heir to the throne of England referring to his mother.

The Prince Regent's piggy eyes swivelled at the motion.

"What the fuck are you looking at?" he demanded of Thomas, who was trying to blend into the wood panelling behind him with limited success.

"I, ah, that is, ya Highness, I, ah–"

"Oh, for fuck's sake, another bloody idiot. Ye Gods, can someone not bring me a sodding solution to this problem?" He glared balefully around the room, his vision settling on the hapless doctor. "Either cure the old goat or fucking send him to his maker."

"George!" A clear, high voice rang out down the length of the corridor. Immediately, the equerry, the doctor and all the other people present dropped into either a bow or curtsy.

Thomas followed suit but, turning his bowed head slightly to the side, saw a middle-aged woman sweep down the corridor, her swishing skirts making the only sound. She was past the prime of her life but still handsome.

Looking up through his eyelashes, Thomas watched as the Queen Consort, Queen Charlotte, regarded her only child.

They stared at each other, eyeball to eyeball, until after a few heartbeats the Prince Regent extended a fat leg and made a shadow of a courtly bow to his mother, which only just stopped short of rudeness.

"George." The Queen Consort said again, in heavily accented English. "Ein Vater est sick, no? You had best attend him, mein Sohn–nein!" She held up a long-fingered white hand. "Deine Mutter asks you, beta, to see to your Vater."

The Prince straightened up, tugging at the points of his waistcoat, pushing his full-bottomed lip in and out, prevaricating whether to obey her or not. His hard eyes darted around the assembly, gauging the mood of those gathered. Deciding that their account of this day would be critical in the days or weeks to come, he decided to appease his mother. "Of course, Mamma, I will attend upon his Majesty."

"Exzellent, he vill be most pleased. Ja?" She nodded up at him. Despite being several inches shorter than her son, the Queen Consort had a presence that demanded obedience.

No one spoke. The seething sound of silence filled the long gallery. Crabbe looked at the highly-polished buckles on the Prince Regent's shoes, trying to breathe as inconspicuously and shallowly as possible.

"Well, quack, don't just stand there; let us go and see my father." With that, the Prince turned and waddled off towards the King's private apartments, followed at a suitable distance by the Queen Consort.

A collective sigh of relief was heard around the gallery. Thomas straightened up and looked sideways at Daisy, whose eyes had gone perfectly round.

"Blimey, there's no love lost atween those two, I reckon." She wiped the palms of her sweaty hands on her skirts.

The footman, Cope, snorted in derision. "You have no idea, dear lady," he murmured.

Neale, bereft of purpose, exhaled strongly through his nose.

"Arsewipe," he said succinctly, his back stiff with barely suppressed rage, finely arched eyebrows drawn into a frown.

Thomas looked thoughtfully at the equerry. He noted the finely formed lips compressed into a slash of disapproval. So, the loyal servant disapproved of the king-in-waiting. Mentally he shrugged his shoulders. It was all the same to him—one Geordie followed another.

Cope turned to Daisy and Thomas. "May I provide you with some refreshments, Madam? Sir?"

Neale snapped out of his brown study and swivelled his dark blue eyes towards the two guests. "My apologies, I have been remiss in my manners. Thank you, Cope; please see them into the Chinese room, and provide them with food and drink. I shall join you shortly once I have checked that all is well with Dr Willis." He bowed smartly to them and strode off down the gallery.

Cope gestured to the guests to follow him. After a couple of turns, he led them into a dark room with lacquered wooden panelling depicting Oriental scenes, which mainly seemed to feature ladies with parasols crossing bridges. The furniture was weighty and dark, with a thick carpet that muffled the sounds of their footsteps.

Daisy found it very oppressive, but Thomas immediately went over to a painting hanging above the fireplace. A wise-looking man in an ornate gown sporting a long beard sat holding something small between his forefinger and thumb. Various hieroglyphics were written on the side of his portrait.

"What's 'e holdin'?" Daisy asked.

"An acupuncture needle," replied Thomas.

"Yew what?"

Thomas turned away from the painting with a smile on his face. "The Chinese use needles to heal. They 'ave certain points in the body that work on different areas to get yew better."

Daisy looked dubious. "I darn't reckon bein' stuck with pins is goin' to make me feel any better."

Thomas sat in the chair opposite Daisy, sighing as he stretched out his bad leg. "A Chinaman on one of 'em trading ships off the coast of Honduras offered to treat me," he gestured at his leg. "I thanked 'im but politely said no."

"I darn't blame yew."

"Later, I mentioned it to Sam and 'e said I were a fool not to take the fella up on it." Thomas looked wistful, whether at an opportunity missed or the mention of his friend.

"Yew miss 'im." Said as a statement rather than a question. Thomas glanced at her.

"Aye, reckon I do at that."

"Yew've no way of findin' out where 'e went?"

Thomas shook his head sadly. "Nay, 'e could be anywhere."

A knock sounded on the door, and Cope appeared bearing a silver tray upon which sat two glasses containing a red liquid and a plate of savouries. He placed this on the table, handed Daisy napkins, and then bade them enjoy the wine and pastries. He then withdrew.

Thomas realised it had been a long time since they'd had anything to eat, and his stomach rumbled in agreement, eliciting a giggle from Daisy. He grinned at her and popped what looked like a vol-au-vent containing some creamy sauce into his mouth. On hitting his taste buds, it revealed itself to be prawns in a mayonnaise flavoured with, he suspected, a pinch of cayenne pepper. Thomas closed his eyes in rapture. He had never tasted anything so good; it melted in his mouth.

Opening his eyes, he saw Daisy munching on a miniature quiche Lorraine.

"Awwmmmhhpphhh, tha's tasty!" she said through a mouth full of pastry.

Thomas sat on the edge of his chair, perusing the savouries. Next, he selected what looked like a small biscuit upon which was a sliver of fish with some little dots on top, accompanied by a sprig of dill. He chewed thoughtfully; salmon with cod's roe, if not mistaken. Well, they *were* spoiled.

As he and Daisy squabbled amicably over who was going to have the last canapé, the door opened again, and the sardonic countenance of Neale appeared. He stood in the doorway, his broad shoulders blocking out a fair bit of light. Thomas squinted at him, watching as Neale shut the door with a soft click and walked over to join them.

Something about how the equerry moved and held himself niggled at the back of Thomas's mind. This niggle he would bring out later to examine more closely, but for now, he inclined his head towards the other man, who took a chair.

Neale stretched out his long legs and steepled his fingers together. "Dr Willis is attending to His Majesty now…we will see what eventuates."

Neither Daisy nor Thomas commented.

"I do not have to ask either of you," Neale continued, "to keep what has transpired here today to yourselves." He fixed both of them with a steely glance.

Thomas drew himself up straight. "Yew darn't need to worry, sir, I've kept many a secret in my time, an' so has my wife."

Neale nodded, tapping his index fingers on his lower lip. He appeared to be considering something. The only sound in the room was the ticking of an ornate grandfather clock in the corner. The silence stretched. Daisy began to fidget. Thomas reached for her hand, and she stilled immediately.

Neale drew a deep breath; clearly, he had decided. "I need to ask your assistance in a…delicate matter." He paused. Daisy glanced at Thomas. Something passed between them.

Getting to her feet, she said, "If ye'll excuse me, sir, I'll be leavin' yew now to chat. I'll have a little wander around the house and grounds, if tha's alright?"

Neale rose and bowed to her. "Of course, Madam." Daisy quit the room, leaving the men to talk.

Chapter 13

After the door closed behind Daisy, the two men regarded each other.

"Ye're not just an equerry, are ye?" Crabbed asked.

"You are correct." Neale steepled his fingers under his cleft chin.

"What are ye, then?"

"I keep an eye on people, Mr Crabbe. Enemies of the crown."

Crabbe looked at Neale, eyeball to eyeball. "Ye mean you're a spy?"

"I leave that to others. I am what you might term… an intelligencer."

Crabbe felt his eyebrows go up.

"I have a talent for organisation and communication, both verbal and written, and the ability to keep my mouth shut."

Crabbe remained silent.

"Added to that," continued Neale, "I can blend into most gatherings, and I have exceptional hearing. I can hear a bat squeak at fifty paces."

Crabbe laughed quietly at this statement.

"Also…" Neale paused, reflecting. "The Queen Consort trusts me, and I speak passable German–not many do, amongst the English staff here."

"So how did ye…?" Crabbe see-sawed his hand.

"The Queen wished me to write a letter to a doctor she had heard of by reputation, but she did not want the King nor the Prince to hear of it. She dictated the letter to me in German, and I translated it into English. However, I realised that it could be intercepted and opened, so I offered to take the letter in person to the physician, Dr Willis, whom you met today. He has had some success in treating the condition that affects His Majesty. The Queen has tasked me with fetching Willis on previous occasions, so I did so again this time.

When His Majesty recovered, the Queen informed him of my involvement, and he came up with the idea of my…shall we say, secondary function."

"But ye are first and foremost the King's equerry?"

"Indeed! I oversee all vehicular transport for the royal family; the royal stables, etcetera." Neale smiled thinly.

"And under cover o' this ye can move freely, passin' letters an' gatherin' information an' so on."

"Just so." Neale spread his hands.

"Not a bad idea, that." Crabbe nodded, acknowledging the King's ingenuity.

"When His Majesty is lucid, he is intelligent and wise. Unfortunately, those moments are becoming fewer." Neale looked sadly at the remains of Daisy and Thomas's tea.

"So, the Prince Regent will become king afore too long?"

"We all hope His Majesty will recover," Neale replied glibly.

"O' course aye, I just meant–"

"The Prince Regent will succeed his father when the time comes, which we all hope and pray will be some way off." The equerry lowered his eyebrows, warning Crabbe not to say anymore.

Crabbe picked up on the other man's tone and let the matter drop. Neale seemed to be contemplating his navel, so Crabbe had a chance to observe him surreptitiously. He was tall, broad shoulders straining the seams of his jacket; long legs stretched out in front of him, crossed at the ankles. His reddish-brown hair was pulled back in a neat ponytail, and he was clean-shaven with a hint of a cleft chin. His appearance overall was one of quiet masculinity, yet…long lashes swept over the downcast blue eyes, manicured fingernails rapped an absent-minded tattoo on the arms of the chair, and a subtle scent of pomade emanated from him.

During his naval years, Crabbe encountered sailors who gravitated towards other men. Some did it from brutal need, forcing themselves on others weaker than themselves, while others made overtures to those they knew were of the same persuasion. After a while, Crabbe developed an inner compass that could define those who preferred their own sex. That compass was now pointing towards True North–in other words, at Richard Neale. The equerry hid it well, but Thomas Crabbe would have bet his beloved cat on the fact that Neale was attracted to men, not women.

Belatedly becoming aware he was under scrutiny, Neale's

eyes flicked up as Crabbe's dropped. Not quickly enough; Neale saw a look of conjecture in the grey depths. He realised with a jolt that the younger man sitting opposite him was highly perceptive, despite his mundane appearance. The thoughts swirling around in his brain began to coalesce into something more concrete.

Neale took a deep breath and prepared to make a proposal. Before he did so, however, he needed to find Thomas Crabbe's wife.

Chapter 14

Daisy wandered through a door into one of the warmest rooms she'd ever been in. The whole room was made of glass, wall to wall, floor to ceiling. In this room were plants and flowers she'd never seen–brightly coloured trumpets, glossy dark leaves, every colour of the rainbow. She felt the sweat break out on her upper lip and bead her forehead, pungent scents filling her nostrils.

Pushing aside various leaves and tendrils, she became aware of a noise–clear at first, then muffled, as if someone had stifled it quickly. She rounded a group of what she later discovered was Birds of Paradise, and there in front of her was the Queen Consort, eyes red-rimmed, a lace handkerchief folded over her mouth. Daisy stopped abruptly, unsure what to do–embarrassed that she had chanced upon Queen Charlotte in a moment of private grief.

The Queen raised her head on hearing Daisy's approach, hastily wiping her eyes.

Daisy immediately dropped into a curtsy, her brain rapidly riffling through various opening conversational gambits. She was spared having to think of one by the Queen beckoning her over.

"Die ist Daisy, nein?"

Daisy nodded, for once in her life, completely speechless. But of course, Neale would have briefed the Queen. She curtsied again.

"I am grateful, danke to you and dein Ehemann." The Queen's eyes filled with tears again. "Mein Koenig is krank, he is not well…"

Daisy moved forward and knelt before the Queen, startling her by taking her hand. "Your Majesty, may I be helpin' yew? Yew seem sore troubled, and I should like to help if I can."

Queen Charlotte looked down into the earnest, upturned face. A good face, a strong face, a kind, dependable face. Should she trust her? An ordinary woman she hardly knew?

"Mein leibchen–George, he is…dying. Herr Doktor Willis he helped before, ja?"

Daisy nodded encouragingly.

"But now I am, how you say…keine hoffnung…no hope." The tears began rolling down her face once more.

"There is always hope, your Majesty. If yew have faith, there is always hope. Darn't be too downcast; the good doctor knows what 'e be about."

Daisy could tell that the Queen didn't understand everything she was saying, so she gently squeezed her hand to reassure her.

"Mein Sohn ist…schwierig." She saw Daisy's incomprehension. "Ist…hard, difficult?"

Daisy nodded again. That was the understatement of the

year. That overweight, arrogant, rude man who would be their next King, God help them.

"He does not mean…nicht grob…" The Queen groped for words. Just then, Daisy heard footsteps, and getting to her feet, she released the Queen's hand just as Neale came around the corner. He bowed deeply to Queen Charlotte and, in fluent German, updated her on the doctor's treatment and the King's state.

Daisy couldn't understand what was being said, but she was a good reader of body language, and she could tell by the slump of the other woman's shoulders and the way her head drooped that the news was not good.

Neale turned to Daisy, giving the Queen a few minutes to compose herself. "Thank you for keeping her Majesty company; I told her that the doctor may have come too late. His Majesty is not well at all and is fading fast."

Daisy looked at the floor, feeling for the Queen but not knowing what to say. She raised her head and asked Neale, "Would yew be kind enough to let the Queen know what I be sayin'?"

Neale's eyebrows went up. "I do not think her Majesty should be bothered with–"

"It's not for me, it's for 'er. I'm a woman, she's a woman; I'd like to give 'er some comfort if I can."

Neale's eyebrows sank back down to their normal level. "Of course. My apologies. What would you like me to say to her?"

"Just tell 'er that I know what it's like to lose a loved one, it ain't easy an' she's not just a wife, she's a mother and Queen n'all."

Neale bowed to Daisy and interpreted for the Queen, whose eyes widened slightly and turning, she smiled at Daisy before replying in rapid German.

"She says thank you sincerely, and if there is anything she can do for you, you only have to ask."

Daisy curtsied to the Queen and was about to ask Neale if he would put in a good word for Thomas when suddenly the Queen gasped and doubled over, holding a hand to her side. Neale shot forward and took her gently by the shoulders. The spasm soon passed, but the Queen seemed shaken by the episode, looking pale and sweaty. She said something breathlessly to Neale, who murmured in reply. He straightened and looked at Daisy. "Her Majesty has been suffering a sickness for some time; it comes on quickly and leaves her weakened. Would you be so kind as to assist me in helping her to her quarters?"

Daisy nodded vigorously, stepping forward and taking hold of the Queen's left arm whilst Neale secured her right. Between the two of them, they slowly got the Queen Consort through a series of winding corridors to her quarters, where a couple of ladies-in-waiting immediately took her into their care.

Neale and Daisy were left standing, looking at the closed doors of the Queen's bed chamber.

"How ill is she?" Daisy asked quietly, although she believed she already knew the answer.

"Very. She has been ailing for some months, and His Majesty's relapse has worsened her condition. She has dropsy, but an ill-advised walk in the rain has caused sickness in her lungs."

Daisy digested this bit of information for a moment. "What happens if she…well…"

"The King must carry on, perforce–which he will, once he recovers." Neale chose his words with care; to even allude to the King's death was treason and punishable by death.

Daisy caught the equerry's tone and nodded her agreement.

"Of course, he will recover," she said more firmly than she felt.

Neale smiled thinly at her. "We all pray so, dear lady."

"The um, the Prince Regent, will he…after the King…?"

"Oh yes, of course, although he has neither sense nor imagination."

Daisy started at his summing up of the heir to the throne.

"He has humour and is a witty conversationalist, but other than that, he is more interested in wine, women, and song than running a country."

A long silence followed this pronunciation. Daisy sincerely hoped there wasn't a servant lurking around a corner eavesdropping. Otherwise, Neale would find himself out of a job very quickly.

Neale saw her expression. "The Prince Regent is a law unto himself and will do whatever he wants when he wants, with whom he wants, irrespective of whatever anyone says."

Daisy thought that, indeed, there had to be some of the father in the son. King George III was known to be abstemious, not taken to drink or swearing, whilst his son seemed to be the opposite. Only last month, he had scandalized polite society by announcing his intention to take another mistress after separating from his wife, Caroline of Brunswick. And that was after he had married Maria Fitzherbert in a secret ceremony several years prior. His father had made him denounce the woman, casting her aside to marry his cousin.

His dissolute lifestyle would not stop him from ruling England, despite the Prince of York being much more reliable and stable. The second in line to the throne had recently given a well-received speech in parliament alongside Peel and the Solicitor-General in the debate against the ten thousand guineas to be given to the Prince Regent as a yearly stipend. Even the country's political unrest and rioting did little to deter the Prince Regent from his hedonistic lifestyle.

Neale exhaled heavily through his nose. "I would be obliged if you would return with me to speak to your husband. I have a proposal for both of you."

Daisy looked at the equerry. He was a handsome man in a brutal sort of way. He didn't appeal to her, as a sense of repressed violence floated around him like a haze, but she could see how he would be attractive to some women. "O' course."

Daisy followed Neale back to join Thomas in the Chinese room where Neale continued, steepling his fingers.

"The King is unwell, as you know, and given recent… hostilities with France, which have weighed heavily on His Majesty's mind, the Prince Regent finds it advisable to—let us say—investigate what is happening in Europe."

Neither Thomas or Daisy spoke.

Neale cleared his throat, crossing one leg over the other.

"We have it on good authority that Napoleon is intending to return from captivity and is intent on regaining his position as Emperor of France."

Thomas started. This was news…Napoleon had been defeated a year earlier, in 1814. An anti-French alliance, including Russia, Prussia, Austria, Britain, and other smaller countries, had overthrown the egotistical dictator. It appeared he was making a bid for his self-appointed throne once more.

"Talking to you just now, you told me about your time in the British Navy–your familiarity with travel and other countries." Crabbe nodded. "Added to that, your– forgive me– but your unexceptional appearance–" he smiled to soften the statement– "makes you an ideal candidate."

"Candidate?" queried Crabbe, rather stung by Neale's comment even if he had no illusions about this looks.

"To blend in, to move undetected, in short…to spy."

The words hung in the air, the silence only broken by the monotonous ticking of the clock.

"Spy?" croaked Crabbe.

Neale inclined his elegant head, fingers still steepled.

"Indeed."

Thomas didn't need to look at Daisy; he could imagine her expression, which was probably the same as his, utter disbelief.

"Just how do yew think I'll do that?"

Neale thought for a few moments. "You work in a public

house in Suffolk, yes?" Thomas nodded slowly, his eyes never leaving Neale's face.

"Well then, how would you feel about a promotion to head footman in the service of Lord Palmer? Palmer is based in Suffolk and is a well-known anti-French activist and politician. I can arrange a position for you there."

At that point, Daisy interjected. "An' what about me?"

Neale opened his mouth to say something, but Thomas cut him off.

"Yew go with me, gel."

Daisy's mouth fell open. "An' what meks yew think I'll go with yew, Thomas Crabbe?"

Neale snorted with amusement.

Thomas glanced at him, then back at Daisy feeling his ears growing pink. "What I meant was–"

"I know wha' yew meant, an' yew can ask me proper like, or not at all!" retorted Daisy.

Neale thought it was about time he brought the meeting to order before total domestic warfare ensued. "Ahem! I think your good lady means you should at least discuss matters with her, sir, which you will have the opportunity to do once I leave you. For now, let me conclude my proposal. I can secure a position for you both in the household of Lord Palmer as man and wife. Mr Crabbe, as I mentioned, you would be the first footman, and you, dear lady, would either be a kitchen maid or assistant cook. I will have to speak to the butler and see where you could slot in most easily." He paused, pursing his lips. "I will speak to His Highness this afternoon and request his approval to write to Lord Palmer." Neale pursed his lips again. More likely, he would inveigle his opinion into the empty shell that was the Regent's brain and plant sufficient seed so that the Regent would conclude that it had been his idea all along. So be it, if it achieved the main aim eventually. "Lord Palmer will take you into his employ, where you will await further instructions."

Thomas and Daisy looked at each other, a whole conversation taking place in a matter of seconds. Thomas blinked once.

"We thank yew, sir, we'd be 'appy to 'elp, an' if it means we can stay together workin' for this Lord Palmer…then, yes, we will."

Daisy thought privately that they probably wouldn't have had much choice in the matter, but Neale inclined his head graciously as if to intimate that they had had the right to refuse.

"Lord Palmer will brief you in due course, but, for now, I will arrange for your safe passage back to Suffolk, where you will probably want to collect those horses. May I write to you care of the Cock and Bull?" Neale raised an eyebrow at Thomas, who nodded in the affirmative.

"I will speak to Cope and arrange accommodation for you both tonight, then I will brief you in the morning." Neale heaved himself to his feet. It had been a long and emotional couple of days, and he needed to rest.

Daisy and Thomas also got to their feet, exchanged a few pleasantries, and wished the equerry a good evening. The door closed, and they were left looking at each other.

"Spying?" Daisy said, eyebrows shooting up. "Aye, well, an' I'll be the least likely spy, no?"

Daisy chewed her bottom lip. It sounded glamorous, but she was worried about what Thomas might be asked to do in the course of his new position. "I reckon tha's what Neale is bankin' on, yew not bein' noticed."

"Aye, reckon yew be right." Thomas grinned suddenly, changing his whole face. "Reckon it'll be fun though, right?"

Chapter 15

Ned was not happy. Thomas had only been with them a short while, and now, not only had he married Daisy, but they'd both served their notices when they'd returned from their mission to London.

"An wha' am I s'posed to do now, eh?" He glared balefully at the newlyweds who sat in front of him, side by side like a pair of naughty children. "Bad enow yew fall in love, get wed, then gallop off to London–an' yew've both got new positions!" Ned puckered his mouth, reminding Thomas of Trim's bottom. He felt a giggle begin to well up but manfully suppressed it. Ned was upset enough as it was.

"So, I ask yew, wha' am I goin' to do?" Ned glanced about the room as if a barmaid and a cook would materialise magically.

"Aw Ned, we're tha' sorry," Daisy assured him. "Thomas 'as spoken to Abel Bedford, 'is neighbour, 'an Abel's got someone in mind, hasn't 'e, Thomas?" She turned to look encouragingly at her husband, who was already nodding.

"Tha's right. Abel's son, who's been working as an apprentice in Ipswich, has a friend, Eustace, who's always shown a love for cookin', an' he'd like to come an' learn here.

Plus," added Thomas, laying his trump card down, "Eustace has a sister, an' she's over eighteen, an' keen to work behind yon bar." Thomas smiled triumphantly.

Ned see-sawed his mouth, weighing the pros and cons of taking on two new people and family members. However, he didn't want all the bother of having to find replacements for Daisy and Thomas so was secretly relieved that the hard work had been done for him. He wasn't about to let either of them off the hook that easily, though. "I s'pose I can 'ave a look. When can they come over?"

Thomas saw Daisy's shoulders slump out of the corner of his eye and knew that she was feeling relieved at Ned's acquiescence. "I reckon on Saturday, 'ow about, say 10 o'clock?"

The two men shook on it–accompanied by the usual spitting in palms, which Daisy thought disgusting, but forbore to comment on.

Eustace and his sister Lucy came over that weekend, and Daisy and Thomas began to show them the ropes. Eustace was a quick study and genuinely loved food, so he and Thomas got on like a house on fire. Daisy found young Lucy to be biddable, if not the sharpest knife in the drawer, but she was willing to do almost any menial task, so Ned was satisfied.

Daisy and Thomas duly left the employ of the Cock and Bull public house and returned to the cottage to pack and make plans.

"Well, he'll 'ave to go in yon crate," Thomas stood, hands on hips regarding Trim. Trim sat looking up at his master. Trim had seen the crate being pulled out of the pantry, and he suspected what was about to happen. Ordinarily he wouldn't have been best pleased; however, having seen Daisy and Thomas packing up boxes of belongings, he realised that he was being packed too, much to his relief. Trim had been with Thomas for nearly four years, and nothing short of surgical intervention would part them.

Naturally, Thomas had written to their new employer, Lord Palmer, requesting permission to bring a cat. He had taken great pains to emphasise the rat-catching capabilities of Trim, his handsome appearance, affable nature, quiet ways, and general all-round appeal. Then had sat back and sweated until the somewhat terse but affirmative letter came back. So, Trim was moving to Long Melford Hall too.

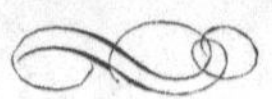

They arrived on a cool, blustery autumn day. The leaves falling from the trees, leaving them naked, their bare branches reaching towards the leaden sky. Something about the way the hall sat, squatting in the middle of open fields, its front windows reflecting the greyness, reminded Daisy of a bleached skull, the windows empty sockets, lifeless. Abel Bedford had offered to convey them to the hall along with their personal effects. They had bumped along rutted laneways, Daisy huddled into her shawl, Thomas and Abel with slouch hats pulled down low over their ears. Trim was in his crate on a blanket, eyes wide as he took in the passing countryside.

The cart pulled up at the side entrance to the imposing edifice. A portly woman in a brown homespun dress opened the door and, throwing a worn shawl around her shoulders, came out to greet them, smiling broadly.

"Alright, boh?" she greeted Abel, who touched his hat in greeting. "I be Mrs Perkins, the cook 'ere. They's told me to expect yew today, yew all must be cold now arter sittin' up there for an hour or so." She continued her cheerful narrative whilst Daisy, Thomas, and Abel descended stiffly from the trap. A young lad of about fourteen or so came shyly forward to take Robin's reins and lead him into the lee of the stable block for a rub down and quick feed before Abel returned home. The journey should only have taken an hour and a half, but with the recent rain, it had been nearer two hours.

They all stepped into the large, inviting kitchen. A young scullery maid was busy peeling potatoes and bobbed a quick curtsy as they entered. Another girl was scrubbing pots in the double sink to her left. The three weary travellers sat down at the worn wooden kitchen table that Thomas thought could have easily seated ten people. He placed Trim at his feet, still in his crate.

"A cat, now? Well, I 'ope the master knows…" Mrs Perkins looked dubiously at Trim, her head on one side.

"Aye, he knows; I wrote to him askin' permission afore we started packin'." Thomas assured the cook.

"Well, tha's alright then." Mrs Perkins beamed at him, then down at Trim, who was sniffing the air industriously, trying to gauge what meat was roasting for lunch. "Do 'e like chicken?"

Trim looked at Mrs Perkins like she had taken leave of her senses.

Thomas laughed at the expression on Trim's face. "Well, bully beef's his favourite, but 'e won't say no to a bit o' roast chicken."

"Well, tha's good then, I'll put a wee bit aside for 'im."

Trim gazed up at the cook, promoting her to his third favourite person in the world.

Thomas grinned at Mrs Perkins. "You've made a friend for life now, missus."

Mrs Perkins chuckled. "Well, as long as 'e keep yon mice down, 'e can 'ave bits o' chicken now an' then."

Daisy coughed politely, bringing the scene of domestic bliss to a close. "Might yew be showin' us where our quarters are?"

"Oh yes, dearie, sorry about tha'–this way, follow me, tha's right, down this passage an' away to the left. Second door on the right, tha's yorn room, both of yew." She stepped back and gestured for the Crabbes to precede her into the room put aside for them.

The room was a little small, but it had a high ceiling and a large casement window that stretched nearly the width of the wall. The walls were painted white lathe and plaster, with stripped wooden floorboards. A double bed squatted against the back wall, accompanied by a small chest of drawers upon which a basin and ewer sat. A commode chair completed the furniture. A board with iron hooks adorned one wall, serving as a wardrobe.

Thomas thought he'd never seen such a large bed. He and Daisy had been sharing a standard double in the cottage, so this was a pleasant surprise. Both of them had few possessions, so the chest of drawers would be more than adequate. They would be spending little time in the room, being part of the staff.

"Well, I'll let yew get settled in, like, an' I'll let Mr Jenkins know you're 'ere." With that, she bobbed a perfunctory curtsy and exited the room, leaving the Crabbes looking at each other.

A slow smile bloomed on Daisy's face. Thomas smiled back. It was ideally suited to them–the house, the bedroom, and the positions earmarked for them.

Mr Jenkins was the butler of Long Melford Hall, and until recently, Mrs Killett had been the housekeeper, but she had been persuaded to retire early. Daisy was now the housekeeper, which had raised a few eyebrows amongst the staff, not least of which belonged to Mr Jenkins. However, Lord Palmer had conducted a quiet conversation with the butler, informing him that the Crabbes were employed at the behest of royal persons and that he, Jenkins, should put aside his inverted snobbery and accept them both into the house. Thomas would be head footman, reporting directly to Mr Jenkins, and Daisy would answer to Lady Palmer with a dotted line to Mr Jenkins. The butler was unhappy about two jumped-up bumpkins from the back blocks being promoted to such senior positions, but if he didn't want to lose his place, Lord Palmer had informed him that he should get the bloody hell on with it.

So, with an uneasy truce existing, Daisy and Thomas began work for the Palmers.

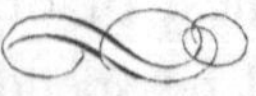

The Crabbes were in their third spring of working at Long Melford House when a soft knock sounded at the scullery door. Daisy frowned. Had she heard correctly? She listened. Yes, there it was again. Daisy stood up, shaking the skirts of her dress down where she'd been kneeling, conducting an inventory of the vegetables with the young scullery maid, Kate. She walked through to the door, opening it to the fine, crisp morning, and a young woman, dressed in plain homespun, a bonnet sat back from her forehead showing dark, centrally parted hair, gloved hands clasped in front of her.

"Good morning. This would be Long Melford Hall?" Daisy nodded, looking the young woman up and down.

"I, ah, that is to say, I wondered if the lady of the house might be available."

Daisy thought it odd that a young woman dressed smartly, wanting to see the lady of the house, had come to the tradesman's entrance, not the front door.

"Yew be wantin' the mistress?" Daisy cocked a dark

eyebrow.

"Ah, yes, that is to say…" The young woman looked down at her feet, shuffled them, then back up at Daisy, who noticed that the stranger's eyes had filled with tears.

"I must talk to her, but not, well, up there." She gestured to the house, presumably referring to the grandeur of the establishment and its rooms.

Daisy cocked the other eyebrow. "The mistress won't want to come all the way down 'ere jest to talk to a young gel," she informed the visitor, not unkindly.

At this point, the girl's head drooped forward, and tears began rolling down her face. Her slight shoulders shook.

"Now, now, darn't upset yourself, lovie, come away in now, that's it, mind the step, there, yew are, in through 'ere,

that's right, now, sit yew down, and I'll have cook put the kettle on." Daisy continued cheerfully whilst showing the girl in and pulling out a wooden chair for her at the huge refectory table.

Mrs Perkins, the cook, turned from stirring a huge pot of soup on the ancient stove and took in the visitor's appearance with astonishment. "Who be this young lass?"

"A visitor, Mrs Perkins. She be wantin' a cuppa and one of your freshly baked biscuits now." Daisy jerked her head at the kettle, widening her eyes and waggling her eyebrows, indicating that she was just as surprised as the cook at the girl's sudden appearance, but there was no help for it but to sit her down, ply her with food and drink and find out what the whole thing was about.

The young woman had removed a handkerchief from her small purse and wiped her eyes. Sitting up straighter, she smiled wanly at the two servants and squared her shoulders.

"My name is Margaret Beardsley. I have come a long way to get here." She paused to take a restorative breath. "I wish to speak to the lady of the house about a personal matter, which may cause her embarrassment if done in the–well, reception area of the house." She swallowed, looking appealingly at the older women.

Mrs Perkins glanced at Daisy. *Is she genuine?* said the look.

Daisy nodded, almost imperceptibly. "And this matter is to do wi' the mistress and not the master?"

Margaret chewed her lip. "It concerns the master, but not in a favourable way, hence my wishing to speak to his wife." The statement hung in the air.

Mrs Perkin's grey eyebrows shot up to her white-frilled cap. She chanced a glance at Daisy, who shook her head.

"The master? Well, that be awkward, an' no mistake."

Margaret nodded. "I know, but I do not wish to embarrass the mistress of the house. The matter I wish to discuss with her will not show her husband in a favourable light."

Daisy looked again at Mrs Perkins, whose eyebrows had almost disappeared into her hairline.

"The master isn't in at present; he went out–but you already knew that, didn't you?" She saw the look on Margaret's face.

"Yes. I waited down the laneway to ensure he had departed before walking up here and knocking on the door."

A silence fell. The three women looked at each other. Daisy

broke it after a few minutes. "I think we should know a little of what yew be here for before I go an' bother the mistress with it." Daisy spoke kindly but firmly. She felt sorry for the girl, but an uncharitable part of her brain realised that if she let this girl talk to the mistress, and all hell broke out, she could likely lose her position.

Margaret looked at Daisy. She appeared kind, but her voice held an underlying note of steel, warning her to be careful. Clearing her throat, she said, "It is a matter of honour, or rather lack thereof, on behalf of the master." She folded her hands in her lap and waited.

Again, an exchange of looks between the cook and housekeeper was not lost on Margaret. She didn't blame the women; they were employed here and probably felt loyal to the people they worked for. Both women looked back at Margaret expectantly.

She looked down at her folded hands, then back up at them. If she was to gain anything, she needed to be honest.

Chapter 16

The gambling had been going on all day and into the evening. Now, it was approaching midnight, and they were still at it. Elizabeth had tried to reason with her husband, but he had merely hauled her onto his lap, breathing wine-sodden fumes into her face, pinching her cheek, and making the group of men laugh.

"By Jove, Palmer, if you want to bed the gel, just take her upstairs, don't mind us!"

They all guffawed loudly, braying like donkeys. Elizabeth felt her face flush with embarrassed colour at the allusion to the bedroom.

Her husband, Lord Palmer, sneered at her reaction. "Maybe I'll just take her over the table," he shouted, and the other men all erupted with laughter. Elizabeth extricated herself with difficulty, running from the room, their laughter echoing in her ears.

She sobbed and stumbled on the stairs, hastily escaping the obnoxious gathering. Picking up her skirts, she took the remaining stairs quickly and ran along the corridor to the nursery where her small daughter was sleeping, watched over by her nurse, Mrs Crooke.

By the light of a single candle on the nearby table, she could see little Margaret asleep, as only young children can be, on her back, arms flung out, head on one side, tiny mouth open, utterly oblivious to her mother's distress. Satisfied that she was sleeping soundly, she nodded to Mrs Crooke and withdrew quietly to her room further down the corridor.

She felt unutterably depressed. How had she managed to get into this situation? She came from a good family, not Suffolk landed gentry like William, but from two generations of successful farmers who had made money through sheep. They had reared a new breed in Bury St. Edmunds, resulting from crossbreeding Norfolk Horn ewes with Southdown rams. The distinctive, black-faced Suffolk sheep was created, raised primarily for its meat, but then its wool became known for its durability, and the family fortunes rocketed.

William's father had been a wastrel, gambling away the Palmer family assets, and his son was proving to be the same. He had a weakness for cards, drink, and women, not necessarily in that order, but all three proved to drain Elizabeth's dowry. Soon the only asset they would have left would be the family home.

She sat heavily in one of the Queen Anne chairs, leaning back and staring at the ceiling. She had tried to remonstrate with William many times, but the discussions escalated into full-blown shouting matches, sometimes culminating in William striking her. He would be the ruin of them; her only hope was that he would either drink himself to death, have a hunting accident, or drop dead of apoplexy.

She gave herself a mental shake. No point in ruminating on what could not be changed–time to go to bed and try and get some sleep. Elizabeth got up and, crossing the thickly carpeted room, rang the bell for her maid.

She awoke the following morning to a grey, overcast day, the lowering skies threatening rain and maybe even a sprinkling of snow. She got out of bed, anticipating a morning of cleaning up the detritus of last night's card game and dealing with her hungover husband.

After breakfast in bed, her maid, Alice, dressed her. After checking in on little Margaret, who was single-mindedly applying herself to coddled egg and toast, supervised benignly by Mrs Crooke, Elizabeth descended to the lower floor.

She expected chaos to greet her, but the servants had quietly been at work, and all vestiges of the bacchanal evening had been dealt with.

Elizabeth walked from room to room, searching for her husband. She eventually located him in his study, sitting in his swivel chair, staring morosely at some papers on his desk. A steaming cup of coffee sat by his right hand, with an uneaten bread roll nearby. She hesitated, not wanting to interrupt him but wanting to know the outcome of the evening. She knocked softly on the door frame, bracing herself for his wrath, possibly some well-chosen oaths, but he didn't react. She knocked again, louder. William's head rose slowly, and he turned in his chair to look at her.

Elizabeth drew a sharp breath. The look on her husband's face was one she'd never seen before. Usually, after his drunken soirees, he was defensive to the point of belligerence, but the expression on his face was one of shame, even sorrow. He looked at her, then down at the floor, looking for the whole world like a naughty schoolboy brought before the headmaster for some misdemeanour.

Suddenly Elizabeth wanted to avoid hearing what William would say. She felt as if the temperature in the room had fallen several degrees despite the cheerful fire burning in the grate.

William sniffed, wiped a finger under his nose, sniffed again and began fiddling with the points of his waistcoat, not meeting her eye.

"William?" she whispered. "William, what is it?"

He cleared his throat with a noise like tearing cloth. Elizabeth could see that he didn't want to tell her what he had to say, and that frightened her more than if he had shouted, sworn, or thrown things at her.

"William!" She hissed his name through frozen lips.

He slowly raised his eyes to meet hers, and to her horror, she saw tears in them.

"Oh God, what have you done?"

He shook his head, and the tears overflowed, spilling down his florid cheeks.

Elizabeth felt numb. A ringing had started in her ears, and the light in the room seemed to flicker.

"I'm sorry, Elizabeth."

"Sorry, for what?"

"For what I have done to you and Margaret." He gulped, wiping a finger under his nose again.

"What did you do?" Elizabeth shouted at him, fists clenched against the front of her skirts.

William clasped his hands over his head and began rocking backwards and forwards.

Elizabeth shot forward and grabbed his hands, forcing him to look at her.

"Beardsley," he said. "You're his now."

Elizabeth could barely make out the words. William's head slumped forward. "I sold you to Beardsley."

Elizabeth released his hands as if they burned her. She staggered back until the wall brought her up short. She stood, feeling the solidity of it behind her, thinking she would vomit on the spot. She laid the palms of her hands on the plaster, the coolness seeping into her hands. If she let go, she would spin out of control.

William continued to weep, covering his face with his hands, his elbows resting on his knees.

Elizabeth heard the clock ticking on the mantelpiece, the crackling of the fire, and the snuffling sounds made by her husband. Her face felt clammy, perspiration had broken out on her forehead. Dust motes swirled in a beam of watery sunlight breaking through the window, and she knew that life would never be the same again. She swallowed with difficulty, running her tongue around the dryness of her mouth, trying to generate some saliva before speaking.

"Beardsley?" she croaked.

William nodded, still weeping, not looking at her. "Septimus Beardsley?"

He nodded again, wiping the back of his hand under his nose.

Septimus Beardsley. One of her husband's gambling friends. A man of medium height, dark wavy hair, thick black eyebrows framing dark brown eyes above a hooked nose and a close-clipped beard. The first time she met him, she had been aware of those dark eyes sweeping up and down before finally resting on her face. Whenever he had visited she had felt that scrutiny. He had never done anything improper but she had always been uncomfortable in his company, aware of the dark gaze following her around the room. He had spoken less than half a dozen words to her in the nearly three years she had been married to William, always polite and deferential, but the weight of his regard had made her skin prickle. They only touched when he kissed the back of her hand one Christmas, holding onto it for a trifle too long. In her memory, she could still feel his breath on her skin as he had placed his lips on her knuckles. She had resisted the urge to snatch her hand away, instead fixing a smile upon her face, hoping that the dislike didn't show in her eyes.

This man, this stranger who had made her feel uncomfortable, owned her. A thought flashed into her mind.

"What is to become of Margaret?" she demanded.

William slowly sat up in his chair, his face contorted with grief. "She is to go with you."

Elizabeth felt her knees buckle with relief. For one terrible moment she thought she was to be separated from her only child. "Beardsley wants her as well?" Not that she wasn't grateful, but she was surprised.

William said nothing, just nodded miserably. "How could you?" she asked.

Her husband winced as if she had shouted the words. His shoulders slumped in shame. "I was drunk, I lost count of the cards, and I, I…" He spread his hands, palms upwards in a helpless gesture.

"I'm your *wife*, for God's sake! Not your horse! Margaret and I are not chattels to be bartered away! Do we mean *nothing* to you?" She spat the last words.

"I was insensible with drink, woman! These things happen!" Now he was shouting, angry.

"These things happen? These things *happen*?" She felt capable of murder at that moment, and William, correctly divining her thoughts, leapt up from his chair and took a few steps towards the window.

"I'm your husband, and if I say you go, you go–or stay, and you stay. Therefore, you will–"

"No! You are no longer my husband, remember? You have no dominion over me, so I do *not* have to obey you!" Elizabeth strode to the bell rope hanging to the left of the fireplace and pulled it hard. The footman appeared.

Elizabeth turned to him. "Brownlow, please be so kind as to get one of the lads from the stables to saddle a horse. I have a note to go to Mr Beardsley's house. Thank you."

Brownlow disappeared whilst Elizabeth walked over to William's desk and, pulling a sheet of paper towards her, dipped the quill in the ink pot and dashed a quick message to Mr Beardsley. She stuffed an envelope, applied sealing wax to the back of it from the mould sitting over the candle next to the writing implements and, rising, rang the bell again.

The ubiquitous Brownlow reappeared, collected the note, and immediately gave it to one of the stable lads ready to ride the few miles to the Beardsley estate.

Elizabeth looked bleakly at William. "I have requested that Mr Beardsley ride here this evening for dinner. I shall have a private interview with him then and hear in his own words what transpired last night. No!" She held up her hand as William began to argue. "I wish to speak to him. As you say, you were insensible with drink, so how do I know what you say is true?" She nodded once at him briefly and departed with what little dignity she had left.

For the remainder of the day, Elizabeth kept to the nursery. She played with Margaret, even teaching her a few colours. Mrs Crooke seemed puzzled at first by this attention; usually, her mistress went for a walk in the mornings, leaving the little one in her charge, only popping her head in around lunchtime. Still, she was pleased to see mother and daughter chattering together; dark heads bent over a small slate on which the mistress was writing words.

In the early evening, Elizabeth heard the sound she had been dreading all day, the clop of horse's hooves coming up the gravel driveway, and she fumbled with the necklace she had selected to wear to dinner. Her maid came forward and tied the ribbon behind her neck, smiling at her mistress in the mirror. Elizabeth nodded her thanks, then gathered her gloves, dimly noting how badly her hands were shaking.

On descending the stairs, she could hear the murmur of men's voices coming from the sitting room. Taking a deep breath, she pushed the door open. Both men got to their feet as she entered, Mr Beardsley more quickly than William, she noted. Mr Beardsley bowed politely, glancing at William as he did so, then back to her. He came forward to greet her.

"Good evening, Lady Palmer; what a lovely surprise to receive your dinner invitation." Beardsley smiled at her without any trace of irony.

She gave him what she hoped was a believable smile and gestured for him to resume his seat.

Once they were all settled, she thought she would grasp the proverbial nettle and get straight to the point.

"My husband tells me you had a game of cards last night where he made a stake he couldn't honour. In place of this, I understand that the wager offered was myself and my daughter. Is that correct?"

Beardsley shot a look at William, but the latter merely looked at a spot on the thick Persian rug. Beardsley took a deep breath, then blew it out. "That is correct, Lady Palmer. Unfortunately, your husband made a wager that he couldn't meet. To avoid welching on that, he offered me this house." Beardsley waived a long-fingered hand at their surroundings. "However, I proposed an alternative payment. You." Beardsley's dark eyes fixed on Elizabeth's.

She felt the hairs on her forearms ripple. "Surely this cannot be legal?"

"The wager was made before witnesses, and so was the agreement."

A heavy silence descended upon the room.

Elizabeth couldn't believe her ears. Just like that, her fate and that of her daughter had been discussed and sealed over a game of cards. "I wish to consult with our solicitor. This is reprehensible; it cannot–"

Beardsley held up his left hand, reaching into his breast pocket with his right withdrawing a piece of paper, folded three times. Without speaking, he leaned over and handed it to her.

Elizabeth unfolded the paper with trembling hands. It was a contract, short and to the point. It was a promise to transfer herself and Margaret over to Beardsley as their new owner in place of a wager on a game of cards. The document was signed by both men and dated last night.

She felt as if she would be sick. Lights began flashing before her eyes her hearing became muffled as the room swam before her.

She came around a few minutes later, lying on the thick carpet, Beardsley kneeling beside her holding her hand. She could dimly make out William pouring himself a glass of claret. How typical of him to think of himself first. Beardsley, conversely, never left her side, rubbing her cold hands between his and murmuring insignificant nothings to her as you would to a skittish horse. Some dim recess of her brain was impressed with his attention.

"William, you might wish to attend to your wife."

"She's your wife now," Palmer rasped, "not my problem."

Beardsley exchanged a meaningful look with Elizabeth. The statement was not lost on either of them.

"Do you feel well enough to get up?" He smiled kindly down at her.

To answer his question, she pushed herself into a sitting position and got to her feet, taking his outstretched hand. The room tipped on its axis, wobbled, and then righted itself. Elizabeth became aware she was still holding Beardsley's hand and hastily detached herself, smiling at him to take the sting out of the gesture.

Beardsley bowed to her, then resumed his seat.

"So," William said roughly, "you will take her then?"

"Of course," Beardsley replied, smiling at Elizabeth as he did so.

Inside she was seething. How *dare* they? Trading her like she was a horse, a cow, or a sack of grain. These arrogant, ignorant, unfeeling men. She dug her fingernails into her palms so hard that later she would muse upon the crescent-shaped marks.

They left, under a leaden sky, the branches of bare trees reaching to the sky as if in supplication to the Gods who would give them leaves. She and little Margaret jolted along in the carriage sent by Beardsley, bundled up with what little possessions they had, bound for London.

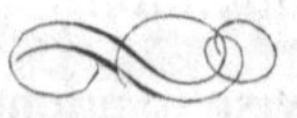

Three years. Three surprisingly short, sweet years. Septimus Beardsley had travelled to Suffolk to fetch the last of her things from her previous husband–her previous life–a few weeks after they had left. The three of them had settled in London in a modest townhouse a short carriage ride away from Beardsley's office.

"Daddy!" Margaret ran down the hallway and threw herself into Beardsley's outstretched arms. He walked towards Elizabeth carrying the little girl who, by now, had her arms and legs wrapped around him, and kissed his wife.

"Welcome home, Sep."

"It's wonderful to be home, Lizzie, back with both my girls."

As Elizabeth linked arms with her husband and turned to walk with him and her daughter, she smiled.

She had won the wager.

A silence descended, only broken by the whistling of the kettle. Mrs Perkins jumped as if stuck by a pin, then bustled over to retrieve the kettle and make a pot of tea.

Daisy concluded they all needed a restorative drink of strong tea and a biscuit. Curiosity got the better of her, and she couldn't resist asking, "What were your life like with Mr Beardsley?"

"We were well treated. My mother was resigned to her fate, and in time I think she and my adopted father came to view each other with genuine affection. To me he was always very kind, I wanted for nothing. I was well educated, for a woman, and after my mother died, I continued to live with him until his death only a few weeks ago."

Mrs Perkins plonked the teapot on the scarred table with three cups and a plate of biscuits. "Help yaself, dearie."

Margaret nodded her thanks whilst Daisy poured the strong tea out. When the ladies helped themselves to milk and sugar, they sat silently, munching the freshly baked ginger biscuits.

Daisy was putting two and two together. "So, I'm thinkin' your adopted father told you the truth about…?"

Margaret brushed crumbs off her lap. "Yes, he told me before he died. Until then, I had no notion of him being my adopted father. I think he thought I should know the truth. What I did with that knowledge was up to me."

Daisy digested this bit of information. So, now Margaret had returned to confront her natural father. And how would that go down with the mistress? And with Lord Palmer? Did Lady Palmer even know that her husband had a child? The Palmers had remained childless, a constant source of sadness for them both. There was a living child fathered by Lord Palmer sitting in the kitchen. A thought occurred to her.

"The contract both of 'em signed…where is it now?" Margaret opened her purse and withdrew a much-folded piece of paper, that looked rather worn around the edges. Mrs Perkins glanced at Daisy, then back at the paper. Margaret placed it on the table, smoothed it out, and turned it for both women to see.

Mrs Perkins deferred to Daisy, as she couldn't read, so

Daisy skimmed the document. Yes, it was all there, dated and signed by both her employer, whose signature she recognised, and that of Mr Beardsley. It was dated some twenty-odd years prior. Daisy blew out a breath, well then. She thought for a moment. This had to come to light, if not now, then sometime–no time like the present.

"I'll go and have a word with the mistress. But first–" Daisy fixed Margaret with a firm eye–"I need to find my husband and talk to him." She stood up and walked purposefully out of the scullery door towards the outbuildings, where she knew Thomas, now the butler of Long Melford House, would be conferring with the head gardener about the sad state of affairs in the vegetable department.

It took her a few minutes of searching, but Daisy had keen hearing, and she heard the rumble of male voices in the vicinity of the herb patch. Sure enough, as she rounded the privet hedge, there were Titmarsh and Thomas. Daisy didn't realise until she set eyes on her other half just how tense she was, but she felt an easing in her shoulders when she saw the slim frame of her husband standing, favouring his right leg to take the pressure of his bad one as he talked.

She called across a row of leeks. "Thomas!"

He turned in surprise to see his wife striding towards him, looking like a brigantine in full sail, her skirts puffing out around her, her white-frilled cap waving in time with her gait, the cream-coloured kerchief around her neck a little awry at the top of her bodice.

"Hullo, my love–what's to do now?" Thomas smiled at his usually cheery wife, but then he noticed her serious expression, and his smile faded. "What is it?" he asked in a different tone, walking towards her.

They met in the onion patch. Daisy laid her hand on his arm, looking earnestly up into his weather-beaten face. "A visitor, up at t'house. A girl, no–young woman, come to see the mistress."

"An' who is this girl?"

Daisy took a shaky breath. "The master's daughter." Her words fell into the resultant silence like a stone into a millpond.

"The *what?*" Thomas stared at her stupidly. A daughter? No mention of any offspring had ever been uttered during the time they had worked at Long Melford House.

"How do you know she be genuine?"

"She 'as a contract, signed by both the master and the man who took 'er in."

Thomas ran his hand through his thinning hair, thinking rapidly. He turned back to Titmarsh, saying some urgent business had arisen, and he was needed at the house. Titmarsh raised his hand in acknowledgement and turned back to his tilling.

Thomas grabbed Daisy's hand, and together they walked quickly back, Daisy having to trot to keep up with him, even though Thomas still limped quite heavily.

On Thomas' entrance, Margaret looked up and then rose from her seat, making her go up in his estimation. He nodded by way of greeting, to which she responded with a curtsy, surprising him even more. No woman had ever curtsied to him in his life. He glanced at Daisy to gauge her reaction and smiled to see her mouth hanging open. Turning back to the newcomer, he introduced himself, then added, "The master's not 'ere; he's gone into Ipswich on business."

Margaret nodded once. "Yes, I know, I saw him leave."

Thomas felt his eyebrows go up at this statement. So, this was well planned then. He sensed Daisy make an impatient gesture.

"She knows, Thomas, she waited until 'e left, then come knockin' on the door."

Thomas regarded Margaret carefully. She squirmed slightly under his intense grey gaze. He was the sort of man with eyes that looked right into you, weighing you up, balancing the pros and cons. Eventually, he came to a decision as he turned to his wife.

"Daisy, go up to the mistress now and break it to 'er. Then if we hear the bell ring, we'll know she be wantin' to see the lass."

Daisy looked at Thomas, conducting a whole conversation with him in seconds. She smiled briefly at him, smoothed her skirts, then turned and left the room.

Mrs Perkins, wide-eyed as a rabbit, asked Thomas if he'd like a cup of tea, which he accepted and took a chair at the table, running an index finger over the scars left by decades of kitchen knives. No-one spoke. They waited, the silence stretching until Margaret thought she would scream with frustration. Then, a bell which hung on a board with several others tinkled shrilly above a small sign marked 'sitting room'.

Mrs Perkins jumped as if stung. Thomas looked at Margaret.

"Guess that be for you, m'dear. I'll accompany you up thar." And with that, he rose, holding out his hand to her.

Margaret took his outstretched hand gladly. The discovery of her true identity, the loss of her beloved papa, her long journey here, and now the prospect of meeting her natural father's wife came crashing in on her. She involuntarily squeezed Thomas Crabbe's hand. He looked down at her, not unkindly.

"Courage, lass, she won't bite you." Not hard, anyway. He led Margaret up the lower stairs to the ground floor, through the main hallway, down a corridor, and through a door on the left, feeling the stock around his throat tighten at the prospect of the impending conversation.

Lady Palmer was sitting in a wingbacked Queen Anne chair in front of a window that stretched from floor to ceiling. Her hands were folded in her lap, her back ramrod straight. Even in repose, she had a severe expression, and under stress, her mouth drew up into a point like an owl. Her pale blue eyes fixed on the newcomer, dislike showing clearly. Thomas couldn't blame her, but hoped she would hear the girl out before eating her alive.

Margaret let go of Thomas' hand and sank into a deep curtsy, before straightening up and smiling tentatively at the mistress of the house. Standing behind Lady Palmer, Daisy winked encouragingly at her, which gave her courage.

"Well? Who are you, and what do you want?" snapped

Lady Palmer.

"I wish to speak to you, my lady, about a…personal matter. It is…very delicate, and I hoped that I could–" Lady Palmer cut her off. "How much?"

"What?" Margaret blinked stupidly.

"I *said* how much for you to go away and leave us alone."

Margaret glanced at Daisy, whose eyes had widened at her employer's words. "My lady, I do not want money; I only wish to–"

"Your type *always* wants money," hissed Lady Palmer.

"My lady, I don't! All I want is to speak to your husband–"

"My husband is an important man and does not want to be bothered by the likes of *you*."

Margaret heard Thomas' sharp intake of breath. She could feel her legs starting to shake. This was different from how she had envisaged it. She tried again.

"Lady Palmer, it is not a question of money, it is a question of honour–"

"Honour!" The older woman spat the word at Margaret.

"You use the word honour when you force your way into my house, confront my household staff, dupe them into bringing you up here, then try to spin some fairytale to me?"

Margaret's mouth fell open. She couldn't believe this woman wouldn't even hear her out. "I came here in good faith, only wanting to speak to your husband. I have it on good authority that he is my fa–"

"Get out!" Lady Palmer shouted.

"But, my lady, I–"

"I *said* get *out*!" Spittle flew from Lady Palmer's mouth, landing on the polished floorboards. "Thomas, you will escort this, this jumped-up trollop, to the scullery door and throw her out. Now!"

Daisy looked with distress at Thomas, who stepped forward and gently took Margaret by the elbow and turned her around, steering her towards the door.

Out in the corridor, Margaret burst into tears. "Why wouldn't she even hear me out?"

Thomas patted her gently on the back and guided her gently down the hallway to the stairs to the lower level and back to the kitchen.

"Another cup o' tea please, Mrs Perkins." Crabbe eased Margaret into a chair.

"All I wanted was her to hear my story, to acknowledge what her husband had done, what he–"

"Lass, lass, now then, you 'ave to look at it from 'er point o' view. You come 'ere, unbidden, accuse 'er husband of God knows what, an' she only 'as to tek a look at your face to know you're his Lordship's daughter. Oh yes," he nodded as Margaret jerked her head up in surprise, "I see it as soon as I saw you; Palmer's ya father."

Crabbe felt Mrs Perkins stiffen behind him. So she'd noticed the likeness as well.

"Is there a chance, any chance at all, that I may see my father?" Margaret wiped her nose, appealing to Crabbe.

"I doubt it, lass. Even if 'e agreed to see you, what good would it do? You've got a new life up in London, be 'appy with that. Forget all this."

"But Suffolk is where I come from, where I belong. I mean to settle here." Margaret's jaw set in a stubborn line.

Crabbe sighed mentally. That could be problematic. He thought he'd try one last time.

"It'd be awkward like, you bein' in the area, on'y a matter o' time afore you bump into her ladyship or lordship."

Margaret's eyes took on a hard-boiled look. Crabbe recognised it immediately. His employer often gave him the same look when he sensed he wasn't being obeyed. *Good grief, did the girl have nothing of her mother in her?*

"I *will* settle here, despite my father and his wife. Mr Beardsley left me comfortably off, so I will see whether I can rent a room in a respectable establishment and begin to put roots down." She chewed her lip thoughtfully.

The door opened, and Daisy came in.

"Well, you should 'ave 'eard her after you left, Lord above." She plunked down in a chair, blowing her cheeks out. "She didn't 'alf rant an' rave."

Mrs Perkins placed a cup of tea in front of her and another in front of Margaret before taking a chair, leaning her elbows on the worn table.

A quiet descended, punctuated only by slurping and munching noises. Daisy exchanged looks with her husband and Mrs Perkins, who wisely kept silent, burying her nose in her teacup.

"Thar's an old lady over Woodbridge way; she's on 'er own, no children an' in a big 'ouse. I 'eard she's been lookin' for a paid companion. You might want to write to 'er." Crabbe rubbed the side of his nose. "Reckon I can get 'er details for you if you'd like?"

Margaret smiled for the first time since she'd arrived. Her whole face transformed when she did so, so answering smiles bloomed on the others' faces in response.

"That would be wonderful, Mr Crabbe! I should so like to be useful, and it would allow me to stay in the area." She placed her teacup in its saucer with a rattle. "May you please furnish me with her particulars, and I shall write to her on my return to the inn where I am staying."

Daisy widened her eyes at Thomas, trying to catch his eye, but he studiously ignored her in favour of rising and getting a piece of paper from the sideboard. He grabbed the inkpot and quill and, retaking his seat, quickly wrote the address of the dowager he had mentioned, passing it to Margaret. She quickly scanned the address, folded the paper and tucked it safely into her purse. Rising from her chair, she bobbed a curtsy to them all and headed for the door.

"You goin' already?" Daisy exclaimed in surprise.

"Oh yes, I need to return to the inn and write my letter, then arrange for a stable boy to ride over to–" she glanced at the paper– "Farrier's Went, and deliver my introduction." She beamed at them, eyes shining with the remains of her earlier tears, now drying rapidly.

Thomas recognised determination when he saw it and rose from his chair to extend his hand to the young woman. "Best of luck, lass. May you let us know 'ow you get on, eh?"

"Oh, I should like that, yes. You have all been kind to me; I shall not forget it." Margaret beamed at them again, putting her small hand into Crabbe's larger, workworn one. They shook, once, firmly but friendly. Crabbe released her hand and opened the door, letting in a stiff breeze and watery sunshine.

"You'll be right to walk back?"

"Fine, I thank you, the fresh air will do me good and 'twill help to clear my head." Margaret turned, stepped over the flagstone door sill, and trotted off down the driveway.

Thomas shut the door with a snick.

"Well, I never did!" Mrs Perkins looked amazed. "Just like tha' she took off."

"Single-minded, that one." Daisy nodded at the closed door. "I reckon the county oughta look out."

"Reckon you be right, my love." Thomas grinned at his wife. "They won't know what hit 'em."

Chapter 17

Lord Palmer buttoned his breeches up. An ageing bladder and too much Earl Grey tea at his meeting in the village had forced him to make a call of nature on the side of the road. He sighed with relief, returning to where he'd hobbled his horse.

As he emerged from the small copse of trees, his horse turned its head and whickered softly. Following the animal's gaze, he saw a small figure in the distance. It sported a neat bonnet, a plain homespun dress, a medium-sized purse, and stout boots.

His first thought was, what was a lone woman doing in a quiet country lane? Then he remembered that the late, great Duchess of Devonshire had encouraged young women to be more independent, which, he supposed, had resulted in the newest mania for country walking exhibited by the current female generation.

Old habits die hard, however, so he waited for her to draw nearer so that he might enquire about her well-being and offer assistance should it be required.

After a few minutes, the young lady was within talking

distance and, spotting Palmer standing next to his horse, slowed her pace.

"Good afternoon!" Palmer raised his Derby hat.

"Good afternoon, sir."

She was level with him now, and a heart-shaped face looked up into his. Dark blue eyes, framed with long lashes above a small nose and bow-shaped mouth. She seemed familiar, yet he was confident they had never met before.

"May I enquire where you are headed, young lady?"

She hesitated, then replied, "I am returning to the village, but I have just been to Long Melford Hall."

Palmer raised his eyebrows. "I wasn't aware we were expecting any visitors today. If I'd known, I–"

"You weren't, and you wouldn't."

"I beg your pardon?"

"You weren't expecting any visitors, and if you had known, you probably would have absented yourself."

Palmer's initial curiosity changed to annoyance. "Just what do you mean by that?"

"It was Lady Palmer I wished to see."

"Indeed?"

"Yes, my lord, on a private matter." She chewed her lower lip.

"What private matter?"

Margaret ceased assaulting her lip, took a steadying breath and replied, "You."

Palmer stared at her.

"What the Devil do you mean by that?" Although a cold sensation in the pit of his stomach was providing an inkling.

Margaret was still smarting from her audience with Lady Palmer. Only the kindness of Thomas Crabbe, accompanied by the address he had given her, had prevented her from breaking down entirely. Now, fate had dealt new cards in the form of Lord Palmer. "I am Margaret Beardsley."

With horror, he realised why the young woman appeared familiar. Elizabeth. "You are lying," he croaked.

She shook her head slowly. Reaching into her purse, she removed a much-folded piece of paper. She shook it out, holding it out to Lord Palmer. All at once, he very much did not want to read it. She was standing, holding the paper out to him, not speaking. Gingerly, he took it between the forefinger and thumb.

The ink had faded, but he read the long-forgotten contract, complete with the two signatures–Beardsley and his own.

His first reaction was to tear it up, then he realised he was too late. She would have shown it to others. He broke out in a cold sweat, imagining his wife's face when Margaret had told her. "Who knows about this?"

"Your wife, Mr and Mrs Crabbe, and the cook, Mrs Perkins."

Palmer closed his eyes. Well, the whole district would know by the end of the week. He could trust the Crabbes, but Mrs Perkins couldn't keep her mouth shut if her life depended upon it. "Elizabeth?"

"Dead, several years ago."

"And Beardsley?"

"Also dead, only a few weeks past. He told me about you and gave me the contract before he passed." She looked at him keenly, waiting for a further response.

He didn't know what to say. This young woman had grown up believing that Septimus Beardsley was her father.

He folded the contract and handed it back to her. "What do you want from me?"

"For you to acknowledge that I am your daughter."

"Nothing more?"

"Nothing more."

He laughed, but it was a mirthless sound. "You don't want money?"

Margaret pulled herself up to her full height of five feet three. "No, I do not. My beloved Papa left me comfortably off."

Palmer started but refrained from commenting. "Well then?"

"I just want to hear one word…" Palmer arched an eyebrow.

"Sorry."

"Sorry?"

"For how you mistreated my mother, how you gambled away everything she owned, how you sold both of us, never enquiring as to how we were faring–"

"Why would I? You belonged to–"

"She was your wife! I was your daughter! Have you no decency? No sense of–"

"*Enough*!" he roared.

She subsided, chest heaving, fists clenched by her sides. They stood glaring at each other. Palmer thought quickly. She was known on sight now, and she was in possession of the signed document. Margaret could make life very difficult for him, and he had worked hard to get where he was today. She didn't want money; all she wanted was an apology. That wouldn't cost much, simply some humble pie. And he needed to keep the overall picture in mind. He had no heir nor any hope of one. This young woman before him had proven to be resourceful, intelligent, and courageous–there was a lot to be said for those qualities. Added to this, she was his flesh and blood. "Do you still play cards?"

Her question startled him out of his reverie. "What?"

"I asked if you still gamble at cards."

"No. No, I do not." The gambling had gone the same way as the liquor. He abstained from both and had done so for many years.

"Good," was all she said.

They looked at each other, waiting for the other to speak. Curious as to these newcomers, a wagtail flew down,

sitting on a low-hanging branch, twittering at them. Margaret smiled up at the little bird.

A memory popped into Palmer's mind. Margaret, as a little girl, sitting in her highchair looking out of the window at a bird. Her smile was just the same.

He felt the deep shame he'd experienced the day he'd watched Beardsley ride away with his wife and child. He'd buried it deep over the intervening years; it only surfaced in the wee hours of the night when the demons came to torment him. Every time he considered reaching out, cowardice overtook him, burying it all once more. Now, he had a chance to make things right–heal old wounds, apologise, make reparation.

Margaret turned away from the bird and looked at him, her smile fading.

"How did Lady Palmer take the news?"

"Not well," she said flatly.

No surprise there. "Let me deal with her; as for you, can you ride a horse?"

Margaret looked wary. "Yes, why?"

"Would you be able to ride astride in front of me on my mare?"

Margaret and the horse exchanged glances.

"She has a kind eye."

Palmer snorted. "My hunting days are over; I simply want an animal who can comfortably get me from one place to another without mishap."

"I think I can manage."

Palmer untied the reins, looping them over the mare's neck. He mounted, bending down to offer his hand to Margaret.

"Put your foot on mine and take my hand."

Margaret hitched up her skirts, put her foot on her father's and, taking his outstretched hand, allowed him to haul her up in front of him.

The mare snorted slightly at the extra weight but adjusted quickly.

Margaret felt very shy, sitting in such proximity to the man who had given her life, his arms around her, holding the reins.

Palmer kneed the mare gently, and she started for home at a gentle walk.

"What do you intend to do when we get to the hall?"

"First, appease my wife. Second, send for my solicitor."

"But the contract has your signature on it! It names my mother and me as–"

"Not for that. To change my will. I'm naming you as my heir."

Margaret quietened. She felt overwhelmed by the turn of events. All she could manage was a whispered, "Thank you."

She heard him laugh drily.

"My dear girl, that is the least I can do."

Neale eyed the dresses in the Queen's closet. She wouldn't be needing any of them now, he thought sadly. She had been tall for a woman and, in later years, had become a little overweight–no matter, they would fit. He walked to the door of the chambers and shut them, turning the key in the lock. If anyone requested admittance, he would state that he had locked the door by mistake, being in the grip of grief.

Returning to the closet, he chose a grey silk with chiffon

sleeves; lifting it down from its hanger, he placed it gently on the back of the nearest chair. Sitting down, he slipped off his shoes and breeches. Shucking off his jacket, he left his shirt on before lifting the dress over his head. It descended on his shoulders comfortably. Unfortunately, he couldn't lace the dress at the back, but gathering the skirts, he walked up and down the room, hearing the satisfying swish of skirts. He removed that, then next chose a red brocade, heavy with panels down the side and front, feeling like a princess in the heavy material.

Walking to the window, he looked out upon the knot garden, imagining he was a damsel in distress waiting for her lover to come and rescue her. As his eyes strayed to the long driveway, he saw a substantial cloud of dust and realised that the Prince Regent and his entourage were approaching the house. Whirling, he tore off the dress, returned it to the wardrobe, quickly donned his breeches and shoes, threw his jacket on and, unlocking the door, clattered down the stairs just in time to reach the front door, where Cope was waiting; the door open to the summer's morning.

The Regent's carriage pulled up at the front of the palace, Cope leaping forward to open the door and pull down the stairs to allow the Prince to descend, wheezing as he did so.

"Well, the old bitch is dead, eh, Cope? How is my father? Still ailing? Take me to him. Where's Willis? Fetch the damn man, don't just bloody stand there!" This last to Neale as he waddled past into the cool interior of the palace. Neale could smell the sweat on the Regent, with an underlying tang of triumph. The time was getting closer. Queen Charlotte, God rest her, was gone, and it was likely that her husband would follow soon. Grinding his teeth, Neale spun on his heel and walked briskly through to Doctor Willis's quarters.

The impasse was broken by the Regent simply sacking the doctor and appointing a new one who would do as he was told.

The Regency Act had been passed in 1811, which granted the Regent full powers, aided and abetted by Lord Liverpool, now Prime Minister, after the assassination of Prime Minister Perceval. King George III remained incarcerated at Windsor Castle until his death, less than eighteen months after the death of Queen Charlotte. George IV ascended the throne, and the country waited to see what sort of monarch he would be.

The new King spent the first weeks of his reign desperately ill. He had a bad cold he caught in Brighton, the treatment for which (according to the locum physician, Tierney) was letting eighty ounces of blood. Afterwards, he had severe congestion in his chest, almost to the point of suffocation. Everyone held their collective breath. Tierney removed another fifty ounces of blood from the King, and he began to recover. His temper, however, remained the same, and he flatly refused parliament the wish to pray for the late Queen in the liturgy for his departed father. He had disliked his mother in life and was continuing to punish her in death.

Neale heaved a sigh of relief as he shut the door, leaving the King resting in his quarters. He felt his jaw muscles sag from the effort of having to keep a pleasant expression plastered on his face when what he wanted to do was pick up the nearest fork and plunge it into his Majesty. Neale imagined him deflating like a pig's bladder, emitting flatulent noises as he did so. He snorted with mirth as he walked wearily down the corridor back to his room. He detected a slight movement out of the corner of his eye and, snapping his head around, saw a young man leaning lazily against the wall. It took him a couple of minutes to dredge the man's name out of his memory–Benjamin Audley, valet to Lord Liverpool, that arch-mediocrity of a man who was now their Prime Minister.

Neale eyed Audley with barely concealed dislike. His natural prejudice towards Lord Liverpool encompassed anyone in his retinue or immediate sphere.

Audley, conversely, smiled sweetly in return, his liquid brown eyes gleaming at Neale from the dimness of the corner in which he was standing.

Neale suddenly felt as if the stock was too tight around his neck, noting Audley's long, dark eyelashes and white hands fluffing his newly washed chestnut hair; Neale could smell lye soap.

"What has caused you such mirth, sir?" Audley asked softly, moving closer to Neale.

The feeling of tightness around his neck passed to his scrotum. Audley stood in front of him. He was shorter than Neale, with narrow shoulders and slim legs. His full-lipped mouth was very red. Neale couldn't tear his eyes away from Audley's rosebud mouth, watching as his pink tongue delicately licked his lower lip. He could smell the soap more strongly now, along with, what was it? Vetiver, a part of his brain not immediately occupied with Audley's mouth, told him. The warm, deep notes of the herb filled his nostrils as Audley moved closer and placed his whole mouth on his.

A frisson of shock shot down his spine into his groin, where his penis, so long neglected, began stirring happily. His brain sounded a warning note, but his penis told him to ignore it, and when Audley began gently kneading his testicles, the resultant surge of lust blotted out all coherent thought.

Neale shoved Audley back against the wall, thrusting his tongue into the younger man's mouth whilst ripping at his buttoned fly, seeking to free his penis to allow Audley better access. Audley helped him simply by disengaging his mouth, sliding down the wall onto his haunches, unfastening the last button and taking Neale full into his mouth. Neale thought his brain would explode as he thrust repeatedly until he climaxed, a starburst of lights behind his eyes.

Eventually, he returned to the corridor and Audley, standing again, wiping his mouth with a lace-trimmed handkerchief, his brown eyes twinkling mischievously.

He replaced the handkerchief in his breast pocket. "I think someone needed that, hm?"

Neale hastily tucked his limp member back into his breeches, ducking his head with embarrassment. A long, perfectly manicured finger reached out and lifted his chin so that he was eyeball to eyeball with the younger man. "There is no shame, mon amour."

"There is, particularly if we are discovered."

"Then let us be discreet in future."

"In future?" croaked Neale.

"You didn't think this was to be our only encounter?" murmured Audley. "Besides, a true gentleman would return the favour, n'est pas?" He gently placed Neale's hand on his groin, where Neale could feel a respectable swelling. He almost threw all caution to the wind thinking he would throw Audley down on the parquet floor and do rude things to him, but the faint sound of approaching footsteps made both men snap to attention.

"Tonight, my rooms, nine o'clock, *don't* be late." Audley turned smartly on his heel and marched down the corridor, leaving Neale open-mouthed, staring at his retreating back.

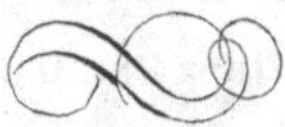

Neale spent the rest of the afternoon in a lather of sweaty anticipation. He couldn't get the image of Audley's mouth out of his mind. He went through the rest of the day like a sleepwalker, not concentrating on what he was doing or saying. Like goldfish, people's mouths opened and closed, but he didn't hear the words. A running debate raged in his mind. He argued with himself whether or not he should go to Audley's rooms, coming up with all sorts of excuses and reasons for not going, but that other, more visceral part of him kept saying, *why not*?

After dinner, having had a quick wash and change of clothes, he found himself standing in front of his looking glass, anointing himself with cologne, brushing his reddish-brown hair until it gleamed, plaiting it in a neat queue that sat on the back of his neck. He had been told he was handsome in a somewhat arrogant way. Regarding his reflection dispassionately, he noted the high cheekbones, dark-blue eyes on either side of a slightly crooked nose above a pliable mouth. He had always thought his hair was his best feature; he was vain about his hair, but the rest of him…well, he hadn't given it much thought. Audley found something attractive about him. The thought of Audley made the hairs lift on the backs of his legs, and his scrotum tighten.

Of course, Benjamin Audley could be a molly boy, a mouth for hire. Neale knew of molly houses in London, establishments catering to men of a particular persuasion. He had visited one such many years ago and had been at once repelled and aroused by the casual nature of the encounters there. Walking through the door, he had been accosted by a languid young blonde, a real-life David, who had introduced himself simply by parting his robe and displaying his genitals, kneading himself until a substantial erection had been achieved. At that point Neale hadn't known what to do– turn and run, or grab the boy and shove him over the nearest couch. In the end the young man had taken his hand, led him up the stairs to a room, where he'd bent over a four-poster bed, displaying strong, muscular buttocks and begged Neale to take him.

Neale promptly had. He could still feel his hands around the younger man's hips as he'd thrust repeatedly. He couldn't explain why, but he always liked to be the more dominant one–he'd never felt comfortable being submissive. Until today.

Tiptoeing along the long corridor towards the back of the palace, he ascended a servants' staircase that led to the upper level. At the top, he listened carefully. No sound emanated from any of the rooms to the left or right. He wasn't sure which was Audley's chamber, so he crept softly along the wooden floorboards, keeping his ears open.

He was about three-quarters of the way along when a door opened quietly, and a curly, dark head appeared, beckoning him by the dim light of a candle. Neale's heart sped up, and the sweaty feeling returned, plus interest. If they were discovered, if anyone even suspected what they were doing, they'd both be hanged.

Pulling level with Audley, they regarded each other in the candlelight.

"What is your pleasure, sir?" Audley softly asked.

His pleasure? His mind went completely blank. Audley smiled sweetly at him. The younger man reached out, took hold of his hand, and pulled him slowly into his room, shutting the door softly behind him with his foot. He held Neale's hand, placing the candle on a nearby table.

They stood, looking at one another, drinking each other in, waiting for the other to make the first move. Neale felt a buzzing in his head and a stirring in his breeches, but still, he didn't move. He licked his lips, suddenly dry. Seeing the gesture, Audley walked over to a bureau and filled two glasses from a carafe. Turning back, he handed one to Neale, clinked his glass against his and took a sip. Neale did the same while trying to figure out what else to do. A rich burgundy soaked into the membranes of his mouth, surprising him. He'd expected some rough gut rot, but this was very good–excellent, in fact.

Audley smiled at his expression. "I raided the wine cellar–it is alright!" He held up his hand at Neale's look of horror. "No one witnessed it; I concealed it in my jacket and smuggled it up here. It will never be missed."

Don't wager on it, Neale thought, his mind going to Cope, who usually counted the bottles of wine jealously as if they were his children. Well, it wasn't his problem. If the theft was discovered, they could always blame a miscount due to the comings and goings of the house following the death of the old King and the confusion that had ensued.

Neale drained his glass in three gulps, anticipation making him nervous.

"Be careful, darling; otherwise, I'll have to go and filch another bottle."

Neale detected a slight accent in the other man. "You have French blood, sir?" He hoped to delay the proceedings slightly by enquiring about Audley's background.

Audley shrugged. "On my mother's side," he said.

Neale placed his glass on the table and then wiped the palms of his hands on his breeches. He coughed, swallowed, then coughed again. He opened his mouth to say this was a mistake and he really should go when Audley stepped forward and placed his warm mouth over his, inserting his tongue gently, flicking it around.

Immediately he grasped the back of Audley's head, kissing him deeper. In response, Audley broke away, pushing him in the chest with both hands. He dropped to his knees in front of

Neale, deftly unbuttoning his flies, taking him fully in the mouth. Neale thought he would spontaneously combust as his nerve endings jangled at the sensations jolting up and down his penis whilst Audley ran his hot tongue up the shaft. He released himself in a hot spurt of liquid, not caring where it fell.

Belatedly he came to, leaning against the wall, his breeches puddled around his ankles, breathing like a cart-horse. He heard a soft chuckle and, cracking one eye open, saw Audley sitting upon the floorboards, nonchalantly sipping another glass of wine whilst stroking the front of his breeches.

"Audley," he rasped, "now it is my turn."

"Oh darling, I can barely contain myself! What did you have in mind?"

Neale pulled his breeches up and crawled across the floor to where Audley sat. He insinuated himself between the younger man's legs, his chest meeting the other man's and lowered his mouth on the other's, biting down on his lower lip. He felt Audley draw a breath under him, bracing himself. For what? A full-frontal assault? A degradation? He pulled back and looked Benjamin Audley full in the face.

"I will not hurt you, only if you want me to."

Audley's brown eyes widened. Clearly, he had never heard *that* before. "I want you to hurt me, but…slowly, gently, until I scream out your name." The words hung upon the air, a promise given and accepted between them.

Neale heaved a deep sigh. He had been given permission. Well, so be it. He bent his head to his work, a happy slave to the purpose. He made Benjamin Audley scream out his name before losing himself in pure sensation.

They lay spent, limbs entwined, Audley's head resting on Neale's stomach. He could hear the gurgles it was making. He giggled at one particularly loud noise.

"What is so amusing?"

"Your stomach, darling. We need to feed you." Audley rolled onto his knees, got up and walked towards a small cupboard. Opening the door, he commenced rummaging.

Neale admired the roundness of his buttocks, the muscles flexing as he brought items out and placed them on a nearby tray.

The items were a loaf of bread, a round of cheese and a bunch of grapes. Neale was astonished.

"Where in God's name did you obtain all that?"

"The kitchens, silly boy. I begged them from one of the kitchen girls. She thought I had had no meat or drink all day, so in exchange for a kiss, she gave me all this–et voila!" He waved his hand with a flourish.

Neale laughed at his boyish enthusiasm.

Audley carried the food over to where Neale reclined, hand behind his head. Audley cut a couple of slices of cheese, laid them on a hunk of bread, halved a grape, placed it on top and held the whole lot out to Neale. The latter sat up, taking the food. Suddenly, he found he was ravenous. His physical efforts of the last hour had worked up an appetite. They munched in companionable silence.

It was wonderful to lie naked with another man, eating, drinking, just being. He had never felt so free. No one to see, no one to judge–he could just…be.

Audley smiled at him now and then. Whilst handing him more food, their fingertips touched ever so briefly, but they both felt and revelled in the contact. It was as if the lightest touch heralded something deeper. It would happen eventually, but for now, the anticipation was as pleasurable as the act itself.

"Tell me about yourself."

"There isn't much to tell, chéri. I was born in France to a couple who were, how you say, upper-middle-class?"

Neale nodded, chewing vigorously.

"My father was a lowly courtier; my mother always had an eye for social climbing; it ran in her side of the family." Audley's mouth twisted down. "Her sister, my aunt, was worse. She married an Englishman–they lived here for a while. Had a daughter, my cousin, then returned to France." Audley popped a grape into his mouth, thinking. "Yes, my aunt liked the finer things in life–perfume, dresses, jewellery, good food, fine wine, the list goes on." From the tone of his voice, Neale deduced Audley held a dim view of his aunt.

"And your parents?"

"Father dead, ma mère remarried. My stepfather and I do not get along."

Neale realised that Audley did not wish to elaborate, so he let the subject drop.

They'd finished the food, Audley licking his fingers. As he

got to his thumb, his gaze locked with Neale's. A glint showed in the dark eyes as he continued sucking the digit. Neale never thought he could achieve an erection so quickly. He grabbed the younger man, pulling him roughly towards him. Their mouths met with an audible smack.

"Ow!'

"Sorry, are you–"

"You bit me!"

"Sorry, sorry! In my haste, I–"

"It's fine, it's fine! I'll live!"

Neale looked at Audley's lower lip. The blood was already drying, but he gently put out his tongue and licked his lip, startling Audley.

"Darling, I didn't have you marked for a vampire."

"You have no idea," he grinned fiendishly. "Now, let's try that again, shall we?"

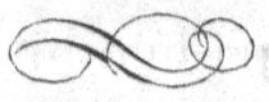

Neale and Crabbe had a meeting pre-arranged–but he had been so preoccupied with his *amorata* that he had missed the allotted time. Belatedly realising his error, he had thrown his clothes on in a haphazard fashion, exited Audley's room, and clattered down the back stairs into the corridor below, nearly colliding with Crabbe.

Having waited for a full fifteen minutes, Thomas had grown bored, and stomach complaining due to a missed breakfast, had gone in search of sustenance. Typically, rather than summon a servant, he had struck out in what he hoped was the direction of the kitchens. Whilst following his nose, he had run slap bang into Neale.

They grabbed each other, performing an odd pas-de- deux whilst apologising. During this exchange Audley, now

appropriately attired, hair hastily tidied, had tumbled down the same flight of servants' stairs, and by the time he spotted the two other men it was too late to turn around and creep back up the way he had come.

Neale and Crabbe were now bowing to each other and enquiring about each other's health.

An awkward silence fell. Crabbe's eyes cut from Neale to Audley, then back again. The silence stretched. And stretched. Audley recovered first.

"Monsieur Crabbe! Enchanté! Neale has told me about you, sir. What brings you to the palace? Oh, mais bien sur, a meeting, how foolish of me. Well, I shall leave you now, maintenant. My esteemed regards." Audley executed his finest courtly bow and departed with indecent haste.

Neale studiously avoided Crabbe's eye. He could feel his face growing hot. He didn't know why, but Thomas Crabbe's good opinion meant a great deal to him. He fiddled with his cuffs, coughed, shuffled his feet, and smoothed his hair.

"It darn't bother me."

"I beg your pardon?"

"I *said* it darn't bother me–each to their own, aye?" Neale's shoulders eased. He took a steadying breath.

Thomas smiled. "'Judge not, lest ye be judged.' So, who am I to judge, eh?"

"Thank you."

Crabbe glanced down. "Yer welcome. Although next time mebbe button yer breeches properly, aye?"

Chapter 18

10th May 1815

To my brothers in arms. I write to you all in haste to look to the incarcerated one. He will rise like a phoenix from the ashes to sit upon his throne once more. The Golden Eagle will spread its' wings again.

9th September 1815

My brothers! I implore you to stand by. The day of judgement cometh, and that right soon. He will come again. Already the Tides are Turning in our favour. Be vigilant! Be ready!

1st October 1815

Its' time. The Winds of Change blow in our direction, and the Ship of Fortune steers its' course away from a solitary island to a land of sun and splendour. The time is now! Stand guard!

The King spat out the lamb bone he'd been gnawing on, wiping his chin on his sleeve. "Well, sir, do you deny it?" He waved a plump hand at the pile of letters on the table.

"Yes, I bloody do deny it!" snapped Neale, forgetting etiquette in his indignant rage.

"That is your hand, is it not?" The King threw the papers at Neale's head, but due to the distance and angle, they fluttered to settle at Neale's feet like an injured swan.

Neale picked them up. He examined the writing closely. Fuck, the script was identical to his–every curlicue, downstroke, upstroke, tail and frigging apostrophe. Someone had made a very close study of his hand. Someone had taken great pains to– Wait a minute. Thank God! The humble apostrophe. He went weak at the knees with relief.

Neale's English master had almost torn his hair out over it. Neale could hear the exasperated shouting echoing down the years. *It's, boy! Not its'! For the love of Christ, learn the difference between singular and plural! What in damnation is wrong with you?*

Even a wooden ruler applied across his knuckles couldn't drum the difference into his head for years. And now he almost wept to see the incorrect application of that humble grammatical mark that he constantly checked and double-checked in his correspondence. He smiled for the first time all day.

"What is so bloody funny?" demanded the King.

"The apostrophe, Your Majesty."

"What the *fuck* are you talking about?"

Neale explained briefly to his sovereign about his childhood confusion over the correct apostrophe usage. Then, leaning over the table, he pushed the last letter to the King, pointing with a shaking finger at the damning words.

"That's no frigging proof, Neale." The King raised his bloodshot eyes to meet his.

"Oh, but it is Sire; I still have some of my catechisms from school, just to remind me." Neale grinned triumphantly back at the King. "I can fetch them for you if you wish."

King George continued to eyeball his equerry, trying to decide whether he was taking the piss. Evidently, he decided he wasn't as he leaned back in his chair, folding his hands over his substantial paunch. "So, if you didn't write the damn letters, then who did?"

Neale could only think of one person who knew him and his handwriting so intimately. Audley. God rot him. He said as much to the King. Then throwing all caution, shared experiences, and any vestige of feelings to the wind, he filled the other man in on Audley's preferences and habits– omitting his own involvement.

"What is that to me? So, he is a sodomite…"

"He sells his arse to the highest bidder, Your Majesty; he–"

"And what are you?"

"What?" Neale was so startled by the question that, again, he forgot to address the King as he should.

"I said, what are *you*?" The King located his napkin, fixing

Neale with a basilisk stare.

Neale stuttered, "I am a loyal, faithful servant, Your Majesty, I–"

"And a molly." The words hung in the air like a foul smell.

Neale could feel sweat breaking out on his top lip. He thought quickly. How the *hell* had the King worked it out? He'd been discreet, secretive to the point of obsession.

"Like playing dress-ups with my mother's clothes, hm?"

"I–ah, that is, I…"

"Oh, for God's sake, man, do you think I wouldn't find out? That day when I arrived shortly after my mother's death, you came to the door, all dishevelled and flustered. I asked Cope what you had been about, and he told me that you'd locked yourself in the Queen's rooms."

Neale felt sweat trickle down his back into the crease of his buttocks.

"You think you're the only spymaster, eh? I have a whole army at my disposal–eyes everywhere." The King chuckled, dipping his chubby fingers into a water bowl, then wiping them on his breeches. "So, find a dress you liked then? Ah, I see you did. Tell me you didn't wear the damn thing when you buggered Audley."

Neale opened his mouth to reply, but nothing emerged. "For fuck's sake, I don't give a tinker's cuss what you get

up to in your own bloody time, but don't do it on *mine*!" The last word was shouted.

"Sire, I–"

"Be quiet!" Spittle flew from the King's mouth. He picked up his glass and took a restoring gulp of claret. "Now you bloody listen to me, you cunning fag, you will kiss and make up with Audley–let me finish!" He held up a fat hand. "You will, as I say, make peace with Audley. We need to keep him close. What's that saying? 'Keep your friends close, but your enemies closer.' Well, we need to keep him close." He took another slug of claret. "When we move against the French, we need that molly boy to lead us to the heart of Napoleon's camp." He tapped a fat index finger against his glass. "What's the name of the cook Palmer is sending?"

"Crabbe, Sire," Neale managed to get out between frozen lips. "Thomas Crabbe."

"Crabbe, yes, should remember a name like that–love crustaceans. Well, let Palmer instruct him on contacting this Shegoe, and then we'll see where it leads us." Another slurp, another tap on the glass. "Does the crustacean speak French?"

"No, Sire, but I have it on good authority that Shegoe speaks several languages, including English."

The King narrowed his eyes. "No one's ever seen the damn man; how the hell do we know what he looks like, let alone what lingo he speaks?"

Neale shuffled his feet. "Audley told me that, ah, he had heard from a reliable source that the agent speaks more than one language."

The King's eyes narrowed further. "A reliable source?" he asked silkily.

Neale could feel his face growing hot. The 'reliable source' had been a cross-dressing molly that Audley had bent over a couch in his rooms whilst Neale looked on. The young man was a dark Frenchman, fresh from the continent, brimming with confidence. And the latest sexual techniques. Neale's face grew hotter still at the memory.

The King stared at his equerry, making Neale squirm even more.

"Very well. See the crustacean has all the information he needs." He gestured to Neale in dismissal.

Neale bowed low and backed gratefully from the room, feeling the sweat drying on his top lip. He'd just reached the door when the King shouted, "Wait!"

Reluctantly he straightened up.

"When you corner Audley, you have my permission to do whatever it takes to destroy the little turd, savvy?"

"Yes, Your Majesty." And with that, he reversed out of the room, closing the door behind him with a soft snick.

"You bastard!" spat Neale.

"Oh, darling, don't be like that, we all—"

"No, we bloody don't! You've just jeopardised the entire organisation and put a man's life—no, several men's lives in danger!"

Audley's usual urbane, slightly haughty expression

underwent a change. The lips compressed into a thin line, and his dark eyes narrowed to slits. Neale suddenly saw a glimpse of the real man. Neale had been taken for a fool, and a middle-aged fool at that. He'd allowed lust and hubris to get the better of him and cloud his judgement. Well, no more.

"You complete cunt," he hissed through stiff lips.

"Flattery will get you everywhere, mon chéri," Audley replied softly, his dark eyes shining brighter.

"I have the ear of the King, and should he–"

Audley broke out laughing so hard he began coughing.

"That oversized windbag? You think anyone gives a flying fuck what that empty-headed idiot thinks?"

"You are talking of the King of England, sir!"

"I don't care if he's the bloody Pope. He's a cantankerous, gluttonous, foul-mouthed lecher who cares more about his dinner plate than the kingdom. What this country needs is a true leader, strong and honest, like his father was–"

"His father? His *father*? He didn't recognise his own wife, for God's sake! How the *hell* can you compare the two monarchs?"

"But he knew how to lead his people, not like that overblown, syphilitic alcoholic who is his son." Audley fixed Neale with an icy stare. "You are completely naïve if you think the King will be any match for the French."

Neale took a steadying breath. The next few minutes would be crucial. "You are right, of course. I have begun to realise that I am serving a man who doesn't deserve to sit on the throne. Whenever I am in his presence, I find him utterly repellent." He paused for dramatic effect. "I do not know if I can continue in my present capacity." He chewed his bottom lip, not daring to meet Audley's eyes.

Silence followed this statement. Neale felt his heart thump in an irregular rhythm. "I believe the time has come for me to make up my mind once and for all."

Still Audley didn't say anything. The silence stretched until Neale believed the other man could hear his heart pounding.

"So, it is with great reluctance that I join your cause." Neale raised his eyes to watch Audley's response.

Audley sat stock still. Then he laughed a short, sharp bark.

"What is so amusing?" demanded Neale stung.

"You chéri, first you splutter expletives, then call me names, and now you want to *join* us?" Audley laughed again, longer and louder.

Neale hoped the desire to throttle him with his bare hands didn't show on his face. "I realise that this comes as a surprise, but I have been thinking about it for some time now, and–"

"Since when?" interrupted Audley.

"For a while, as I said–"

"Since *when*?"

"What does it matter?"

"It matters to *me*. I have to decide whether you are genuine or not."

Neale thought quickly. He rapidly flipped through several possibilities but settled on something approximating the truth. "Since the King found out I had worn some of the late

Queen's dresses. He found out and…humiliated me." Half the truth, enough to sound convincing, anyway.

"Tsk, tsk. How could you be so careless, my sweet?" Neale shrugged, not trusting himself to speak.

"You must learn to cover your tracks a little better than that."

Neale couldn't disagree with him. Yes, he would need to cover his tracks much more carefully, not from the King, but from the arrogant dandy who had slid off his chair and was now standing before him.

Audley put a well-manicured finger under his chin and tilted his face to the light. The dark eyes swept over his features, and it took every ounce of willpower to keep his face straight and meet Audley's gaze.

Audley stepped back, straightened his cuffs and said, "Well, darling, I'll believe you; thousands wouldn't."

Neale felt something unclench in his stomach. He'd convinced him. The King would be pleased.

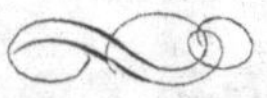

"And he swallowed your story?" The King belched loudly, wiping his mouth on the back of his hand. He'd just polished off an entire plum duff with a bowl of custard and felt magnanimous.

"Yes, Sire, he was doubtful at first, but then he believed me." Neale was still reeling.

George IV rapped a tattoo on the polished dining room table with his fingertips. He belched again, then farted loudly, causing the footman behind his chair to close his eyes as if in pain. Neale just managed to control his face. The King's bodily eructation was the stuff of legend. Privately Neale thought that the sovereign's guts must be rotten on the inside, considering the stench now wafting through the room like a purple fug. One of the dogs, who had been lying peacefully in front of the fire, rolled over, sat upright and looked reproachfully at his master. Neale thought he'd lose control altogether, so instead of looking at the dog's expression, he stared fixedly at a point on the opposite wall.

"Hmm, well, we'll believe it, eh? I'll inform Palmer, you speak to this…Crabbe, and we'll give Audley enough rope to hang himself with." He chuckled, making his double chins wobble. The footman made a moue of distaste. Dear God, if the man didn't learn to control his features, he would lose his position and possibly his head.

"And he's of French descent?"

"Yes, Sire, on his mother's side, it would appear."

The monarch belched again. "Watch him closely and keep Palmer advised." He lifted his chin in dismissal. Neale reversed out of the room, smiling gently.

Lord Palmer pulled the bellrope to the right of the mantelpiece. He didn't have too long to wait before he heard the irregular footsteps of Crabbe.

The morning was fine, crisp, cold, and the pale winter sunshine gilded Crabbe's auburn hair and eyebrows.

Despite having the Crabbes imposed upon him, Palmer had grown to like Daisy and Thomas, although Lady Palmer still had to thaw out towards either of them. Mind you, she still had to thaw out towards him.

"Ye rang, sir?"

"Yes, Crabbe; sit, please." Palmer gestured towards a wingbacked chair.

Crabbe looked politely expectant.

Palmer fiddled with the points of his waistcoat and collected his thoughts.

"Neale has written to me–finally." Crabbe's wispy eyebrows slowly went up.

"He writes that you are to travel to Kew with me. He wishes to discuss the next stages of the campaign whilst I meet with the King."

So, at last, the time had come. Crabbe felt his belly somersault. After all this while. Working hard, proving himself worthy of trust, the moment had arrived. He drew himself up higher in the chair, waiting patiently.

"Whilst I have an audience with His Majesty, you will be briefed by Neale, understood?"

"Aye, sir–I mean, m'Lord."

"Very good. We leave tomorrow morning. You will need to be ready at first light."

"Aye, m'Lord."

"Your wife will remain here."

Crabbe nodded, envisaging Daisy's face when told

the news.

"Billy will take us in the carriage. Please be punctual."

"Yes, m'Lord."

"Well, I'll let you get on." Palmer nodded once in dismissal.

Thomas found Daisy in the scullery with Kate, the kitchen maid. Kate wasn't the sharpest knife in the box, but she was pleasant and willing, so Daisy had taken her under her wing. Daisy couldn't resist a lame duck, so Kate was her new duckling.

"Allo, my lover!" Daisy dimpled at Thomas as he approached.

"I need to speak to ye, lovely."

"Oh, aye? Well, Kate, you carry on cleanin' up here; I 'ave to speak to Thomas."

"Aye, mistress," Kate replied softly, bobbing a curtsy.

Thomas put an arm around Daisy, leading her into the herb garden.

"I've got to go to London."

Daisy widened her eyes at him. "When?"

"Tomorrow."

"Tomorrow!"

"Aye, at first light."

"Oh heavens! I darn't know if I can be ready that early!"

Thomas coughed. "Ye darn't 'ave to be. I'm goin' alone."

"You what?" Her tone was icy.

"It's not my choice, lovely; the master wants me to go with him alone."

There was a pregnant pause. "Just you an' him?"

"Ah, yes, m'love."

"Why?" She asked crisply.

"I darn't know, lovely–I'm just followin' orders." Daisy made a rude noise.

"Now now, sweetheart, darn't take on so–we must do as we're bid, whether we like it or not."

His wife snorted, indicating what she thought of *that* statement. "Yew be careful, Thomas."

"I will, an' *you*," he tapped her gently on the tip of her nose, "be good."

On his arrival at Kew, Thomas found Richard Neale in the Chinese room, where they had taken tea almost three years ago.

"Crabbe! Good to see you; come in, sit down."

After shaking hands with Neale, he took the chair opposite.

"So, how is life at Long Melford?"

"Good, busy. Daisy an' I have our work cut out."

Neale smiled at the thought of the ubiquitous Daisy, all hustle and bustle around the hall. "I can imagine Lady Palmer would keep her on her toes." He raised a plucked eyebrow at

Crabbe.

"Yer not wrong." Crabbe grinned at him.

"Well, I asked you here to tell you that we have secured a low-level intelligence contact in France, specifically Paris. He is known to Lord Palmer, who trusts him, and is ideally placed to introduce you around and obtain the necessary invitations."

Neale looked at Crabbe for a reaction. Crabbe had the most unusual expression on his face, one Neale had never seen before. It was a mixture of horror, surprise, and disgust. However, his gaze was not on Neale but some inches over his left shoulder.

Turning slowly in his chair, Neale made out a boa constrictor, about six feet long, bright yellow, making its way nonchalantly across the Persian rug.

"Oh bugger, Hermione has gotten out again." Rising slowly from his chair, he tip-toed over to the empty fireplace, gently pulling the bellrope that hung there. Glancing at Crabbe, he saw that he had pulled his feet up and was now clasping his knees, not taking his eyes off the snake who was tasting the air with her forked tongue.

"Is it…is it…dangerous?" croaked Crabbe.

"No, no. Well, not venomous. It is a Jamaican Boa. So, you are safe unless you are a rat or chicken."

The only thing that moved was Crabbe's eyeballs, which swivelled slowly towards Neale. "Chicken?"

"Ah yes, the boa squeezes its prey to death."

Crabbe did not look at all reassured at this statement.

Neale, despite the younger man's discomfort, was enjoying the scene. "They are said to hang in trees, dropping upon their intended prey and wrapping their coils around their meal."

Crabbe was now pushing himself back in the chair, almost sitting on the back in his efforts to get away from the snake. Hermione, conversely, seemed to see something attractive in Crabbe as she changed direction, leisurely undulating towards him.

"Neale!" A note of panic sounded in Crabbe's voice.

Neale was grinning by this time, finding the situation funny. He, unlike Crabbe, was used to exotic animals, reptiles and birds appearing unexpectedly in various parts of the palace. In contrast, poor Crabbe was not and probably had never clapped eyes on a snake before, let alone a boa.

"*Neale!*"

"It's alright, Crabbe, truly, she will not harm you; she is quite–"

"I don't bloody care!"

Hermione, hearing the shouting, hesitated. Snakes are sensitive creatures, prone to sensing changes in taste, touch, sound, and even temperature. Hermione hated noise. She appeared to be thinking. On the other hand, Crabbe was now squatting on the chair, the whites of his eyes showing all around his pupils.

Neale couldn't help it; he started laughing.

"It's not bloody funny, man!"

"Oh, but it is!" Neale was holding his ribs; he was laughing so hard.

"Shit–"

Confident that the shouting wasn't threatening, Hermione now had her face over the edge of the seat, about two inches from Crabbe's toes.

"NEALE!"

At this fortuitous moment, the door opened, and Cope appeared. Taking in the scene, he swiftly walked over, grabbed Hermione firmly behind her head, and lifted her with his other hand, draped her body around the back of his neck and shoulders. She looked surprised at first, then settled comfortably, feeling his warmth.

Neale subsided, giggling. Cope turned to look at him, smiled, and left the room with a relaxed Hermione.

Crabbe, on the other hand, was far from relaxed. "Ye bugger! Ye just left me there, with that, that…"

"As I said, she is quite harmless to humans. Something must have disturbed her, as she's usually nocturnal. Probably got a bit cold, I expect." Neale resumed his chair, still chuckling at Crabbe's discomfort.

Crabbe shot Neale a dirty look and slowly eased himself into a normal sitting position.

"As I said, we now have the contact details in Paris. Here is the address." Neale reached into his breast pocket, drew out a piece of paper and leaned over to hand it to Crabbe. "Write to this address. Mark it for the care of the housekeeper. In the letter, write, 'Request for accommodation in a few months.' Then sign it John Watson. The contact will know that you are in my employ."

Crabbe accepted the paper with a shaking hand. He looked at the address written there. So, it was all falling into place. He would write as bid, then wait.

"Have your nerves sufficiently recovered?" Neale murmured.

Crabbe eyed him with a mixture of amusement and irritation. "Aye, I'll do."

"Well then, let us have a drink to settle you and wish you luck in your future endeavours!"

Chapter 19

Some months later, the two men sat, watching the dying embers of the fire. Neale glanced at Crabbe, watching the flickering flames gild his auburn eyebrows. He was not a handsome man, but something about him engendered affection. His nature, perhaps? His sound moral compass, his proper ethics? Maybe his sense of duty and honour?

Neale compared his visceral lust for Audley to his warm attraction for Crabbe. The men were polar opposites. Fire and ice. Chill and warmth. Darkness and light. Audley was the night to Crabbe's sunshine. Even their colouring was the opposite. Audley was dark and cunning–Crabbe was golden and steady. From his auburn hair to the pale grey eyes set in freckled skin, bronzed by the sun and ending in the stubble that sparked copper in the firelight, Crabbe was flame, fire, light and sparkle. He cast light into the dim recesses, turned a shadow into a paler shade, and shone a lantern into the dark corners.

The clear grey eyes lifted and fixed on his. Neale saw the embers reflected in their depths, the flames mirrored in the irises. He sat, transfixed by the rough-hewn beauty of the man opposite him. For an insane second, he saw himself kneeling on the carpet at Crabbe's feet and lay his head in his lap. He imagined how it would feel if Crabbe laid his hand gently on his head, stroking his hair. Time stood still, the only sound was the crackling of the fire and the crusty ticking of the grandfather clock.

Neale thought for a moment. "We could make a formidable partnership, you and I."

"Aye, tha' we could." A twinkle formed in Crabbe's eye.

"Mebbe not the partnership *you* were hopin' for, but a solid an' true one, nonetheless."

Neale tugged at the points of his waistcoat, chewing his bottom lip. He stroked his chin.

"You're thinkin' you should warn me 'bout Shegoe.

"How the *hell* did he do that?

Crabbe laughed softly at Neale's expression. "I been friends with you long enow to know tha' look."

Neale's face softened at the word. "Are we, then? Friends?"

"Aye, reckon we are at that." Crabbe smiled.

Neale felt like he'd been punched in the gut. A hidden part of his innermost soul wished with every fibre of its being that he could be this man's companion. He wanted more, much more, but knew that was impossible. He would take what he could get. That had to be enough–it must suffice.

Neale swallowed the lump that had formed in his throat.

He cleared it and fiddled with his cuffs.

"Shegoe. Yes, well, where do I start?" He stroked his chin again, feeling the stubble rasp under his fingers. He must visit his barber soon. "No one has ever laid eyes on the man. He is a ghost, an apparition, a will o' the wisp. Nebulous and phantasmic. When you think you have discovered him, revealed his identity, he vanishes, disappears into the ether like a waif–half-formed, feral and fairy-like. The stuff that dreams are made of." Neale's voice trailed off.

Crabbe watched the equerry pause, looking inwards. For himself, he didn't believe in ghosts, phantoms, or fairies. He believed in the duplicity of humans, the deceit, the double-dealing. He had seen the dishonesty and two-facedness of his fellow men, and it had left him very jaded. There were only two people he truly trusted in life–his wife Daisy and his friend Sam, the latter sadly lost to him. Added to that, his beloved Trim, who never strayed far from his side, but he was a cat without the capacity for deceit. Naughtiness, yes; disobedience, definitely, but dishonesty? Never.

Neale raised his head, smoothing his hair. "You will have to go to France. Infiltrate the ranks of Napoleon's supporters–become one of them."

Crabbe nodded, waiting for Neale to continue.

"What pretext can we use?" Neale asked the room, pacing the floor like a caged lion, backwards and forwards.

He'd wear a path in the carpet if he carried on like that.

"Mebbe askin' if I can be of service to the cause?'

Neale stopped in his gyrations, thinking. "No, too obvious." He resumed his pacing, muttering to himself. Crabbe caught the words "trust," then "infiltration," and finally, "freedom."

Neale stopped dead in his tracks and, turning to Crabbe,

exclaimed, "That's it!"

"That's what?"

"It!"

"What is?"

"The reason!"

"For what?" Crabbe queried, feeling exasperated.

"For infiltrating the ranks and connecting with the French. Freedom."

Crabbe blinked stupidly at Neale. "Who for?"

"Bonaparte, you idiot, who else?"

And the penny dropped. Of course, the promise of freedom and release from his captivity in Saint Helena, where he was currently incarcerated. A chance to regain his throne.

Crabbe took a huge breath, blew it out, and rubbed his face hard–bloody hell, a gaol break for the former Emperor of France.

"I will get Audley to contact Shegoe on the pretext of having connections with local people of certain sympathies.

I will ask Audley to tell him that the same people would do *anything* to restore their Emperor to his former position. I will hint at having a considerable amount of money in the form of donations from rich beneficiaries who would like to see a…restoration."

Crabbe tapped his chin thoughtfully. "Aye, go on."

"That's it. Money, position, timing, intent. Perfect." Neale smiled triumphantly, his usually taciturn countenance lightening. "By God, Thomas, I think we've cracked it!"

Thomas found Neale's enthusiasm infectious, but, as usual, his practical nature was uppermost. He had been told by Neale that Shegoe was a master spy, an expert in deceit; double-dealing and duplicity were second nature, so how on *earth* would they convince him they were genuine?

Thomas nodded slowly, a cautious smile forming on his face.

Neale caught the smile and arched an enquiring eyebrow.

"Vanity," stated Thomas.

"Meaning…?"

"Offer Shegoe the chance to be a part o' history. The only one to break the Emperor of France out o' prison and restore 'im to his former glory, outwittin' the English to boot." Thomas concluded with a grin. "The Frenchies love givin' the finger to the English."

Neale grinned back, suddenly looking ten years younger.

"Well, Thomas, I think you have your work cut out. I'll inform the King in the morning." A yawn took him by surprise, making his jaw crack.

Crabbe laughed, then yawned himself widely, blinking like an owl. He heaved a deep sigh, blinked, wiped a finger under his nose and said, "It be late. I should be leavin' you now." With that, he hauled himself to his feet, suppressing a grimace as he stretched his bad leg.

The gesture was not lost on Neale, who walked over and extended his hand. Crabbe clasped it in his own dry, warm grip. They stood, eyeball to eyeball, trying to get accurate measure of each other.

"I love m'wife," Crabbe said softly.

"I know," Neale replied just as softly, feeling an unwelcome stab of jealousy.

"An' you should know she's carryin' m'child."

Neale manfully suppressed another sharper stab. "Congratulations, my dear fellow!" He pumped Crabbe's hand, hoping he sounded sincere.

Crabbe laid his left hand over Neale's, whether to halt the overly hearty movement or to convey his appreciation of Neale's sentiment. Either way, Neale stopped abruptly, suddenly feeling like bursting into tears.

"You'll find your half of the apple," murmured Crabbe.

"My half of the apple?"

"Aye, everyone has another 'alf, you just 'ave to find it."

"And what if I don't find it?"

"Then you learn to live with just yaself."

Neale had already learned to do that, but his relationship with Audley (if it could be called that) had opened his eyes to having a significant other–a soulmate, companion, and friend. Or at least he had thought. His mouth turned down at the corners.

"Yon arsewipe will get 'is."

Neale glanced at Crabbe. So, he knew as well. How many other bloody people knew about his ill-advised liaison with Audley?

"Darn't you worry, only me an' Daisy know…an' the King, o' course," Crabbe added, almost as an afterthought.

Neale broke out in a cold sweat when he remembered the last interview with His Majesty. Crabbe clapped a hand on Neale's broad shoulder, squeezing hard. "Darn't worry! It'll all come right."

Neale wished he shared Crabbe's certainty. Privately he thought he'd be lucky if he got away with his neck, let alone his position.

Crabbe said, "Reckon it's time for me to turn in." He bowed to Neale, wishing him a cordial good night, and left quietly.

Neale stood looking at the flock wallpaper on the wall opposite. As he did so, a door opened soundlessly and a pudding-faced man with a balding head, large sideburns and an obsequious manner oiled his way into the room.

Obidiah Slope was a spy in the pay of Richard Neale. Born to a workhouse drudge who died giving birth to him, he had grown up in various institutions for the poor, becoming a product of the system. Weaned on neglect and ignorance, he developed a sly and cunning nature and learned at a very young age the power of information. His unremarkable features and servile demeanour made him invisible; folk looked straight through him, dismissed and ignored him. Rather than being hurt or offended by this attitude, he relished the lack of observation, affording him passage through the ranks of society, until one day, he was noticed, truly noticed, by the equerry to the then George III.

It could have ended badly. Slope was riffling through some state papers on Neale's desk under the guise of a lowly footman serving at a state garden party. He didn't hear the soft approach of Neale. Neale had spent all day on his feet at Kew Palace in Moroccan heels on one of the hottest days of that summer. Finally, he had managed to extricate himself from the buzz of the court, shucked his jacket, loosened his stock, kicked off the pinching shoes and was enjoying the feel of the cool parquet floor under the hot soles of his stockinged feet when he padded into his rooms surprising Slope at his roll-top desk.

Slope had tried to bluster his way out of the situation, claiming he'd lost his way, taking a wrong turn down labyrinthine corridors, but Neale knew a polished liar when he saw one. Rather than shouting for the nearest guard, he asked Slope what he had hoped to achieve and, gradually, drew him out. As he questioned Slope, he realised that the young man had a real knack for survival and a nose for intrigue. Added to that, Slope's extremely pedestrian appearance, and Neale concluded he would make a perfect agent.

Neale had employed Slope, paying him out of his own pocket, and had managed to inveigle the young man into the household hierarchy without any questions. Slope was invaluable–and once a snitch, always a snitch, so he didn't even have to ask for updates from Slope; the other man readily volunteered information. Privately, Slope made Neale's flesh crawl, but his usefulness far outweighed any discomfort he might feel.

Now, Slope was tasked with monitoring Crabbe, known associates, meetings, and any little bits of information that would aid their cause. But above all else, Slope had it on strict authority to see that no harm came to Crabbe whilst the latter was in Paris.

It was an irrevocable flaw in Neale's nature that he fell in love with those who did not reciprocate his feelings. Mistakenly he had believed that Audley had felt the same way about him, but eventually, he'd faced the bitter truth that Audley only wanted to suck his cock whilst sucking information out of him.

"Well? Did you get a good look at him?" Neale enquired.

"Oh yes, sir, surely I did." Slope smiled, revealing a snaggle tooth in his upper jaw. "Not a handsome cove, is he, sir? But a pleasant enough face."

"It is for that reason that I chose him," snapped Neale.

"O' course, sir, o' course. You 'ave your reasons, I do not doubt."

Neale didn't like Slope's tone or his avuncular expression, but studiously ignored both. "You will follow him and his wife to Paris and see no harm comes to him."

"O' course, sir, o' course." Slope spread his hands, palms upwards and bowed to the equerry.

"If anything untoward happens to him…" His voice trailed off.

"Rest assured, sir, it won't."

"Whatever it takes, Slope, you understand me?" he said softly.

"O' course, sir, o' course, stand on me." Slope placed his left hand over his heart and bowed again, his bald pate shining in the candlelight.

It made Neale's skin crawl to think that his dear Crabbe would be in the care of Slope, but what choice did he have? There was no one else. Slope was the only person for the task. Swallowing his instinctive dislike, he smiled in what he hoped was an encouraging manner. "Well then, keep close to him. Be his second shadow and report back."

Neale nodded curtly and Slope bowed his way out of the room.

Neale always found he felt slightly soiled after being in Slope's presence. He got out of his chair, walked over to a glass-fronted cabinet inlaid with mother-of-pearl, and poured himself a generous whisky. After a healthy gulp he felt partially cleansed. After a more conservative sip he began to relax.

Resuming his seat, he ruminated on the task he had set Crabbe. That his new recruit would execute it to the best of his ability he did not doubt, but what if his ability was insufficient? He was reasonably educated, well travelled, had been a prisoner of war, had endured hardship and suffered loss–but how equipped was he to deal with low cunning? Only time would tell. Neale downed the rest of his whisky in one gulp, sending a prayer up for the protection of his new friend.

Chapter 20

Neale rounded the corner just in time to witness Obidiah Slope reversing out of the King's day room. He jumped back to avoid detection. Slope did not notice him, tottering off down the corridor in his odd ballet-like walk.

What was that odious creep doing having an audience with the King? Neale thought that he had provided full instructions in his meeting with Slope a month earlier. Slowly he approached the double doors that led to the inner sanctum, his mind whirling with possibilities. Neale had never been one to shy away from a problematic situation–instead, he grasped the proverbial nettle. Thrusting open the doors, he entered the room. The nearest footman looked startled at his sudden entrance, as did the sulphur-crested cockatoo sitting on the back of one of the chairs.

George IV was a man who generally disliked most human beings but loved animals. One of his more eccentric habits was collecting them, even exotic species from the far-flung regions of the Empire. Neale was entirely used to monkeys jumping off the top of doors, peacocks on the table, and skunks strutting across the room.

"What the fuck do *you* want?" the King snapped. He was

in a bilious mood; he'd suffered from acute flatulence all day and now had stabbing pains in his abdomen. Neale glanced at the footman, who widened his eyes in warning.

"I *said* what in God's name do you want?"

Rather than prevaricate, Neale decided on a full-frontal assault. "What was Slope doing here, Sire?" The last word was said almost as an afterthought. The brief hesitation was not lost on the King.

"Leave us!"

Various servants made their obeisances and left, leaving George IV and his equerry glaring at one another.

"Out with it!" spat the King.

Neale ran his tongue around his dry mouth. *Careful now.*

"As your Majesty is undoubtedly fully aware, Obidiah Slope is in my employ. I was not aware he reported directly to you."

For nearly a full minute, Neale thought he had gone too far. The King just glared balefully at him. Then he began to vibrate. His chins wobbled with mirth. Throwing back his head, he roared with laughter, tears filling his eyes.

"Oh Neale, Neale, Neale." He wiped his hand over his eyes, still snorting with amusement. "You think you are the only intelligencer in this palace. I didn't wait for *years* to become King and learn nothing!" The King uttered the last word like an expletive. "I was taught by the best. My late father and my conniving, controlling cow of a mother–not to mention tutors, teachers, and ministers. I would have to be the local village idiot not to have learned something."

Neale looked at the King–truly looked at him, as if he was seeing him for the first time. Had he so misjudged the man? Was the corpulent, decadent buffoon merely a façade? Did a shrewd brain sit behind those piggy eyes?

George IV smiled slowly, resting his chubby paws on his barrel chest. "Well now, what have we here? A man in a quandary. A man with a conundrum, not knowing what to think!" The King chuckled loudly. "I would be a poor ruler if I did not keep several fingers in various pies. Knowledge is information; knowledge is power. I make it my business to *know*." He steepled his fingers under his chin. "You, my friend, are merely a cog in a wheel, a link in a chain. You fit where I say you fit, and you go where I say you go." He pointed a chubby finger at Neale. "You serve *me*. I do not serve *you*."

Neale swallowed audibly.

"Did you think for one moment that I would be stupid enough to leave the fate of this country in the hands of minions?"

Neale felt a response was required, but the King continued.

"The populace believes me to be a syphilitic, alcoholic, obese, empty-headed windbag. And they would be correct, up to a point." The piggy eyes narrowed whilst a cunning smile spread across his face. Neale couldn't believe that the man he was looking at was the same man he had been serving for the past few years.

"Oh yes–even you have been led to believe I am nothing more than a figurehead, an empty shell, signifying nothing. I lure people into a false sense of security, then–!" He snapped his fingers, making one of the royal dogs sit up, looking expectant.

If Neale hadn't been so taken aback he would have smiled. Instead, he couldn't stop staring at his sovereign. The latter was openly grinning now, enjoying Neale's discomfort.

"I warned you once before about trying to pull the wool over my eyes when I mentioned the dresses." The King wagged a finger at Neale. "Don't think I haven't looked into the crustacean, where he comes from and who he's connected with."

Neale felt sick. Not Crabbe, please, no.

"Stop panicking, man! He's as straight as an arrow–bloody boring, if you ask me. What's the story with the cat, though?"

Even Neale, accustomed to his sovereign's mercurial turn of mind, was caught off guard. "Ah, the cat. Um–was the ship's cat, Your Majesty. Crabbe, he–well, he–"

"Pinched him, eh? Not so honest after all." The King snorted. "Well, he probably saved the creature from death or starvation."

As if divining the change in her master's mood, the dog who had sat up padded over to the King to have her ears rubbed.

"Animals, Neale. They are the only things you can truly rely on. Honest, loyal, don't ask for much in return, eh girl?"

The dog's eyes began to close slowly under his gentle ministrations.

Apart from that and his mistress, Maria Fitzherbert, the King's only other passion was architecture. In 1787, he commissioned Henry Holland to develop a design for a pavilion that would provide an escape from London. George IV chose Brighton, which afforded him a private space to take the sea air but also where he could conduct clandestine meetings with Maria. Adjacent to the pavilion were riding stables and an enormous onion garden that fed the King's well-known addiction. On the grounds, the King had a lake dug on which he occasionally was rowed about, sipping cherry gin with his pet cockatoo on his shoulder. The same sulfur-crested cockatoo was now sitting on the back of the King's chair, its expression mirroring that of its owner.

It's bad enough he's looking at me in that tone of voice, but do I have to put up with the bloody bird as well?

"Oh, come now, Neale! Swallow your pride and come down off your fucking high horse! No man is an island, least of all you." The cockatoo bobbed its head in agreement. "You've done well so far. I am pleased with your progress with Audley. Keep it up, man, and we'll succeed in our infiltration." The cockatoo cocked its head on one side as if weighing Neale up.

Neale smiled thinly. He didn't like being hoodwinked, especially by a man he'd mentally compartmentalised and dismissed as a nincompoop.

"Slope reports to you with a dotted line to me. I need must check and double-check the loyalties of *all* my servants." He beetled his eyebrows at Neale. "No one is immune, understand?"

"Yes, Sire."

"Keep the correspondence clandestine with the crustacean. Provide encouragement, let Slope keep a close eye on him and his wife. Report to me on *every* detail, understand?"

"Yes, Sire."

"Now bugger off."

They were decanted at the Port of London, and after a refreshing pot of tea and a slightly stale scone, Daisy and Thomas stood upon the quayside watching as the ship docked and sailors threw the lines ashore. Thomas was used to such sights, but Daisy was astounded at the crew's speed and efficiency as they cast their lines to the waiting stevedores who tied the ship to the enormous bollards that dotted the quay.

After a brief period during which the gangplank was lowered and secured, they boarded the ship. Thomas's heart lifted to feel the dip and swell of a ship beneath his feet once more, and he began to anticipate the journey across the Channel to France and onward to Paris.

Lord Palmer had arranged a small cabin for them which they shared with another couple, and to this they retired, as it was to be a night-time crossing. Daisy barely had time to undress and complete a minimal toilette before she rolled into her bunk and sank into a deep, dreamless sleep. Thomas stayed up on deck for a while, watching the sunset and the coast of England fade into the distance.

The first thing Daisy registered on waking was the scream of gulls and the shouting of men as the ship tied up alongside the quay in Le Havre. Sitting up in her bunk, she peered through the small porthole in the vessel's side and perceived several pairs of feet running to and fro in front of her nose. Realising that they had docked and that disembarkation would begin shortly, she hastily got up, dressed alongside Thomas, who gathered their belongings and joined fellow passengers awaiting further instructions. A rough sailor came down the gangway stairs and shouted, "Disembarkation in five minutes!" before disappearing up the stairs again to carry on unloading the ship.

After a short wait, they began filing off the vessel and got their first look at the port of Le Havre. Being adjacent to the fish market explained the number of herring gulls that filled the sky above them, and in the distance, Thomas noted a small row of 'diligence'–French coaches waiting to convey passengers to Paris and other destinations. He left Daisy minding the bags and walked over to obtain their tickets.

They boarded a 'diligence' along with six other passengers. Thomas, thanks to Neale's bag of coins, had managed to negotiate seats for them in the cabriolet at the front, fixed to the coach's body. They shared the interior with three other people–a couple like themselves, and a corpulent Frenchman who proceeded to stuff the little pockets surrounding his leather seat with bread, snuff, a bottle of wine, and several pocket handkerchiefs.

Up top with the driver sat two less fortunate souls who were not protected from the rain and had to make do with the space available between hats, swords, bandboxes, and portmanteau.

Thomas was surprised that seven horses pulled the diligence, the most he had ever seen attached to a carriage. Once they got underway, he calculated they were achieving a top speed of six to seven miles an hour.

They bumped along in the carriage to the first rest stop, where they changed horses. They made good progress, and after another stop and fresh horses, the outskirts of Paris began to appear. Thomas could see the Seine winding its serpentine way into the city and, faintly, the Ile de la Cité with the spires of Sainte Chapelle pointing skyward.

"It's cleaner than London," Daisy remarked as she bounced up and down beside Thomas. She reckoned she'd be black and blue by the time they arrived in the city and was glad of several layers of petticoats to protect her bottom. Her main concern was the baby, though; she spent most of the journey holding on to her abdomen while clutching her husband's hand.

The cries of street vendors became louder, horses whinnying, geese quacking, and pigeons' ubiquitous cooing. Wherever you looked, there were grey pigeons—on rooftops, in the street, splashing through puddles, pecking leftovers. The diligence had slowed to a walking pace, dodging other vehicles, pedestrians, horses, and geese. Daisy noticed the feet of the poultry were black, having been tarred to protect them as they walked from the city's outer regions into the centre to either be slaughtered or sold.

The diligence turned into the Rue Saint-Denis, where the coach terminated. They were both as stiff as boards after the long journey, and it took a while for the circulation to return to Thomas's bad leg. Fortunately it took some time to unload the baggage, so whilst they waited, they eased their cramped limbs. Finally, in possession of the bags, they hailed a small hansom pulled by a resigned-looking pony to take them to the Rue de Rivoli where they had rented a house. Within fifteen minutes they reached their destination, to be greeted by the housekeeper, Madame Crecy.

Madame Crecy did not speak English, and Daisy did not speak French. Thomas had a smattering learned from some of the French traders he had had dealings with whilst on the Donegal, but it is incredible what can be achieved with smiles and hand gestures. In a very short time they had been welcomed, their bags taken upstairs, a pot of strong coffee delivered, along with a plate of little meringues sandwiched with buttercream. Thomas had eaten macaroons before, but it was a new and delightful taste experience for Daisy. Instantly she was addicted. Thomas had to take the plate away from her after she'd quickly demolished four.

"I'm hungry!" she protested.

"Aye, well ye can eat somethin' healthier than *those*," Thomas chided her.

"But they're only small!"

"An' full o' sugar," he countered.

"So? I'm eatin' for two." She dimpled at him.

Thomas snorted, indicating what he thought of that excuse.

"I'll ask the cook to prepare ye a hearty soup for lunch."

Daisy made a rude noise and stuck her tongue out at him. He chuckled as he left the room, eating the remaining two macaroons whilst descending the narrow stairs to seek out the resident cook.

Madame Margarita de Castro y Sousa was a freed slave proud of her Portuguese heritage and cooking. She also hated white men in her kitchen. White men smelled like 'le cochon'. Thomas thought this rather harsh, considering he was very particular with his hygiene, but Madame Sousa wouldn't budge. They therefore engaged in a conversation with Thomas standing in the doorway yelling at Madame, with Madame yelling back. The entire thing would have been funny if not for the considerable noise already in the basement kitchen over which Thomas had to shout. Madame refused to speak English, although Thomas suspected she could, so by the time he had communicated his request, he had a headache accompanying his rumbling stomach.

Despite the strained exchange, a soup was duly provided; a hearty onion stew richly flavoured with tomato and complete with croutons. Thomas thought he detected a touch of red wine in the soup but couldn't be sure. Daisy ate the lot and the crusty bread and slurped the rest of the broth straight from the bowl, much to her husband's amusement.

"Like French cookin,' do you?" He smiled at his wife, now replete.

"Dunno what it was, but it were delicious." She suddenly yawned widely, making her eyes water.

"Why darn't you have a lie-down, love?" Thomas nodded at the bed behind her.

"I will, at that." She heaved herself to her feet and padded over to the bed, kicked her shoes off, elevated her feet, and curled up on her side like a shrimp. Within five minutes, she was fast asleep.

Thomas drew the counterpane up over her, smiling at the soft snoring. He resumed his seat and mopped the remnants of his broth up with the last hunk of bread. He thought of Trim with a pang. At a time like this, he would have put the bowl on the floor to allow his beloved cat to lick the rest of the liquid up. He hoped the housekeeper at the Palmer estate was looking after him. Thomas had contemplated bringing Trim with them–the cat would have loved the sea voyage, but the thought of him in a busy city like Paris, where, if he escaped, he'd never find him, dissuaded him from doing so. He hated being parted from Trim, but it was safer this way. At least he had Daisy. She should have stayed in England, in her condition, but she'd flatly refused, insisting she go with him, much to Thomas's secret relief.

Neale had persuaded Audley to write to his French connections, making introductions. Audley had received a reply, and Thomas had been told to sit tight to wait for further instructions. The rented house was a front for their stay in Paris. Crabbe had identity papers personally signed by George IV in case things went to smash. Part of him was nervous about the mission he had been given, but another, more significant part, was excited. He loved travelling again, the sea voyage had been like a tonic, and the sights and smells of a new city were tantalising. If he could experience a new place, helping to prevent a dictator from taking control of France while serving his King, then why not? Additionally, the fat stipend he received would set him and Daisy up to buy a small business of their own, perhaps when they returned to

England. Whilst Daisy slept, Thomas continued to happily dream.

Chapter 21

"Crabbe!"

Thomas halted at the sound of the stentorian tones. His subconscious had recognised the voice before his conscious had. He was not surprised, therefore, to turn and come face to face with the chiselled countenance of Captain Knox.

"Sir!" He knuckled his forehead, feeling his spine straighten through the force of habit.

"Able Seaman Crabbe. Well, seaman no more, I suspect, as I am a captain no more." The ocean spray-coloured eyes crinkled at the corners as he looked down at Crabbe.

"No longer a Captain, sir?"

"No, I resigned my commission. My wife Arabella was tired of my seafaring and wished me to plant my feet upon *terra firma* rather than the deck of a yawing ship."

The two men smiled at each other in perfect understanding.

"Arabella wished to experience the continent, so we are spending the summer in Paris. So, Crabbe, what are you doing with yourself these days, hm?"

And there lay the rub. Should he tell the truth, or should he prevaricate? He had been told to stick to the truth where possible; if interrogated, he wouldn't get caught out telling half-truths. After all, you never knew if the other fellow had the other half.

"Well, sir, I find myself in the employ of, ah–a servant in the household of the King of England."

The green eyes widened. "The King?"

"Tha's right, sir; his equerry to be precise."

Knox digested this bit of information for a few seconds. He stared hard at Crabbe. Crabbe felt his ears turning pink under the scrutiny.

"Crabbe, you are a terrible liar; I wonder if you even bother with it." Knox's eyes twinkled.

"It's true, sir, I am employed by the equerry–well, an' partly a colleague of 'is. Daisy and I be in 'is service at the request of ah, Neale." Crabbe finished lamely.

Knox's eyes continued to bore into Crabbe's face, making him grow redder.

"Neale, you say? Would that be Richard Neale? Tall, saturnine, reddish hair and blue eyes?"

Crabbe nodded like an automaton.

Knox wiped a finger under his straight nose, took a breath, and said, "Neale informed you of a low-level intelligence contact in Paris with whom you were supposed to meet today?" Crabbe nodded again.

Captain Knox smiled again, waiting patiently, hands clasped behind his back.

"It be you, sir!"

"Indeed, Crabbe. It is I."

Crabbe was delighted. What were the chances of not only meeting his old captain again, but working with him once more?

"Be careful, Crabbe—Neale is not what he seems."

Now it was Crabbe's turn to make Captain Knox uncomfortable. "If you mean about 'is sexual…nature, I already know."

Knox's finely shaped eyebrows shot up at that statement. "I wasn't aware of his sexual preferences; I was referring to his political leanings."

Crabbe could have kicked himself. Damn, now he'd let the cat out of the bag. Neale would *not* thank him for that. He closed his eyes, then reopened them to see Knox looking at him, head on one side like he couldn't decide whether he was feather or fur.

"I trust you do not share Neale's…orientation?"

"No, sir, I do not. Not that there's anything wrong wi' it, but it ain't for me."

Knox snorted. "I beg to differ with you, Crabbe, but you seem more broad-minded than I."

Crabbe wisely kept quiet. Knox was an old-fashioned type of man, one who believed men were men and women were women, but Crabbe had developed a friendship with Neale and had learned quite a bit from him about how the lines could blur when it came to relationships. And he believed in his heart that love was love, no matter who it involved.

Then his brain caught up with Knox's comment. "Political leanings, sir?"

"Yes; that is to say, his allegiances aren't clear cut." Silence hung upon the air between the two men. "Rumour has it that he has French sympathies."

Crabbe felt something cold slither down his back. No, he couldn't, could he? Had he so misjudged the man? "I can't say as 'ow I've seen tha' in him, sir."

"Well, you seem to know him better than me, so that I will defer to your experience of the man."

Knox sounded dubious to Crabbe's ears, but there wasn't much he could do about it under the circumstances. However, at the first opportunity, he would write a letter to Neale and arrange a meeting with him on his return. He needed to see the other man's face up close to make up his mind.

"So, my dear fellow, this colleague of Neale's in whose employ you are in now…?"

"Lord Palmer, sir, he's a–"

"By Jove, I know Palmer!" Knox exclaimed. "He was on a naval committee a few years ago. We were tasked with the investigation of an officer, and Palmer was a member of the Commission of Inquiry."

Knox explained that he had been a military member of the tribunal; the rest had been civilians, one of whom was Lord Palmer. They had struck up a conversation after the proceedings, which had led to a late dinner at Palmer's club, and their paths had crossed over the years in London. "Is he still living in Suffolk?"

"Aye, sir, me and m'wife both work for 'im. We live in the big 'ouse."

"Well, what a small world it is." Knox smiled fondly at Crabbe. "So, then, Thomas, may I call you Thomas? Fine, where are you headed today?"

"I have been tasked with an errand for Neale–that is, 'e were hopin' I would trace a certain personage," Crabbe finished lamely.

"And that personage would be…?"

"Allus I know, sir, is that they're called Shegoe." A pregnant pause followed this statement. "Shegoe?"

"Ah, yes, sir, that is what I have been told they're called."

Knox considered the man before him. Earnest, honest, and straightforward, with a good moral compass and sound ethics. What the *hell* did he have to do with Shegoe? Knox thought rapidly. It had to start with Neale. That slippery, two- faced, double-dealing courtier. He must have given Crabbe instructions. Wound him up, pointed him in the right direction and waited to see what he could achieve–the arsewipe.

Out loud he said, "Well, Thomas, I've never heard of this personage, but I can certainly ask around. I am not without influence in this area of Paris." He smiled thinly at the younger man whilst keeping a bland countenance. "Where are you headed now?"

"I thought I might 'ave a spot of lunch in one of the eateries around 'ere." Crabbe looked around him, hopefully.

"Nonsense, man! You will dine with me at my townhouse;

it is but a short walk this way." Knox gestured down the street.

Crabbe accepted the invitation with alacrity, and the two men strolled together, making for Knox's house.

Neither was aware of a figure standing in the shadows, watching them both.

The man stood motionless, watching the retreating backs of Knox and the other English man, the one called Crabbe.

He took out a snuff box, applied a healthy amount to the back of his hand snorted the tobacco up one nostril, then the other. Shutting the lid with a decisive snap, he replaced it in his breast pocket. Withdrawing a large, red silk handkerchief from his waistcoat, he wiped his putty-like nose, folded it into a small square, and returned it.

Reaching behind him, he reclaimed the silver-topped cane reclining against the dank wall and, straightening his top hat, slowly emerged from the Stygian gloom into the bustling street.

He joined the tide of humanity ebbing and flowing around him. No one gave him a second glance as his appearance was, well, ordinary. With a chinless pudding-like face and balding pate, he had short legs with smaller than usual feet which made him walk like a ballet dancer, almost balancing on the balls of his feet. The cane prevented him from wobbling out of control and lent him an air of gentility.

Slope followed Crabbe at a discreet distance, as instructed. In his heart of hearts, Richard Neale would die if anything happened to Thomas Crabbe. And his wife, of course.

Slope strolled leisurely after the retreating men.

Later that evening, as the sun set like a bruise in the sky, a soft knock sounded at the tradesman's entrance to Knox's house. The door was opened to admit a tall person, swaddled in a thick coat with a felt hat pulled down low over the brow. The lower footman took the visitor to the upper footman, who passed them over to Duval, the butler. Duval led the latecomer down the main corridor to the room Captain Knox called his study.

Knox was sat in his old Captain's chair, which had been unbolted from the floor of his cabin and reinstated in his house (minus bolts) but now sporting small wheels which allowed him to zoom backwards and forwards across the polished wooden floorboards, much to the annoyance of the housemaids whose job it was to clean said floor. Currently, though, Knox was sitting still, anticipating the clandestine visitor.

The visitor was ushered into the room, lit only by a few candles and the flickering firelight. Duval shut the door softly behind him, not offering to take the visitor's outer robes. He had seen this personage before and therefore knew his assistance was unnecessary.

Knox waited whilst the newcomer divested themselves of coat, hat, scarf (which had been pulled up to obscure most of their face), gloves, and a large pistol concealed in a deep pocket sewn into their clothes.

"Finally! God, that lot makes me so hot!" The woman drew a sigh of relief, taking the seat opposite Knox, fanning herself with a long-fingered, white hand.

"Whisky?"

"Please. No water, as you know." She took the preferred drink, leaning back in the chair.

"Were you seen?"

"Seen, yes; recognised, no. Followed, definitely not." She downed the drink in one gulp, dabbing her mouth with the back of her hand.

"Another?" She nodded.

"How is that bastard of a husband of yours?"

"Still a bastard and still my husband, more's the pity."

"Do you want me to call him out and shoot him?"

She laughed, a husky, throaty sound. "Pistols at dawn? As entertaining as that would be, darling, I can shoot him myself." She snorted.

Knox resumed his chair, nursing a glass of brandy. He raised his glass to the woman in salute. "What are we drinking to?"

"Us. You." She smiled at Knox over the rim of her crystal tumbler.

Knox gazed at her. He was an unusual creature–a man who genuinely liked women for themselves. Of course he appreciated the usual aesthetics, breasts, buttocks, hair and the rest, but he was more interested in what lay between their ears than their legs. The woman who sat now sipping her second drink fascinated him. Her personality, force of will, and indomitable spirit attracted him more than a well-formed arse. Not that he would turn a well-formed arse down if it were offered to him.

"Harriet."

She glanced up at him. "Yes?"

"I asked you to come this evening to discuss a…friend of mine."

She arched a well-plucked eyebrow.

"He was a man I served with whilst in the navy. He reported to me before privateers apprehended our ship. He was indentured onto another ship whilst myself and my officers were imprisoned."

Harriet nodded once, remembering Knox telling her of his time on the high seas.

"He now finds himself in the employ of Lord Palmer, tasked with finding the master spy trying to free Bonaparte." I know that you have certain…connections. I would be very grateful if you would keep a weather eye out for him."

"Does this man have a name, dear one?"

"Crabbe. Thomas Crabbe. He is a simple fellow; I mean not soft in the head, but rather innocent. I would appreciate it if you and your people could make sure he comes to no harm."

Harriet gave it some thought whilst finishing the rest of her whisky. Her husband was high up in the French government, and unbeknownst to him, she had formed some very useful contacts over the dining table during many of their candlelit soirees. Harriet was an intriguer by nature; she couldn't help herself, and she had learned that information was very valuable. Her husband, although a wealthy man, was tight as a fish's arsehole, God rot him, and only gave her a trifling amount for her allowance. She had to find other ways of earning her own money. Information, blackmail, and conspiracy were good ways of obtaining some ready coin, as long as she was careful and clever.

"What does this man look like?" Knox provided a brief description.

Harriet placed the now empty glass on the table beside her, fixing her dark eyes on Knox's. "And what is this service worth, my love?"

Knox felt as if the stock around his throat had tightened.

Without taking her dark eyes off his, she leaned forward slightly and began drawing the hem of her gown upwards, parting her legs, revealing the dark triangle between them.

Knox's breath caught in his throat. He slid off the chair onto his knees and bent his head to make full payment.

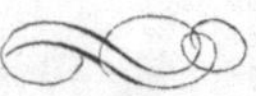

Harriet Deschanel wrote several messages to her contacts around the city. She alluded to a man who matched Crabbe's description. Pieces of paper were passed from hand to hand, quietly, quickly, until Crabbe was known on sight. The instructions were to follow him and observe his movements, but under no circumstances was he to be harmed.

In the meantime, her instructions from Lord Palmer were to contact Crabbe quietly. A note arrived at the Crabbe's house, instructing Thomas to present himself at the Rue St Honoré the following day.

That night Crabbe sharpened his knife, eventually sheathing it in its holster. He believed in preparing for the worst but hoping for the best.

Chapter 22

Thomas paced nervously back and forth, ignoring his protesting leg. His palms felt sweaty at the prospect of meeting Palmer's contact. All the letter had alluded to was that this personage had information on the possible whereabouts of Shegoe. He had been instructed to wait in the Rue St Honoré, at the top of the street, off the Rue L'Opera. He had no idea who he was meeting or what they looked like, but apparently, they knew what *he* looked like.

Thomas turned in his perambulations to see a tall figure moving towards him. The person had a long stride with broad shoulders and long-fingered hands. As the stranger approached, Thomas realised with a start that the person was wearing a gown over which was a sleeveless, full- length cardigan in heavy brocade. A tasselled cap completed the ensemble.

The woman stopped before Thomas, topping him by a good two inches. Her almond-shaped eyes were heavily lined with black kohl, and the wide, full-lipped mouth sported scarlet lip paint. She had high cheekbones and a broad, cleft chin. At first, Thomas thought she might be a man, but then his eyes dropped to the visible swell of bosom, encased as it was within a bodice.

"Like what you see, Monsieur Crabbe?" The voice was husky and held a note of amusement.

Thomas felt his face grow hot. "Ah, no, I mean, tha' is…" He trailed off, looking helplessly about him for reinforcement.

"It is just you and I here, Monsieur Crabbe." The deep voice sounded slightly crisp.

"Of course. I, ah–I thought p'raps you would have… friends, protectors…"

"Do I look like I need protection?" she asked with some asperity. Thomas could see the spark of annoyance in the deep brown eyes. "Rather, *they* should fear *me*."

Thomas realised that this lady probably had a powerful husband and that she operated under his auspices and protection. "I didn't mean to insult you, ma'am; I'm assumin' o' course tha' your husband would make–"

"I *beg* your pardon?" The brown eyes took on a hard-boiled appearance.

Thomas cast about for a suitable response, trying desperately to choose his words with care; he'd put a foot wrong, but he honestly didn't know what to think of this most unusual woman.

"My husband, such as he is, is completely ignorant of my activities. He assumes, like most pompous members of his sex, that I spend most of my time playing cards, sewing tapestries, and bouncing friends' various offspring on my childless knee." She fixed Thomas with a gimlet eye, the full mouth now like a slash in her handsome face. "What I engage in couldn't be further from the truth. However, my gender allows me to move undetected within the polite circles of French society…so there is something to be said for being a woman." The gimlet eye had developed a slight twinkle.

The penny dropped like a rock into a pond. Dear God in heaven, it was *her*. Smiling dryly down at him, one eyebrow arched–this woman was the spy to George IV, the informant, the go-between, posing as a French agent. She was Shegoe. Thomas felt his mouth fall open.

Now she was openly grinning at him. "Quite a disguise, hm?"

He nodded, not trusting himself to speak, but examined her closely–from her black, wavy hair pinned up under the soft cap to her feet, clad in leather boots if he wasn't mistaken. He could see their toes peeping out from under the hem of her gown. What sort of woman wore boots under a dress? His mind supplied the answer. *A prepared one*.

"I'm a practical woman, Mr Crabbe; it would not behove me to wear high heels if I needed to run at a moment's notice." She had followed his gaze. "Also, the over jacket that you see me wearing hides the fact that my gown is not a gown at all, but a skirt fastened at the waist, which I can untie and lose quickly, enabling me to run in the thin calfskin breeches that hide beneath."

Thomas felt his jaw drop even further.

Shegoe laughed, a rich, warm chuckle. Had Thomas been a different kind of man, he would have stepped forward and placed his mouth upon hers. This woman had an earthy, almost animalistic quality about her that made the hairs on his forearms stand up under his cotton shirt. There was an air of danger and a whiff of brimstone about this unusual lady, which might have been repellent, but Thomas warmed to her. She looked at him as if she could see into his soul and liked what she saw.

He passed some test as she extended her right hand to him, the gemstone on her third finger winking in the pale sunlight. He grasped it by reflex, feeling the hairs on his arms stand up even more as she rubbed her thumb over his palm, her eyes never leaving his. The secret signal. She had just given it to him very subtly.

Thomas rubbed his thumb against her palm, noticing the slight smile lurking at the corners of her mouth.

"So, then, we are members of the same group. Here to serve one who has only just gained his position?" The last word was said as a question.

Thomas felt his mouth go dry. He nodded slowly, looking into her eyes, waiting for a flicker, anything indicating she wasn't genuine. The dark eyes never wavered or looked away but continued boring into his own.

"And how is our employer?" The words almost a caress.

"Well. The last time I saw 'im." The Prince Regent, now King George IV, was getting fatter by the day, swilling buckets of claret, using even more obnoxious language than ever. Privately Thomas couldn't stand the man, but he had sworn an oath, so he took his position and his loyalties very seriously.

"That is excellent news. So, you have your instructions from Lord Palmer."

Thomas nodded. "And here you are."

"Aye," croaked Thomas, "here I am."

He was subjected to further scrutiny, the dark eyes sweeping him from head to toe. Then she did an unusual thing. She leaned forward and very gently sniffed him.

Thomas took a step backwards, trying not to look affronted.

Shegoe smiled slyly. "'Tis a habit of mine. I come from a long line of 'nez' and my mother taught me to smell fear on a person." Catching his look, she smiled more broadly to take the sting out of her words. "I am happy to tell you that you are a brave man, straight and true."

Thomas was utterly baffled by this statement.

"And, although not handsome, attractive in your way."

She cocked her head to one side, looking intently at his face.

"Are you married?"

Thomas coughed, patting his chest to dislodge a non-existent blockage. "Aye, I'm wed to Daisy. My wife," he added unnecessarily.

Shegoe laughed, showing very even, white teeth. "Of course, she's your wife if you're wed to her, no?"

Thomas wished with every fibre of his being that Daisy stood beside him. He felt tongue-tied and gawky, like a teenage boy in the presence of this self-possessed woman.

As if divining his thoughts, Shegoe tucked her arm through his, despite the height difference, and towed him slowly down the Rue St Honoré. "Let us find a quiet auberge where we may have a glass of champagne and discuss matters."

"Er, I don't drink champagne, ma'am."

Shegoe stopped in her tracks. "Blasphemy!" she cried, then threw her head back and laughed loudly, startling a couple of pigeons from a nearby rooftop. Turning back to Crabbe, she asked, "What *do* you drink, Mr Crabbe?"

"Beer."

"Beer? *Beer*?! In Paris?" Shegoe looked horrified. "I shall introduce you to a nice Burgundian. A wine, not a man." She chuckled, towing Crabbe along once more.

A saying floated through Crabbe's mind. *An immovable object meets an irresistible force*. That meant he was the object, for Shegoe was a force to be reckoned with.

They reached a quiet wine bar, with the obligatory round tables and wicker chairs placed outside. Shegoe took the table furthest from the main entrance, Crabbe noted, and sat in the chair facing the street. He turned the other chair slightly so he could see the street out of the corner of his eye.

A waiter came out, took their order, and oiled his way back into the dim interior.

Neither Shegoe nor Crabbe spoke a word. The waiter returned with a metal tray upon which sat two glasses containing a red liquid which, after placing on the table, he bowed unctuously and withdrew.

"To what shall we drink, Mr Crabbe?" Shegoe raised her glass, looking at him in anticipation.

"I, ah–that is…"

"Oh, come now," she said crisply. "Do not be so feeble."

"Um, new beginnings?"

Shegoe poked her tongue out and made a rude noise. "How about new alliances and the success of our enterprise?"

Crabbe nodded like an automaton, gulping the wine. His brain registered it as a dry, oaky red before the membranes of his mouth caught up, and he swirled the liquid around his mouth. It wasn't to his taste, as he much preferred full-bodied, smoother wine, but he dared not say so to the commanding woman sitting opposite him.

Shegoe fixed him with a basilisk stare, making him shift in his seat.

"So, Mr Crabbe—or Thomas. May I call you Thomas? Good, you may call me Harriet. We are here to discuss a certain…personage who is currently not at liberty." She took a sip of her wine, licking her lower lip. "This…person wishes to return to their homeland; however, it is not in the common interest for said person to be at liberty, n'est pas?"

Crabbe nodded, his eyes never leaving hers.

"Well then, we need to call a meeting of like-minded people to put plans in place to stop this bird from escaping its cage." Her eyes sparkled over the rim of her glass as she took another sip. Crabbe left his; he didn't like the taste, and he wanted to keep a clear head.

The sounds of Paris swirled around them. Street vendors shouting, the metallic tang of forks and knives on metal plates, the clopping of hooves as carriages passed by, the chiming of church bells, but all Crabbe could hear and see was Shegoe. What was her background? How did she come to be a spy in the service of England? Why was she opposed to Bonaparte, considering her husband was high in the French government? These questions and more ricocheted around his brain.

"My mother."

"I beg ya pardon?"

"The connection."

"The what?"

"You were wondering how a woman married to a French Government official living in Paris could be an English agent." Said more as a statement than a question.

Thomas gave up marvelling at her powers of mind reading and merely nodded.

"She was French, from a long line of perfumiers–her father was a famous 'nez', a nose highly sought after for blending essential oils for distilling into perfume. My mother married an English man, and they naturally moved to England following his career." Harriet made a moue of disapproval at her mother's obedience and her father's perfidy. "I was born and educated in England, but the old alliance was always there, so I was sent to finishing school in Paris at eighteen. Whilst attending there, I met my husband, and… well, the rest is history, as they say." She paused to finish her wine. She eyed Crabbe's nearly full glass. "You do not like Burgundy, Monsieur?"

"Um, no, ma'am, it be not to my taste."

"The person currently not at liberty is an arrogant, egotist who nearly won Waterloo. If it hadn't been for the Prussians, the outcome would have been very different to what it was. Even Wellington reckoned it was the 'nearest run thing you ever saw in your life'." She allowed this information to sink in.

Crabbe nodded again, not trusting himself to speak.

"A third attempt to return would be disastrous for everyone."

Crabbe removed his handkerchief and wiped his nose, more to gain time in formulating a suitable reply than because his nose was running. Plus, he could hide his facial expression in the voluminous cotton folds.

"Mr Crabbe?"

"Aye, I heard you." Crabbe folded the handkerchief carefully, keeping his eyes down the whole while. "We need to call a meetin' then, get certain folks together to talk about strategy." Finally, he raised his eyes to hers. Harriet's eyes had narrowed slightly and it took every ounce of willpower to stop his face from reddening.

"Hmmm. As you say, monsieur, we must arrange a meeting of like-minded people. Leave it with me; I will send out messages quietly around the city. Give me two days, then meet me here again at 3 o'clock; I will tell you where we go from there."

She stood abruptly, surprising Crabbe. He stood more slowly, feeling his calf muscle, or what was left of it, twinge.

"You are in pain?" Harriet asked softly.

"An ol' war wound, ma'am, got in the service of His Majesty's navy." Crabbe grimaced, not bothering to control his expression this time.

"I'm sure our grateful benefactor thanks you for your sacrifice." She smiled at him, the gesture transforming her face. Unlikely, thought Crabbe, but forbore to say so.

They parted amicably, promising to reconvene in two days.

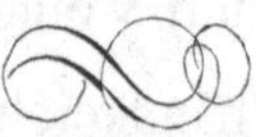

15th October 1819

My dear sir,

I have delayed writing so long under the expectation of making contact with the person you indicated. This has been achieved, and a meeting has been arranged between Interested Parties. I hope to learn more in due course.

Your humble and obedient servant, The Cook

30th October 1819

My dear sir,

I congratulate you on making contact. Keep a 'weather eye out,' as you would say. The claret drinker wishes you Godspeed in your Endeavours. I wish you much more.

Your humble and obedient servant, The Dresser

8th November 1819

My dear sir,

We continue in the same lodgings and pass our time comfortably and peaceably, receiving much attention from the Gentlemen and Ladies about us. Tomorrow certain guests will be attending a dinner party held by a New Acquaintance. I shall write the very next day to advise you of the proceedings.

Your most humble and obedient servant, The Cook

20th November 1819

My dear sir,

The dinner was Fruitful. Things are in place. I have one last meeting tomorrow and hope to report Good Tidings.

Your most humble and affectionate servant, The Cook

Chapter 23

Britain's corpulent monarch was reclining on a day bed surrounded by his beloved dogs. As Neale entered, all the dogs raised their heads, looking enquiringly at him.

"Come in, man, and shut the bloody door." George IV had suffered a severe episode of gout overnight, which had resulted in a short temper this morning. "Damn drafts, come in every frigging direction," he grumbled, drawing a thick woollen blanket higher over his chest. He glared at Neale, who stood patiently before him. "What is it, man?"

Neale cleared his throat. "Lord Palmer, Your Majesty, he-"

"What about him?" snapped the King.

Neale drew a deep breath.

"Your Majesty, he has written to me to advise that Captain Knox has formed an…ill-advised relationship with one of our informants."

"Which informant? Spit it out, man!"

Neale swallowed, commended his soul to God and said,

"Harriet Deschanel."

Complete silence greeted his statement. A log dropped and

fizzed in the open fireplace, one of the spaniels yawned, and a floorboard popped. The silence stretched.

"That conniving little tart," hissed the King.

Neale let his breath out surreptitiously, striving for a bland expression.

"So," the King said softly, "she thinks she can play with us?"

Another log popped in the hearth, sending a few sparks up the chimney.

"Or is she playing Knox only?"

Neale wiped a finger under his nose. "Palmer's spies inform me that the relationship appears purely physical."

"Nothing is purely physical with that woman," snarled the King. Then his expression changed. "Although, I once heard a story about her gambling habits. She likes a flutter, does Harriet. Oh yes. Cards, dice, horses, flies crawling up a bloody wall, she'll bet on it. One of her more notorious bets, *allegedly*–" here George IV waggled his eyebrows– "was on two young men, as to who could take his togs off the quickest. To the winner, the spoils, because she apparently had sexual intercourse with him in an adjoining room."

Whilst Neale was casting about for a suitable comment, the King continued.

"So, she thinks she is a match for most men. She seeks to outwit us all with a feeling of superiority, but her vanity will be her undoing, mark my words." George IV nodded sagely. "Well, give her enough rope, as they say."

Neale agreed with his sovereign, although he failed to see how it would come to pass.

"How's the crustacean faring?"

Neale snapped out of his brown study. "He has met with her and is hopeful of gaining her trust."

The King narrowed his eyes. "You rate this man?"

"Indeed, Sire, I do."

The piggy eyes narrowed further. "Why?"

Neale felt the sweat break out on his hairline. Because he loved Crabbe? Because he was his friend? Because he thought a world without Thomas Crabbe was no world at all? Perhaps all of the above.

Out loud, he said, "He has proven himself to be honest and trustworthy. He has been privy to several secrets and has kept his mouth firmly shut."

The King's eyes didn't leave Neale's face. The latter hoped sincerely his face hadn't turned red under the scrutiny.

"Hphmph. If you say so, we will trust him then, eh?" Neale bowed, hiding his face for a few seconds.

"So, do we let Knox dig a hole for himself?"

"I think he is innocent about Deschanel's true intentions, so we need not worry about the captain."

The King snorted in derision. "He won't be the first man to fall for a ready cunny."

Neale twitched slightly but kept quiet.

"Well, let the crustacean flush 'em out. We have our man ready?"

Neale nodded.

"Good, let the dice fall where they may, and let's see how Harriet picks 'em up."

Chapter 24

Harriet watched her overweight, overbearing, sweaty husband slurp his coffee and gobble his pain au chocolat. He was still in his banyan, sporting a nightcap with a tassel that swung in time with his masticating. The only sound that filled the room was munching and slurping. She thought about picking up her fork and plunging it into his fat neck, imagining all the partly digested food spilling out onto the table, but then thought about the resultant mess and reluctantly pushed the image to one side.

"I am meeting a gentleman today, ma chéri, so I will not be back until–"

"If you are fucking him, I don't want to know. What time will you be back?"

Harriet drew a deep breath. She would *not* rise to the bait.

"He is an ex naval man who once sailed with Captain Knox. Arabella Knox thought he would be amusing and might have some interesting anecdotes that I could use for my novel. I am meeting–"

"What time?" barked her husband, wiping his wet mouth with a stained napkin.

"I will be back before the dinner gong," Harriet replied sweetly, hoping the hatred she felt for him didn't show on her face.

"Good. We are expecting the Minister of the Interior and his wife," he reminded her for the tenth time; "*don't* be late." With that he heaved his bulk out of the chair and lumbered from the room without a backward glance.

Harriet gripped the edge of the table. She loathed her husband with every molecule of her being. What the hell had her father been thinking when he had announced him as a prospective husband? She had only been eighteen, and of course, being female and young, had had no say in the matter. Antoine had been slim then, although beginning to display signs of gluttony. Over the years his girth had widened, and his sense of humour had disappeared along with his erectile function; she had been reduced to a decoration at the interminable soirées and dinner parties they threw for various ministers and their wives.

However, those social gatherings had introduced her to some remarkably interesting people. Subtle undercurrents would ebb and flow around the dinner table. A glance would hold and linger. Whispered words in corridors, paper passed from palm to palm. Always the frisson that she might be found out, exposed, punished.

But as time went on, with no reprisals, Harriet grew in confidence and boldness. Now she found herself in the employ of Lord Palmer under instructions from the King of England. Right under her husband's nose. She smiled, hugging that knowledge to herself, and her mind drifted to Knox. He was an additional bonus. Handsome, educated, intelligent, witty—fascinated by her. He had a lot to recommend him. Usually she preferred younger men, ones she could teach and mould, but Alexander Knox had a certain boyish charm about him that appealed to her. Plus, he knew how to pleasure her.

The real truth was, however, that Harriet Deschanel was brittle. In her own mind she was hard as flint, unyielding as granite, her soul made of steel. Her childhood had been one of duty, diligence, a decoration for her French mother. Mère had been a toxic, narcisstic manipulator who used her little daughter as an externalisation of her own hopes, dreams, and thwarted ambitions. Harriet had been taught to sing, play the pianoforte, dance, paint, and appreciate perfume. And her mother had a lot of perfume—bottles and bottles of the stuff, all encased in different shaped and coloured bottles. As a child, Harriet would watch the sun shining through Mère's bedroom window, turning the bottles into glass jewels, the light refracted onto the whitewashed walls.

Her mother had viewed her as a nuisance, to be seen and not heard, only trotted out at social soirées to be shown off to her various, vacuous friends like a paper doll. Often after one of these showings Harriet would muse over the half-moons on the palms of her hands where she had dug her fingernails into the soft flesh. Her heart became an obsidian thing, hard with ragged edges like a serrated knife. She got used to the throw-away comments Mère would make about her hair, her posture, her face, how she wore her clothes, how she spoke, or didn't speak. She was an accessory, a tick in a dutiful box as far as her glamorous mother was concerned.

Sometimes, she would imagine she was a knight of yore,

bedecked in a suit of armour that no arrow or barb could penetrate. And yet, she had a soft underbelly. She was sensitive, artistic, sentimental, fragile, with a deep love for animals–the only thing that loved her for who she was, not for what they wanted her to be. But even Mère had ruined that.

She adored next door's cat, a large ginger male, who used to sit on her lap whenever she was able to slip out of the house and perch on the front stone steps. Mère found out, and after several days of looking out of the front windows, checking under the stairs to the root cellar, combing the garden and checking every nook and cranny, Harriet found him dead under a magnolia tree. He had had foam around his mouth which, the cook informed her, the frills of her white cap nodding in time with her head, was indicative of poisoning.

In a rare fit of temper she confronted Mère, who merely shrugged her elegant shoulders and said that the cat had probably eaten rat poison. After all, there were always hoards of mice and rats, and cats ate both, *n'est pas*? So, what did she expect.

At that moment, Harriet knew rage. Blinding rage. Murderous rage. Rage that blotted out all reason, causing a red mist to descend allowing her to do whatever she wanted. She saw herself as if from outside her body. She watched her other self walk calmly over to Mère's dressing table, pick up a curved bottle in pink glass, and throw it on the wooden floorboards, shattering glass and spraying expensive scent all over her mother's new dress.

She'd spent a night in the root cellar for that one. Not even bread and water to keep her company. She had hugged her bitterness to herself like a warm blanket.

The following day she had emerged from the dank space, blinking like a mole, only to face a wooden ruler across the knuckles for good measure, meted out by her father.

Ah yes, her father. A man utterly captivated by his dark-haired, brown-eyed French wife. Mère could do no wrong. Her father would have pulled the moon down and hung it about his wife's neck if he could. She used all her feminine wiles upon him so that, in the end, he was besotted and believed every lie she told, every tale she spun, every web she wove to the exclusion of his only child. Harriet bore the brunt of his displeasure, his stern censure, his disappointment. The girl child became the whipping post upon which he inflicted punishment.

The only ray of sunshine in this miserable existence were her grandparents. Her mother's parents lived in the countryside, about an hour and a half south of Versailles. Her grandfather, or 'Poppy', loved gardening. During school holidays she would help Poppy. They would be out from dawn until dusk, tilling the soil, pulling weeds, pruning trees, picking fruit, and collecting eggs from the talkative chickens that ran free on the property. Eventually they would come indoors, tanned, scratched, sporting insect bites. Then grandmere, or 'Nan', with the help of the housemaid, would pull the old copper bathtub out to sit in front of the fire. The bath would be filled only enough to cover Harriet's ankles.

"Water is precious," her beloved Nan would say. "We rely on God for the rain, so be an angel and don't use too much!"

Even to this day Harriet never overfilled a bath, especially as she knew that Poppy would have simply been sluicing cold water over himself in the yard outside.

Once clean, now clothed in a soft muslin smock dress, they would sit down to dine. Nan and Babette, the kitchen maid, would prepare the dinner together–something her elegant mother would never have condescended to do. It was always simple fare, vegetables or salad from the garden, freshly baked bread and homemade cheese. Sometimes during summer the green, leafy salad would be dotted with hard-boiled eggs, their yolks mustard yellow, adding a splash of sunshine amongst the leaves. Dessert would be fresh fruit or in winter, stewed apples spiced with cinnamon, accompanied by a crème anglaise.

After dinner, she would sew or embroider whilst Nan knitted and Poppy read the broadsheet of the day, reading out loud the most interesting or amusing bits. Last thing before bed, Nan would boil milk and make a small cup of 'chocolat' laced with cayenne pepper, to "keep the fingers and toes warm."

Harriet would sink into the duck down mattress, feeling the vertebrae in her back crackle from the day's work. Her skin would be warm from a day spent in the sunshine, her hair would smell sweet from being outside in the fresh air, but most of all she would feel contentment. No harsh words would have been spoken, no punishment inflicted, no glowerings of disapproval or tuts of disappointment. If she ever misbehaved, Poppy would simply look at her and shake his head slowly. For some reason that made her want to behave even better than if she had received a thrashing.

She learned so much from her grandparents. How to sew, embroider, bake, pickle, preserve, prune a rose to make it grow stronger, how to use soap flakes in a watering can, anointing it to keep the aphids and green fly away. She learned the differences between weeds and flowers, and herbs that were edible and often medicinal. Even to this day she could recall the smell of Poppy's greenhouse, redolent with the fragrance of tomatoes.

"They like to be sung to," he would say, "and tickled."

"Tickled?"

"Mais oui. Pass me that." He gestured to something small and furry tipped with silver lying on the worn wooden shelf. Harriet picked it up and laid it in the palm of her small hand.

"It's a rabbit foot, an' you tickle tomatoes with it." Her grandfather proceeded to dust each and every tomato with the soft paw whilst humming the Marseillaise. Harriet watched him in disbelief.

"You're mimicking a bee, chéri. The bee tickles the fruit with its feet, taking the pollen with it to the next one where it tickles that one. But we do not have bees in here, so we must improvise." His old face creased into a smile, eyes twinkling above his pince-nez. Harriet thought he was pulling her leg, but he carried on until every shiny red orb had been given love and attention. He had the best tomatoes. Big, fat things the size of her clenched fist. Nan would slice them, drizzle them with balsamic vinegar, olive oil, and a twist of salt. Delicious.

The next best thing to Poppy's tomatoes were Nan's ginger biscuits. Wafer thin, so hard that when you snapped them, crumbs flew. Fresh butter heated gently in a pan with brown sugar until it dissolved. Ground oats would be weighed out with a healthy pinch of ginger and a dash of cinnamon. The dry ingredients would be mixed with the wet, rolled into walnut-sized balls and baked. The balls would gently flatten and spread during cooking.

Removed from the heat, Nan would lay them on wire trays to cool and harden. That was the worst bit–the waiting. But

if you took a biscuit too early, they were soft with no crunch. Half an hour cooling time and another ten minutes for luck, then they were ready to eat, washed down with a pot of freshly brewed tea for the adults, a glass of milk for Harriet.

She had baked her Nan's biscuits, sticking closely to the recipe, but she had never been able to replicate them. Perhaps she lacked the required loving attitude that had imbued those long-ago biscuits with that extra something.

Harriet stared sadly at the table. Her grandparents were long dead, as was her father–only her mother was left. Mad, bitter, and twisted, confined to an institution where she ranted and raved using language that Harriet hadn't known she possessed. Harriet had ceased visiting her around two years ago. She could no longer endure the torrent of vitriol directed at her, the poisonous comments about her father, grandfather, grandmother, and anyone in between.

At least she could thank her husband for the money which went towards the upkeep of Mère. That was all *he* was good for.

She became heartless. Cold, hard, cruel almost to the point of monstrosity. Life had shaped her thus. Yet, deep down in her innermost heart she was the little girl who loved cats. Those school holidays with Nan and Poppy were frozen in time, like an insect in amber, golden and halcyon. She had seen a lot of the world, and it was cold and dark–those long-ago days were light and warmth, so she held them close, locking them away in a small casket inside her heart, hiding the key in a safe place.

To the outer world she presented a brittle countenance. She laughed too loudly, she flirted too much, danced excessively, ate, drank, and was shrilly merry. Witticisms crawled out from between her lips like ants. People found her captivating, charming, clever.

She was a fraud. But a convincing fraud. So convincing that she believed it herself. Almost.

Chapter 25

The carriage clopped along the wet streets, cobblestones glistening in the breaking dawn. The first vestiges of a watery sun began shining weakly over the rooftops as the horses turned into the courtyard of the Crabbes' rented townhouse.

Thomas had spent two days and two nights at Captain Knox's house with other associates, discussing strategies for infiltrating the French government and preventing the escape of Bonaparte. His head was spinning with too much wine, tobacco, and intrigue.

When horses pulled up at the front door, Daisy ran out and down the stone steps, almost sobbing in relief. Thomas descended from the carriage, passing a weary hand over his face. As he turned, Daisy reached him, threw her arms around him and burst into tears. This behaviour was so unlike his usually cheerful, easy- going wife that he was taken totally by surprise. She was crying in earnest, the sound coming from her throat like a wounded animal. He could feel the sobs shaking her body and thought that if she carried on like that, she'd do herself and the baby a mischief. He pushed her away from him, holding her by the arms, looking into her face. The tears rolled unchecked down her cheeks as she continued to cry, unheeding his questions, until he shook her gently, imploring her to tell him what was the matter.

"Oh, Thomas, Thomas, I'm sorry, it be my fault." She resumed her sobbing, burying her face in her hands.

"What be your fault, lass?"

"The baby." Her words were muffled, but Thomas heard them. He went cold all over, then hot. Oh, God.

"Daisy, m'love, my dearest, 'ave you lost the baby?"

She didn't answer, just nodded miserably, sobbing as if her heart would break.

Thomas took her into his arms, allowing her to sob her fill until she finally subsided into little hiccups. "How?"

Daisy emerged from the front of his jacket, which was, by now, soaking wet. She pulled a handkerchief from her sleeve and blew her nose, wadding the linen into a damp ball, squeezing it in distress. "Night afore last I were that worried about you an' where you were, I walked around our room. I weren't concentrating on where I was stepping an' as I turned, I caught m'foot on a low stool an' fell to the floor. I tried to put m'hands out but I weren't in time, an' I landed on my stomach. Around bedtime I started getting' pains in my tummy an' they called the midwife. She came around 11 o'clock but I'd started bleedin'–an' then I felt sommat atween m'legs an' when I looked down, my skirts were soaked in blood, an' then…" She burst into tears again, sounding so desolate.

Thomas took her in his arms once more, patting her back, murmuring meaningless platitudes while feeling a crack forming in his heart. How could she have been so careless? Why hadn't she been resting? Just as swiftly as the thoughts entered his brain, another voice pointed out that if he hadn't brought her here, put her through so much worry and uncertainty, she might still be carrying their child. He immediately felt contrite, chastising himself for blaming her. Clearly, she would blame herself far more than he ever would, and that was punishment enough. He must not let this tragedy drive a wedge between them.

"Lass. Now then, give over, you'll mek yaself ill." He put her away from him, gently shaking her and kissing her forehead. "Dry your eyes now, an' let's go inside. You can tell me more over a glass of wine, eh?"

He turned her around, putting his arm around her shoulders. She leaned in and curled her arm around his waist, wiping her face with the soaked piece of linen.

What she didn't tell her husband was that the midwife had shown her the baby. Despite not being full-term, the child was perfect. Little eyes tightly shut, tiny hands like shells and a hint of dark hair forming on her head. Yes, the midwife confirmed Daisy had been carrying a little girl. Daisy held her tiny daughter to her chest, washing away the blood from the baby with her tears. She thought that telling Thomas would not help the situation, maybe make him even more broken-hearted, so she kept the details to herself. Why she lied and said that the midwife had covered the unborn child with a cloth and whisked it away, she couldn't have said. Logic didn't form any part of her silence. It was a purely emotional response, something only a mother could feel. She hugged the knowledge to herself, a secret that only she shared with her unborn daughter. Thomas would never know.

She looked up into his face, seeing the stubble glisten on his haggard face. He'd passed a hard night, and now she had added to his woes.

"How did it go, m'love?" she asked him softly.

"Never mind tha' now, let's go in."

They walked slowly up the stone steps into the house, and Daisy guided him to the dining room where a hearty breakfast had been laid up, complete with a silver coffee urn, the largest Crabbe had ever seen. But he had no appetite after what Daisy had just told him. Guilt, anger, and sorrow warred in his stomach.

"Where is the baby now?"

"The midwife took the body. There's a graveyard in L'Hopital de la Charité where the Benedictine brothers bury babies born afore their time. She's there if you care to visit 'er."

"She should 'ave left her 'ere."

"Thomas, they darn't believe in such things 'ere. They think dead babies attract unwanted spirits an' such."

Thomas snorted at such superstitious nonsense.

"Besides, we didn't know when you were comin' back, an' it didn't seem right to– well…." Daisy's voice trailed off. She felt guilty about not allowing her husband to see their daughter, but the midwife was insistent. A deep-seated part of her hadn't trusted herself to keep the little girl. She knew she would have kept unwrapping the little body and looking at it. No, far better that she had been removed and given a decent burial on holy ground.

"I'd like to go an' see where she is."

"Of course, m'love. We'll go together. I haven't yet felt well enough to go, so we'll ask the brothers to show us where she is. I'll get a little posy of flowers."

Thomas nodded bleakly. They sat quietly, not eating or drinking, just being together. None of this would have happened if they hadn't come to this accursed place. Why hadn't he turned down Neale's proposal and been content to work at the public house in Suffolk, living in their little cottage with Trim? Because he wanted to make the world a better place. Because he didn't believe in tyrants and dictators. Because he didn't like people being enslaved to others. He'd been a prisoner of war and hadn't enjoyed the experience–still, cold comfort for Daisy.

He would make one more contact with Shegoe, and then they would return to England. To their little home in the peaceful Suffolk countryside, where, God willing, Daisy would conceive again surrounded by familiar things and their beloved cat.

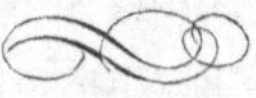

It was a cold, blustery day; the wind plucked at Daisy's skirts, making her irritable. The carriage dropped them outside L'Hopital de la Charité in the 6th Arrondissement. The hospital had been founded in the 17th century by the Brothers of Charity, but during the French Revolution they had been moved on due to the confiscation of properties owned by the Catholic church. However, some of them had drifted back, although the hospital was now strictly a lay institution. A section of the hospital's gardens had been turned into a graveyard for children born dead to women in the hospital or brought there by appointed midwives.

One of the brothers led them to the graveyard at the back, making the sign of the cross over them with a kindly smile before leaving them alone. The grave was barely a foot square, with a little wooden cross engraved with just one word. *Allie*. Someone had carved a tiny flower under the name.

"Ye named 'er after my ma?" Thomas whispered, feeling tears prick the back of his eyes.

"Yes, m'love, I'd allus wanted to call 'er after your ma, even though I never knew 'er. It just seemed right somehow."

It *did* seem right. Completely right. And yet wrong as well. Allie Senior and Allie Junior were lying in the cold, hard earth, miles apart. However, maybe they were together in spirit. Thomas sincerely hoped so. His mother would have loved a little granddaughter.

He heaved a deep sigh as Daisy knelt in a puff of skirts to place the small posy of rosemary dotted with blue flowers on the grave. *There's rosemary, that's for remembrance; pray, love, remember; and there are pansies, that's for thoughts.* Ophelia had been foretelling her own death. Thomas recalled that rosemary was for death and mourning. Something skittered up his spine.

He mentally shook himself. His daughter was not here in this bleak place; she was running through open fields, the sun warm upon her back, hearing her grandma call to her to come in for a cup of milk and a biscuit warm from the oven.

"Daisy, let's away, love. She's wi' us in our hearts and will always be so." He could tell she wanted to stay awhile, but he didn't want to risk her getting a chill from the damp earth on top of the miscarriage she had suffered. "Come, love," he repeated, reaching down to help her.

They walked away, arm in arm, the rosemary leaves stirring in the stiff breeze, waving like hair across the newly turned soil.

Chapter 26

The doorbell dinged as he entered the shop. The resultant echo cascaded through the bowels of the establishment, but no one appeared.

Crabbe stood quietly, taking in his surroundings. Various eclectica sat on shelves of different heights. Here a pot, there an ornament, a collection of books, a cast iron fire-set…all of it bric-a-brac, yet somehow there was a cohesion to it all. These objects said, *we are here because one person placed us here. We belong together because one mind could see us blending as one, complimenting one another.*

Crabbe stepped forward and lifted a wooden carving off a shelf. It was made of dark wood, lacquered with red paint, made in the shape of a frog, squatting with its tongue protruding out of its mouth. Crabbe placed the curious little carving in the palm of his hand, admiring the detail, realising that there was a coin resting on the tongue.

"Bonjour Monsieur!"

He spun around to see a short man, resplendent in Mandarin robes, a long moustache adorning his face, hands thrust into the sleeves of his gown. The man chuckled at his expression, and bowed low from the waist, his pigtail swinging forward over his left shoulder. As he straightened up, he said, "Ni hao ma?"

Crabbe went blank. He had travelled far and wide but had yet to speak to anyone from the Orient, and certainly had no knowledge of their language. "Ah, I…that is…"

The other man chuckled again flapping his hand, "Mei guan xi." He moved towards Crabbe, still smiling and took the money frog from his palm. "You are English?"

Crabbe nodded, smiling in return.

"It is Feng Shui, a money frog. Honourable sir, is said to bring fortune to those who put it in house –however!" He held up a long index finger. "It must be placed at entrance of house facing south, or it does not have full power."

Crabbe was fascinated by the other man. His appearance, his speech were all redolent of a faraway place and an exotic culture. He wished to know more. "Ah, sir, what else would a body place in one's house to, well, bring good health?'

"Honourable sir, Feng Shui is based on elements of nature– earth, air, water, fire. It is based on the 'bagua', the nine squares of life. Each square is area of life which is connected to family, money, health, and so on. You wish this for your house, yes?"

He would like peace and harmony in their cottage in Suffolk. He wished with every fibre of his being that Daisy would conceive again and that their child would be delivered healthy and sound.

Out loud he said, "Aye, I would like that."

The shop keeper bowed and placed the frog upon the

counter top. He cocked his head one side like a bird. "What else I help you with?"

"Um, would ye have anything for a lady to get with child?"

"Ah, your Honourable Wife, yes?"

Crabbe nodded.

"But of course, there is turtle."

Crabbe wasn't sure he'd heard correctly. "Turtle?'

"That is for baby chi. Chi is energy, life, and *heping*, how you say…peace?"

Peace, yes. And quiet. And space to rest and let a baby grow.

"You buy frog, I give you turtle for wife." The little man bowed again.

"Tha's very generous of you, sir."

"Nali, nali, it is nothing." The shop keeper beamed and trotted behind the counter to reach down to a shelf. Straightening up he placed a small carving on the surface to join the frog.

Crabbe limped over to look at the newcomer. It was a tiny turtle, beautifully carved in what looked like brass. It instantly made him smile.

"Ah, you see, Honourable sir, it works already!" The other man smiled as well. "I wrap these for you."

Crabbe paid the shop keeper for his purchases, wished him good day, and left emptier of pocket, but lighter of heart.

Chapter 27

They met in the upstairs bedroom of an almost derelict townhouse on the Left Bank. The room had no carpet; the only furniture was a chair and a single mattress with grimy bed sheets, which Crabbe studiously avoided looking at. Harriet was sitting in the chair, Crabbe perched on the edge of the bed.

Crabbe took a deep breath and decided to roll the dice.

"Knox."

"Yes?"

"He is–tha' is to say…"

"Go on."

"He confided to me that he's goin' to aid Napoleon in getting off Saint Helena." Thomas trailed off, observing Shegoe's face. Not a flicker, her eyes remained steadily on his face, never wavering.

Thomas drew a deep breath. Now was his moment. He coughed lightly, took his handkerchief out, wiped his mouth, folded it neatly and replaced it in his breast pocket, formulating his words carefully. He felt the weight of the dark basilisk stare acutely. He silently prayed for protection as he stared at the faded wooden floorboards. "I were talkin' to 'im the other evenin' an' he informed me that he is currently in secret talks wi' the French."

A sound made Thomas look up. He found himself staring down the barrel of a short musket. Shegoe had it balanced on her forearm, which was propped on her knee.

"Thomas, oh Thomas. I like you very much. You and I could be friends. But know this, I would not hesitate to shoot you in the face if it meant stopping you from preventing Bonaparte's escape."

Thomas felt like a deer trapped in a poacher's gun sights. He waited with bated breath, scarcely breathing.

"Bonaparte *will* return, and he *will* regain his throne. You cannot stop that. The King of England cannot stop that. When they–"

Shegoe stopped at the sounds of smashing glass and shouting. She got up from her chair, the musket still pointed at Thomas, and moved swiftly to the window. She chanced a quick look outside.

"They're coming," she stated flatly.

"Who are?" Thomas croaked.

"The mob," she snapped, "we are both in grave peril. We must leave, now." She uncocked the firearm and stuffed it into one of the capacious pockets of her gown. Drawing a scarf out of her left sleeve she covered her hair, pulled up the collar of her jacket, and made for the door.

"Harriet!"

She turned back briefly, impatient in her haste to be gone.

"Where can I find you?"

"You can't," she replied, "I will find *you*." She tore the door open and, with a swish of skirts, was gone.

Thomas was left standing in the middle of the room, feeling bereft. Despite his successful bluff and her threatening him with violence, he felt as if all the colour had been sucked out of the room, leaving a vacuum.

The sounds of the angry crowd outside intruded on his musings. The urgency of the situation sank into his consciousness. Not all French people agreed with the reinstatement of the emperor. What Shegoe did not know, despite her spider's web of informants, was that Great Britain was in clandestine talks with the French government to stop Bonaparte from returning and seizing power. Even if Shegoe and friends did manage to free the former Emperor, the French would not allow him to take charge once more.

Thomas chewed a torn fingernail nervously. Time to go. He could not be discovered here; even if he managed to persuade the mob that he agreed with them, he could be torn to shreds.

Casting frantically about, his eyes fell on the bed sheets. Quickly ripping them off, he knotted them together, tied one end to the leg of the iron bedstead and, stumbling to the window, threw up the sash, dropping the rest of the sheets to the ground. He heard a pounding on the door downstairs as he slung his good leg over the windowsill. Just in the nick of time he ducked through the window, drawing his bad leg after him, and slid clumsily to the cobbles below. The angry crowd, sounding like a hornet's nest, were so intent on splintering the wooden door and smashing the front windows that they didn't notice a slightly built, limping man with thinning auburn hair making his way in an unhurried fashion into the back alleyways.

Thomas feigned an air of nonchalance but was churning with fear and anxiety. He deliberately kept his pace steady whilst maintaining a calm expression. If anyone stopped him, he would say that he was making for the household of Captain Knox, formerly of His Majesty's navy, to attend a dinner there, which was partly the truth. He felt the reassuring crackle of identity papers in his inside breast pocket, personally signed by King George IV.

The noise of the mob faded into the distance as Thomas made his way down the alleyways. Night was descending, and as he rounded a corner, a lamplighter was propping his ladder up against the lamp post. He wished the man 'bon soir' and, receiving a nod in reply, continued on his way.

Thomas stumbled slightly, and it was then that he heard the extra footfall. Without straightening he swung around just as the assailant brought a large club down on what should have been Crabbe's head. Instead, it glanced off his shoulder, causing him to grunt in pain. Without conscious thought he twisted to one side, dodging the second blow, and ran as fast as his shaking legs would let him, hearing the noise of a scuffle behind him.

As he corkscrewed hurriedly along his brain caught up with his body, and he realised the man who had attacked him was the false lamplighter. The man must have seen him come down the alleyway and, under the pretence of setting up his ladder, had turned and quietly followed Crabbe. That meant he had been told what Crabbe looked like. Therefore, his face was known. The knowledge of this made him jog faster, ignoring his protesting leg.

After some minutes and one false turn, he came to the townhouse of Captain Knox. Grabbing the iron balustrade, he hauled himself up the few stone steps to the front door, banging the heavy metal knocker in a sharp tattoo. Only then did he allow himself to shake, bending over, trying to catch his breath.

The door opened to Duval, the saturnine and unflappable butler.

"Monsieur?" he peered at Crabbe, who was still bent over, wheezing slightly.

"I'm alright, Duval." Crabbe straightened up. "Just a little out of breath. Can you take me to the Cap'n?" Even though Knox was no longer in the navy, Crabbe still referred to him by his naval title from force of habit.

"Mais oui, Monsieur. Please follow me." Duval gestured for Crabbe to enter, shut the door, and led the way down the brightly lit corridor, where freshly polished floorboards gleaming in the light cast by recently lit candles.

Crabbe concentrated on putting one foot in front of the other as lights began flashing at the corner of his eyes. His hearing was playing tricks on him.

Duval showed him into a pleasant reception room decorated in heavy tapestries with large wingbacked chairs sitting upon thick Persian rugs. The air was fragrant with cigar smoke, and a roaring fire in the grate cheered Crabbe's heart.

"Monsieur Crabbe; Capitaine." Duval bowed slightly to Knox, who stood on the hearth rug, legs apart, warming his backside, puffing on a Cuban.

"Ah, Crabbe! Just the man! I was telling Hawkins about the time–" Knox stopped abruptly, cigar forgotten. "Crabbe? What ails you, man? Here, sit before you fall!" He threw the cigar into the fire and shot forward, grabbing Crabbe's arm and gently pushing him into a Queen Anne chair.

Lieutenant Hawkins, also formerly of His Majesty's Navy and a long-standing friend of Knox, got out of his chair, coming forward to peer into Crabbe's face. "You look like you've seen a ghost, man. I'll get you a brandy."

"Put your head between your knees, Thomas." Knox pushed Crabbe's head gently down.

"I know what to do!" Crabbe replied crossly, his voice slightly muffled. In truth, the pattern on the Persian rug was swimming about alarmingly, threatening to slide off altogether.

A large brandy glass came into his view, and he reached out, grasping it gratefully. Slowly he sat up and, leaning back in the high-backed chair, took a cautious sip of the excellent cognac, grateful that his head wasn't bouncing across the floor.

"Good to see some colour coming back into your face," Knox commented, patting Crabbe on the shoulder in an avuncular fashion. "Now, tell us, what brought you here in this state?"

Crabbe took another slurp of the cognac before proceeding.

"We've been discovered," he croaked, eyes watering at the pungent fumes wafting up his nose.

"What?" demanded Knox.

"I met wi' Shegoe, an' barely escaped from an angry mob tha' had gathered in the street. On me way croaked ere I passed a lamp lighter, who were no lighter. He followed me an' very nearly bloody killed me." Crabbe noted with detachment that the hand holding the brandy balloon was shaking. "Through good luck, I managed to get awa' from the bastard an' came 'ere with all haste."

Knox and Hawkins looked at him open-mouthed. The crackling of the fire was the only sound in the room.

"I need to return to England, ain't safe for me 'ere. Or m'wife." Crabbe downed the remainder of his brandy. He looked up at the two men standing in front of him.

"Now, Crabbe, don't lose your head. We can sit and discuss this, after all."

"No." Just one word, but it had a ring of finality about it.

"But Crabbe–"

"I said no!" Crabbe felt his temper beginning to rise. He thought about Daisy and how this quest had cost them their child. No doubt she was back at the house, crying softly to herself. He had to get her away from here, back to England, where they could breathe freely and not be looking over their shoulders every five minutes.

"Will you write to Lord Palmer, sir? Explain to 'im wha's 'appened, particularly with Daisy…" Crabbe trailed off, looking appealingly at Knox.

Two deep lines appeared between Captain Knox's eyebrows. He thought for a moment. "Very well, Thomas." He sighed. "It will be a great shame to lose you, but I understand the concern for your wife. I will write to Palmer now and despatch the letter by private courier this very night."

Crabbe nodded bleakly. He felt he had let the cause down, but Daisy's welfare was uppermost.

Hawkins left Knox to write to Lord Palmer, patting Crabbe's shoulder as he left the room to collect his hat and cloak from Duval.

Crabbe sat before the crackling fire, seeing Shegoe's face in the flames. How could Knox have misjudged her? Had she never given the captain an inkling? Crabbe had called her bluff more from gut instinct than knowledge. Another thought occurred to him. Did Knox know? Was he even now writing a warning to her? With his head spinning from brandy and adrenalin, he heaved himself out of the chair, weaving down the corridor to Knox's study.

Knox had his broad back to the door, head bent, scribbling furiously. He turned at the sound of Crabbe entering.

"What is it, Crabbe?"

"Did you know?"

"Know what?"

"About Harriet?"

"What about her?"

"That she's a double agent."

Knox jumped from his chair, heedless of the ink dripping from the quill he'd dropped onto the paper.

"She wants to see Boney escape."

"Utter rubbish." snapped Knox.

"She shoved a stick in my face an' threatened to shoot me should I get in the way."

"She is one of us; she has been all along."

"I don't feckin' care wha' she's been bloody doin'!" roared Crabbe, brandy making him brave. "Ye thought wi' ya bloody cock an' not ya brain, man!"

"Now, just a min—"

"No! Ye bloody listen! I darn't answer to ye anymore." In his anger and intoxication, his Suffolk accent grew broader. "I'm not an able seaman anymore an' you're not a feckin' cap'n, so ye listen to me!" Crabbe clenched his fists by his side, breathing like a carthorse. "She put you an' me, m'wife an' Neale in danger. She's hung us all outta to dry like yesterday's socks, man, an' ye couldn't see it for the hold she 'ad over you. Oh yes, I had my contacts an' all. Jest when ye thought I was swallowing it all like an old numpty, I took precautions an' had you an' her followed."

Thanks to Neale, his vast network and the King's gold, Thomas had been supplied with a couple of trusty souls, one of whom took great delight in giving a very detailed account of the comings and goings at the Knox residence and the mysterious visitor who would arrive in disguise, stay a few hours, then leave.

Thomas opened his mouth to say more when a soft knock sounded at the study door. Knox bellowed, "Come!"

Duval poked his head cautiously around the corner. "Excuse

moi, Capitaine, but there eez a man at ze back door."

"What sort of man?" barked Knox.

"Er…' e sez 'e wishes to see Monsieur Crabbe, Capitaine."

"How the devil does he know Crabbe's here?" demanded Knox.

Duval gave a Gallic shrug, indicating he had no idea, hadn't asked, and would Knox like to show him in.

"Crabbe, what sort of trick is this?" Knox glared at Crabbe, who was looking surprised at the introduction of a visitor.

"I darn't know, Cap'n, I know of no man who would come 'ere at this time o' night, 'specially to the back door." He looked pointedly at Duval, who shrugged again.

"What does he look like, Duval?" Knox frowned at the butler.

"Like a pudding, Capitaine."

"A pudding?" Knox looked amused.

"Oui, 'olding a cane wiz a silver 'andle."

Now it was Crabbe's turn to frown; he racked his brains, trying to recall a man with a pudding-like face and a silver-topped cane amongst the contacts Neale had arranged. No, nothing.

Knox watched Crabbe's face closely. He genuinely looked at a loss to explain this unwelcome guest.

Even though he'd been ready to throttle Crabbe a few moments before, now he trusted the able seaman that Crabbe had once been. Knox had fond memories of Crabbe's cooking aboard the *Donegal*, particularly his plum duffs, and any man who could cook a steamed pudding light as air enclosing plump, juicy dates, accompanied by perfectly golden custard, deserved a second chance.

"Very well, Duval, show this mysterious man in."

Duval bowed and withdrew his head.

The two men waited silently, eyeing each other like a couple of dogs. Before too long, they heard the murmur of male voices, and the door opened to Duval, ushering the stranger into the room. The butler bowed to Knox and quietly left.

Crabbe and Knox looked at the man before them. Below medium height, narrow-shouldered, wearing a short top hat in brown–dressed in a brown fustian suit, waistcoat straining over a paunch, fawn breeches ending in a disreputable pair of old laced boots. The most remarkable item of his attire was the silver-topped black cane upon which he was leaning, watching the other men with a gentle smile upon his doughy face.

"Gentlemen." He removed the Derby hat, revealing a bald head with straggly mousey hair hanging down to his collar. He bowed, replaced the hat, and resumed leaning upon the cane.

Crabbe and Knox exchanged puzzled looks. "Who are ye?" demanded Crabbe.

"Why, sir, I am your shadow." The man smiled even more broadly, revealing a snaggle-tooth in his upper jaw. His voice was piping and soft, making the hairs stand on the back of Crabbe's neck.

"What the Devil does that mean?" Knox barked.

"It means, Captain Knox, formerly of His Majesty's navy and once commander of the *Donegal*–"

Knox started at the mention of his ship.

"–that I have been watching over Mr Crabbe for the duration of his sojourn in Paris." The man bowed again, making a courtly leg to Knox.

Crabbe twitched. He'd felt eyes boring into his back now and again but had put it down to being in a strange city and nerves about his dangerous task. "You have been followin' me?"

"Oh yes, m'dear sir, I've not let you out of my sight the whole time you have been here. Yes, indeed, sir, yes indeed." He bowed unctuously again.

"What is your name?" Knox asked with asperity.

"My name, sir, is Obidiah Slope, and I 'ave the pleasure and honour to serve who you both serve." He bowed again, spreading his right hand, accompanied by the same courtly leg.

Despite his servile attitude, bland appearance and smile, Crabbe instantly disliked Slope. He wouldn't have trusted him as far as he could throw him, which in his current emotional state wouldn't have been far.

"My dear sir, I followed you 'ere this evening an' saw you bein' attacked. Alas, I was not in time to intervene but, by the grace of God, you managed to confound your attacker an' make good your escape whilst I, well–I completed the despatch."

The last word echoed in the quiet room. Crabbe's eyes dropped to the cane. The silver tip gleamed in the firelight, lending it an other-worldly hue.

Slope followed Crabbe's look and, smiling gently, pulled the tip away from the shaft, unsheathing a long, sharp sword. The rasp of steel grated on Crabbe's ears as the wicked metal winked in the flickering light. He half expected there to be blood on the blade, but it had been wiped clean.

"This 'ere blade saved you more vexation, Mr Crabbe," murmured Slope, openly grinning now. "Why, if it weren't for the kiss of steel on 'im as what attacked you, I don't know where you would be, truly I don't, sir."

"Who was he?" cut in Knox.

"Oh, sir, I can't begin to guess," which meant he knew *precisely* who Crabbe's assailant had been, "but he won't be troublin' you no more, sir." And with that, he thrust the sword back into its hiding place, making Crabbe and Knox jump.

In opposition to his antipathy towards Slope, Crabbe felt a mixture of gratitude, relief and affection directed towards Richard Neale. It could only have been he who had appointed this odious little man to keep an eye on him. Neale had known about Harriet and her true persuasions. Why had he sent him, Crabbe, to meet with her? Surely Knox could have achieved that. Crabbe shook his head like a horse trying to dislodge an annoying fly. "All in good time, sir, all in good time." Slope smiled gently at Crabbe's gesture. "Now, sir, I think it best if you stay wi' Cap'n Knox, an' I will make my way to your house an' pass a message to your good lady tha' all is well an' she will see you on the morrow."

"Be gentle with 'er," Crabbe admonished.

"Of course, sir, of course, no need to mention it, sir, no need at all." With that ingratiating statement, Slope bowed again and slithered out of the room.

Knox and Crabbe exchanged looks. "What do you make of him, Crabbe?"

"He makes my flesh crawl, Cap'n, but I s'pose I have to thank 'im for savin' my neck."

"Mm, well, there is that I suppose." Knox resumed the seat he had leapt out of. "Crabbe, sit down." He gestured to a chair by the window.

Crabbe lowered himself into it gingerly, mindful of his swimming head.

Knox rubbed a hand roughly over his face, trying to assemble the thoughts flapping around in his head like a panicked bird. "Harriet. You say she is a double agent?"

"Aye, sir, she seemed so smooth an' polished. Too smooth an' polished. Somethin' jest didn't sit right. I had m'suspicions, an' one of Neale's contacts alerted me to the comings an' goings at your house."

Knox jerked his head up at that statement.

"I darn't trust anyone, sir, not even you." Crabbe chewed his lip. "But from how you reacted when I told you she were bad, I reckon you didn't know about 'er."

"No, I did *not*." snapped Knox, looking even more annoyed than before.

"Aye, well, Cap'n, you aren't the first culley to be led by the cock, nor the last, I reckon."

Knox reared up, blood in his eye, but Crabbe made quelling motions with his hand. Suddenly he felt tired, so very tired. "Neale told me afore we left England tha' Audley was of

French stock on 'is ma's side. I met wi' Audley jest the once, but when I met wi' Harriet, I saw a resemblance."

Knox's mouth dropped open. "Related?"

"Aye, sir, if not brother an' sister, mebbe first cousins. An' it was then that I realised she were Shegoe. She told me tha' she's French on her ma's side an' all." He recalled Harriet telling him about the long line of perfumiers.

It was a hunch, but Crabbe had learned to trust his gut, and his gut flipped over every time he thought of Harriet Deschanel. She lived for intrigue and deception. On the surface, she was an agent acting for the English crown, but in fact, she was a double agent. She had French sympathies on her maternal side, that had become clear. She also had played Knox like a harp, probably giggling to herself the entire time. Once Crabbe had insinuated that Knox was a French informant spearheading a plan to free Bonaparte, Shegoe's vanity had reared its ugly head. She couldn't have some jumped-up ex captain from the British Navy stealing her thunder. Even if it wasn't true, she had concluded that Knox had served his purpose, and it was time to move on. Neale had been right, her vanity was her weakness. Added to that, the adverse reaction of some of the Parisiens to the news that Napoleon Bonaparte might be returning must have shaken her. She'd done the only thing she could–cut and run.

Knox was now staring at the carpet, a frown between his brows. Crabbe felt for him, he must feel like a fool.

Ah, well, not his problem anymore. He only wanted to collect Daisy and be on the first ship out of Le Havre. He got unsteadily to his feet. "If ye darn't mind, Cap'n, I'd like to avail maself of one o' your beds afore I fall down."

"Of course, Crabbe, of course." Knox got up and pulled the bellrope next to the fireplace. Duval appeared after a few minutes and escorted Thomas up the stairs to one of the guest rooms. He didn't bother undressing; he kicked off his shoes and reeled to bed.

Chapter 28

Daisy packed the last of her dresses into the worn portmanteau. She straightened, easing her aching back. A knock sounded at the front door. She smiled, glancing at the clock on the mantelpiece, glad Thomas had returned from his meeting. Shaking out her skirts, she left their bedroom and descended the stairs.

Just as she reached the bottom stairs, she almost collided with a man taking the stairs two at a time from the landing below. His bald head shone in the light thrown from the overhead candelabra, casting the stubble on his face into shadow. Daisy started, her hand flying to her chest. Something about the expression on this man's face did not seem wholesome. He gave her a grotesque smile, revealing a snaggle tooth in his upper jaw and bowed obsequiously, palms spread upwards.

"Mrs Crabbe, m'dear lady," he murmured. "I am right glad to see you. Your dear husband is the one wha' sent me to see to your welfare." He smiled again, although the action contained no mirth and little warmth.

Daisy felt the hairs on her forearms ripple under the sleeves of her gown. She kept a calm countenance, not wanting to let this stranger see he discomforted her. "An' yew are?" she demanded.

"Oh, m'dear lady, forgive me." He placed a long-fingered hand upon his chest. "M'name is Obidiah Slope an' I have been sent by your dear husband an' Captain Knox to make sure all is well with you."

"Where is my husband?" Daisy asked with asperity.

"At the 'ome of the good cap'n, dear lady. Regretfully, your husband met with a little…accident. He is alright!" Slope held up a hand, forestalling Daisy's protest. "I myself 'elped to extricate him from said incident. As we speak, he is now restin' at Cap'n Knox's residence. Do not fret, dear lady, 'e is safe an' well." Slope's black eyes glinted with a sly light.

Rather than being reassured, Daisy felt fear shoot down her spine, weakening her legs. She grabbed the bannister for support. The gesture was not lost on Slope, who stepped forward and cupped her left elbow in his right hand. The movement brought him closer to her; she smelt tobacco on his breath and noticed a single dark hair protruding from the end of his putty-like nose. It took every ounce of willpower not to step back, snatching her elbow out of his moist, warm grasp.

Slope sensed her dislike but ignored it, smiling benignly at her. *Thomas Crabbe hd done well to win a comely lass like this one.* Slope took in the dark hair peeping out from beneath a starched, frilled cap, dark, long-lashed eyes, a dimple winking in the right cheek. A full bosom bubbled over the top of her bodice, which he studiously avoided looking at but was keenly aware of. He felt, rather than saw, the small, slim bones, narrow waist, and generous hips. *Yes, very comely indeed.*

Her female scent caressed his nostrils, the natural fragrance warming him. Her skin was porcelain, unblemished, peaches and cream. Dark eyes looked into his—a deep brown with a ring of green around the irises. A tip-tilted nose above a perfectly shaped mouth just made for kissing.

Daisy watched Slope's pupils dilate, his breath becoming uneven. A pointed tongue peeped out to moisten lips gone dry. She didn't know what to do or say. She was a rabbit staring down a fox—one false move, and she would be dinner. She remained perfectly still, quiet, showing no emotion, waiting for the predator to grow bored and move on. She did not doubt that if she had struggled, cried out, or spurned his touch, he would have torn her to shreds.

Slope became aware of his surroundings, belatedly returning to the room and the present circumstances. He stepped back from the precipice. The yawning chasm closed—he was safe on the opposite bank. He cleared his throat, wiped a finger under his nose and smiled in what he hoped was a reassuring manner at Daisy Crabbe.

"I'll be wishin' you a good night, mistress." He bowed to Daisy, turned on his booted heel and descended the stairs to the scullery, there to collect his hat and silver-topped cane, disappearing into the inky night.

Daisy felt as if a noxious fog had dissipated, leaving fresh, clean air in its wake. She could breathe once more, unimpeded by fear. *Who was that sinister man? Who did he work for?* Anxiety took the place of fear. *Was Thomas genuinely safe? Had Slope been telling the truth?* It gnawed away at her like a rat chewing wood. She paced up and down the hallway, wringing her hands.

After several gyrations, she halted. This would not do. Daisy was a woman of action–she could not, she *would* not sit idle accepting a stranger's word as to the wellbeing of her husband. She hitched up her skirts, ran up the stairs to their bedroom, grabbed her shawl, threw it around her head and shoulders, and thus attired, descended to the hallway. Checking left and right to ensure no servants were about, she went out the front door into the darkness, now tinged with fog.

Daisy had never been to Captain Knox's house, but Thomas had described it often enough for her to find her way. After several wrong turns and shrinking back into the shadows to avoid passers-by, she found herself at the top of the street. The night was darker now, foggy withal, with a cold that nipped her fingertips and the end of her nose. She began berating herself for her foolishness, a lone woman out late at night. She made her way quietly over the cobblestones until she was within a few yards of the front door. The fog was even denser now, great banks of it roiling down the street, completely obscuring lights shining from windows. As one bank cleared slightly, the front windows of the Knox residence came into view. Silhouetted in the light shining between open curtains was a figure. Tall, hooded, gazing intently up at a bedroom window where a solitary candle flickered upon the windowsill. The figure stood immobile.

As Daisy watched, a man came to the window, peered out into the murky night, licked forefinger and thumb, then pinched the flame out. Before the candle was extinguished, Daisy recognised the dear face of Thomas, tired but whole.

Relief flooded her body. She could return home now and sleep well.

She glanced back at the hooded figure on the pavement, but it had gone, snuffed out like the candle flame above.

Daisy felt the chill of the foggy night begin to settle in her bones. Drawing her shawl closer around her head, she turned back the way she had come, carefully retracing her steps to their townhouse, her mind ruminating on the identity of the silent watcher. Friend or foe? She remembered Thomas mentioning an agent named Shegoe–he had met this person on more than one occasion but had not gone into detail. Thomas had told her that the less she knew, the better. She smiled ruefully–what you don't know can't hurt you.

She reached home to find Maame Crecy and the butler in uproar at her absence. She reassured them as in the little French she had gleaned whilst in Paris. Somebody informed Madame de Castro y Sousa of her return, and she sent up a small cup of *chocolat* with a tot of West Indian rum by way of reproach at her late-night meanderings. Daisy sipped this gratefully whilst being undressed by her maid, Celine, who scolded her in the guttural French of her native Languedoc. Daisy smiled at the girl in her looking glass. Rather than being offended by the telling-off, she felt comforted, oddly touched by the concern shown by the household staff. Realising that and knowing that Thomas was indeed safe and tucked up in bed made her feel drowsy. Celine saw her begin to droop and placed the hairbrush on the dressing table. She gently laid her hands on Daisy's shoulders, admonished her again, then implored her to go to bed.

Daisy swung her feet under the cotton sheets, feeling the warm brick that Celine had placed there earlier. Celine padded softly around the room, snuffing the candles out one by one until the room was dark. She left with a gentle *bon nuit*, allowing Daisy to sink into a dreamless sleep.

Chapter 29

As dawn was kissing the rooftops of the houses lining the Rue de Rivoli, Thomas Crabbe turned into the street. He had spent a fretful night tossing and turning. Too much brandy, adrenaline, suspicion, and physical exertion had led to broken sleep. Captain Knox had offered him breakfast–kippers with slices of fresh lemon, accompanied by freshly baked bread–but he had politely declined. The thought of food made him feel queasy.

The captain offered to escort him to his house, but Thomas said he wished to alone. Now, having spent the last half an hour stumping along cobbled streets, his leg reminded him of his desperate dash the previous evening. He cursed himself for his stubbornness. *Wasn't that always his downfall?* Stubbornness–along with an inability to rely on anyone else except himself. He hadn't wanted to accept the King's protection initially. He hadn't accepted Neale's loyalties, suspecting him to begin with. He hadn't believed that Shegoe could be a double agent. He hadn't wanted to think that Captain Knox had been played for a fool. Most of all, he had brought Daisy with him, believing he could protect her–he had also failed there.

What was left? His marriage, but it might prove a barren one. His position with Lord Palmer? He may not want him back in his employ after this. Money? He had some put by, but not enough to build the life he wanted. Reputation? That was tarnished by Shegoe's escaping. He would return to England with his tail between his legs, hoping that Palmer would give him his place back.

So busy was he in his ruminations, he missed the runaway horses and carriage that rounded the corner at the bottom of the street, hurtling towards him at a rate of knots. Not until the horses mounted the pavement and were almost upon him did he look up, twisting to one side and throwing himself out of their path. His head hit wrought-iron railings, and he blacked out.

Light flickered in and out around the periphery of his vision. God, but his head hurt. Thomas felt as if a knitting needle had been inserted into the back of his skull, exiting just above his left eyebrow. A face floated into view, a concerned frown upon its broad, smooth brow. He groped for a name–a flower, something small and delicate but also hardy. What was it? He could see it in his mind's eye, covering a green lawn like a carpet. Ah, yes, a daisy.

"Thomas? I'm here, m'love."

He felt a small, warm hand grasp his in a firm grip. He tried to reciprocate, but his fingers stubbornly refused to move.

Where on *earth* were his hands? He couldn't locate them—were they even there? Had they floated off altogether?

The pain in the back of his skull intensified, and lights began blinking behind his eyes. Was he dying? He sincerely hoped not; there was so much more to do—he needed to talk to Neale and explain how it had been with Shegoe.

Shegoe, she was a puzzle. A blend of masculine and feminine appealing to both genders, an enigma, disappearing into the ether like a will o' the wisp. She was gone. For now.

Finally, he became aware of his hands. They were holding something—no, someone. He looked down and saw a baby girl, beautiful, soft, smelling of fresh flowers. Her eyes were closed, long dark lashes sweeping the tops of her round cheeks. A little rosebud mouth sat underneath a button nose. The lips parted slightly, emitting a tiny snore. Hands like shells curled on her chest, which moved rhythmically up and down.

She was perfect—a little angel. Thomas became aware of another presence. Lifting his gaze from his daughter, he looked into his mother's face.

"Yew need to give 'er to me now, Thomas."

But he didn't want to relinquish the sleeping infant. He hugged her to his chest, making her squirm slightly. "Now, Thomas, yew give er to me. I'll look arter 'er like I did yew, m'boy."

Still, he held the baby close. His ma reached out and gently prised the little girl away from him. He felt a sudden coolness on his chest where she had lain.

"Ma!"

"Yes, Thomas?"

"She'll be safe?"

"O'course she will. Ye know that, foolish lad." His ma smiled gently at him, boosting the baby onto her shoulder. She touched his cheek in farewell, then turned and walked away.

Thomas felt bereft. He was alone; no mother, no daughter, no friends.

Something nudged against his leg. Looking down, he saw a black-and-white shape leaning against his left calf.

"Trim! Where'd yew come from, lad?"

Bending down, he scooped Trim up, laying him on the spot vacated by his daughter.

A rumbling purr began just beneath his chin. He could feel the pinpricks through his shirt as Trim commenced kneading biscuit dough. Although somewhat painful, he found the sensation comforting. He needed a small, warm weight over his heart. If he didn't have one, his heart might fail altogether.

His heart. He imagined it as a set of bellows, a series of meaty clicks and whooshes, the blood rushing in and out of the chambers. The blood would be rich and red, coursing through his veins, giving life and strength.

Trim's purring began to fade, overtaken by the pulsing of his heart. Where was his furry friend? He needed a friend now more than ever now.

Richard Neale. His friend, benefactor, erstwhile protector. Thomas knew how Richard felt about him—it was acknowledged but ignored. Yet the friendship and warmth of the man remained. Crabbe wished sincerely that he could voice these sentiments to Richard, if only for an instant. He drifted into darkness…

But there he was! Before him, real and solid. Thomas felt Neale's grasp on his, palm to palm. Thomas smelt the scent of pomade from Richard's hair and knew it was him.

"Crabbe? Crabbe? Can you hear me, man?" The pressure on his hand increased. He squeezed in reply.

"He pressed my hand!" he heard Neale exclaim. "He is with us still!"

One smaller and slighter claimed his other hand. Daisy. Her name came quickly to him this time. Two people who meant so much to him, connected by touch. He imagined rather than saw a current pass between them, linking them all.

Another cool, large hand landed on his forehead. An unfamiliar voice stated, "The fever is abating, and I believe the pressure on his brain is lessening." Exclamations of relief and joy filled his ears. He felt a kiss upon his left cheek, light as a butterfly's wing, and a bubble of happiness filled his heart. He was whole, he was well, he would live.

"Thomas, let me 'elp you, love."

"I'm fine," he snapped, although his fingers felt like pork sausages, and he was all thumbs trying to tie the stock around his neck.

Daisy half rose from her seat, then subsided as she realised she must let her husband shift for himself.

In truth, Thomas felt dizzy and nauseous. Sounds were distorted, now seeming close, now at a distance, and it felt like he was on shifting sands when he walked. 'La bon docteur' said he had suffered a severe concussion which had led to a fever. In total he had lain ill for nearly two weeks. How long the residual symptoms would last, no one knew. It could be weeks, months, or even longer.

Daisy couldn't stand it any longer. She got out of her chair and crossed the room to straighten her husband's stock, brushing his hair as she did so.

"There, tha's better."

Thomas smiled thinly. He knew she meant well, but he wanted to shout with frustration.

He felt removed from reality. He was not in control at all, it was driving him mad. He was used to working, cooking, cleaning, organising, and caring for others. The roles were now reversed–he was passive, letting others care for him, unable to do anything for himself. He was redundant, useless, fit for nothing.

"Thomas," Daisy broke into his musings. "Darn't you be feelin' sorry for yourself now." She frowned at him, admonishment written upon her face. "Yew need to think about the future."

"Do I now?"

"Yes, yew do."

"Then?"

"Then we go back to England, to Lord Palmer's estate, an' we begin again."

"An' how do you suppose we do that?"

"Yew best go an' talk to Richard. He's just outside."

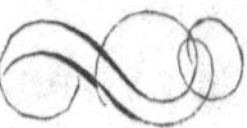

Richard Neale was sitting on a wooden bench, legs stretched out, sunning himself. He could get used to France. The climate was far superior to England, the food was delicious, the wine superb. Perhaps he could persuade the King to allow him to stay.

He was interrupted in his musings by the slow, heavy tread of Crabbe. Opening his eyes, he squinted at Thomas, walking gingerly towards him with the aid of a walking stick. Rather than jumping up to assist his friend, he allowed him the dignity of making his way towards the bench, which after some minutes he did, plopping himself down with an audible grunt.

"Any better?" Neale asked quietly.

"Gettin' there–slowly."

"Mm, hm. Slow and sure wins the race."

Thomas looked wryly at him. "Oh ah? An' which race am I supposed to be runnin'?"

"The one back to good health, Thomas." Richard gave him a wry look of his own.

Thomas snorted in reply.

Richard wanted to broach the subject of the Crabbes returning to England, but it was a delicate matter. Thomas had nearly died twice now–Richard wasn't prepared to risk a third time.

"Lord Palmer," Richard began. "Aye?"

"He feels that you went above and beyond."

"Oh, aye?"

Richard fixed Thomas with a hard stare. "Stop saying 'aye' in that bloody cynical tone! He acknowledges your efforts, for which you nearly paid with your life, and wishes to assure you that you have a place in his household whether you want it or not."

Thomas had the grace to look sheepish.

Richard snorted at his expression. "Just stop being so bloody stubborn and accept what is offered."

Thomas's expression softened. "Aye, then."

Richard rolled his eyes. God, Thomas was frustrating but endearing at the same time. Simultaneously, he wanted to throttle him or embrace him. He sighed deeply. Thomas would consistently engender warring emotions.

Thomas caught the exasperated sigh and smiled ruefully. Well, perhaps he was a thick-headed numpty at that. Well, not quite as thick-headed as he thought, considering the recent concussion and fever. "So, ye say Lord Palmer will 'ave us back?"

"As you would say, aye."

Thomas grinned. "An' what o' the King?"

Richard paused before answering. "The King has been fully appraised of the situation. However, he is not altogether happy with the disappearance of Shegoe."

"I'll bet he isn't."

"His Majesty would like certain…enquiries to take place." Richard glanced at Thomas. "As you were the last person to clap eyes on her, well…" His voice drifted off.

"His Majesty wants me to try an' find her." Thomas finished for him. He remembered Harriet's parting words, "I will find *you*." She would prove very elusive.

"So," Richard interrupted his thoughts, "will you return to England to continue serving your King?"

Thomas considered the question for a moment. "No."

Richard opened his mouth, ready to remonstrate, but Thomas forestalled him with a hand on his sleeve.

"I won't serve the King, but I will help *you*, my friend."

Chapter 30

Yacoumbe sniffed the air, his straight nose twitching like a truffle pig. The smell was the same–stale, fetid with the tang of human misery. He mentally shrugged his shoulders. Every slave ship smelled the same. He felt a sense of déja vu. He was transported back in time. A young boy led in chains down into the dank, dark hold.

The sailor pushed him in the back. "Move."

Yacoumbe's mouth filled with bile. For a split second, he imagined spinning on his heel, wrapping his fetters around the man's fat, sweaty neck, and pulling with all his strength. Common sense prevailed; the moment passed, and he took his place on the wooden boards.

The next man came in, sat down, then another, until Yacoumbe lost count at fifty.

The ship was leaving Boston, bound for France; he'd overheard one of the crew predicting a rough passage. Well, he was used to choppy seas. A memory came to him then.

Thomas Crabbe, Trim and himself on the *Renown* being tossed about like corks. He smiled at the thought of the three of them clutching each other–he muttering supplications,

Thomas saying the Lord's prayer over and over until Yacoumbe knew it by heart.

Where was Thomas now? The last time he'd seen his friend, he'd been gently boosting the sack containing Trim onto his narrow shoulder–disembarking the ship to join the *Alexander*, headed for England. Yacoumbe sincerely wished that Thomas had returned home, found his mother, and settled into a quiet life. Yacoumbe, as he often did, sent up a prayer for his friend's health and wellbeing.

His thoughts went to their destination, his first experience of France. Over the years he seemed to be travelling further west, away from his beloved Africa. He knew he'd never see his homeland again–he was resigned to that fact. What he was *not* resigned to was his indentured state. He longed for freedom, a chance to live his life–maybe a wife and children. He longed to hold a woman in his arms, feel the warm funkiness of her after love-making, the scent of her hair, the moistness of her quim like a split peach in the palm of his hand.

Being close to other men, you became aware of their physical needs, as well as your own. Several times, a sheer brutal need had led him to deal with the urges of the flesh. He had learned how to silence his manacles until he climaxed, hoping that no one heard him. It was no substitute for the real thing, but it would have to suffice for now.

A phlegmy cough jerked him out of his reverie. An older man with grizzled hair and tribal tattoos across both cheeks was coughing spasmodically, his shoulders hunched in pain. Yacoumbe didn't like the sound of the cough–he could hear the congestion from where he sat. His fingers itched for some willow bark. His Pa had taught him how to steep it in hot water, let it cool, drain it, and give it to the afflicted to drink as a tea.

The man coughed again, more painfully this time. Honey, with a squeeze of lemon, would ease his throat–a raw onion, diced finely, sprinkled with some palm sugar. Left overnight, the juice would leech out of the onion to melt the sugar. The resulting liquor could then be given a teaspoon at a time for the cough.

The man coughed, hacked, spat.

"Hey, mun," Yacoumbe called softly.

The older man's head came up. Bloodshot eyes met his. Yacoumbe could see the milky ring of developing cataracts even in this dim light.

"Yeah?"

"How long you had dat cough?"

"Long enough, boy."

"Yeah, tha's what worries me."

"Don't you worry, boy, I's tough."

He'll be lucky if he makes it to France. Yacoumbe kept quiet–no point in making the man feel worse than he already did. They slipped the mooring lines at midday. The captain was sailing with the tide and wind, so they left the harbour quickly. The swell began immediately. Yacoumbe could hear the bleating of the goats and sheep in the adjoining hold.

Apart from the indentured men, the ship was carrying a consignment of seabird guano. The letters S.H.I.T. were painted on a sign hanging from the forward bulkhead. *Stow*

High in Transit. That was in case any water came into the hold. If it mixed with the volatile cargo, methane began to form–not desirable on a wooden ship. Or any ship, for that matter.

The pungent aroma of manure wafted through below decks, adding to the general nausea of the incarcerated men. If they didn't feel sick to begin with, they certainly would by the time they got into the Atlantic. Yacoumbe snorted. The floor would undoubtedly be covered in vomit by the day's end. The sawdust sprinkled on the wooden boards would soak up the worst of it. Then the crew would sluice buckets of seawater over them come morning, the dirty fluid running out of holes made for the purpose into the bilges.

He could feel the ocean waves beneath the ship. The swell built, peaked under the stern, then the vessel rode the wave, shuddering as it exited under the bows. Yacoumbe deduced they were on a stern reach, running before the wind. All the canvas would be out to maximise the prevailing wind.

"You been a sailor, boy?" The rasping voice brought him abruptly to the present. The man with the cough was watching him.

"Yeah, mun–a while ago, but I know my way 'round a ship."

The other man nodded, his eyes never leaving Yacoumbe's face. "Tell us 'bout it."

Yacoumbe became aware of the silence in the hold. Suddenly he felt self-conscious. Various men's eyes were on him now, waiting. As the silence stretched, he realised they were anticipating his story. An escape from their present situation, a welcome distraction from their misery. He took a deep breath. At first, he was nervous, then after a few minutes he got into the stride of storytelling.

"I were on a ship, bigger dan dis one. T'was a warship. One day, young man come, he came to da hold lookin' for someone to help 'im cook for da officers. He picked me. Da man was called Thomas Crabbe. Tom."

As the ship got deeper into the Atlantic, he recounted his history. How he was chosen by Thomas, their time cooking together for the officers, the capture of the *Donegal*, their transfer to the American warship, a further transfer, the capture of the *Renown* by the marrons, and so on. Yacoumbe fleshed out the details of his friendship with Thomas and his trusty cat Trim, eliciting cautious smiles from some men. His memories loomed large through the telling, bringing Thomas and Trim back to life. His heart swelled with affection for them both–he felt warmed by the touch of memory.

He reached the end of his story. A few sighs greeted the end of the tale. He exchanged smiles with members of the company as they shuffled into different positions, anticipating a rough night. Thomas lived on. If not in reality, he continued to walk down the corridors of his mind.

The night passed uncomfortably. As expected, two-thirds of the men had been unwell. Seasickness was one thing. Bronchitis was another.

Yacoumbe crawled over to the older man with the cough. Now, he could hear severe congestion in his chest, which was worrying.

"How you doin', mun?"

"Not so good, boy."

"Yeah, I figured. You wanna blanket?" A blanket was stretching it somewhat. A burlap sack, ragged at the edges, was as good as it got, but he would sacrifice his own for the older man.

"On'y if you don't want it."

Yacoumbe would be cold, but his clear conscience would keep him warm. He wrapped the tatty sack around his companion's shoulders.

A gnarled hand came up and grasped his. "Thank you, boy."

"Yacoumbe–my name is Yacoumbe."

"I be Seka." They pressed hands.

Saying his name aloud sounded strange. He was so used to 'boy', 'hey you', and other choice monikers. It gave him a surge of pleasure to formally introduce himself. "Where you from, Seka?"

Seka pulled the sack closer around his bony arms. "Ivory Coast. Those white fellas grabbed me when I were out fishin'. Didn't even see dey bumboat until it were too late. Arsewipes'd anchored round in da next bay, so I had no warnin'."

They'd tossed the fish back into the ocean, bound Seka hand and foot, and rowed back to the mother ship, where Seka joined the other captives. They sailed to America to the newly founded state of Louisiana, where Seka was put to work cutting cane sugar.

"I know damn squat 'bout sugar. All's I know is fish. But this ol' negro was put to work an' if I didn't want da feel o' the lash on m'back, then I was yessir, no sir, three bags full sir."

Seka nodded, looking at the floorboards, but Yacoumbe

could tell he was seeing another scene altogether. "One day, da overseer he got da shits an' had me dragged out in da noonday sun. Not sure what I'd done but he were mad as a cut snake. Dey tied me to a tree an' whipped me until my bones showed, I reckon. I could feel blood runnin' down ma legs, spots 'fore ma eyes. Den I got water thrown o'er me. I just wanted to die, mun, you know?"

Ycoumbe nodded but remained silent.

"Dey cut me down an' some lady she pour raw spirit on me and bound m'back. I's still feel da pain o' that spirit on me– you coulda heard da screams for miles."

Half out of his mind with pain, the other workers carried Seka to the slave quarters. The woman who had treated him tended his wounds until they healed–at least good enough for him to return to the cane fields.

Unbeknownst to him, the overseer had met an unpleasant end, hanging from the same tree where Seka had been whipped. Those responsible were never caught.

"Tings were better after dat. We got us a new overseer, he not so wicked as the first white fella."

Seka worked in the cane fields for a total of twelve years. The owner eventually retired, so the house and plantation were sold. The buyer decided that sugar was not the crop for him, so instead, they turned the land into arable. The existing workforce were reduced in numbers. Thus, over sixty percent of the indentured people had to be moved. The new owner sold them to a French slave trader. So here they were, bobbing around in the Atlantic Ocean, bound for a market and who knew what.

"You is strong, mun. I's old and weak."

Yacoumbe started to protest, but Seka held up a weathered hand. "I know I's not long for dis world. Yo'll go on. Know dis, you do it for both of us, yeah?"

Yacoumbe couldn't speak–his throat closed with emotion. "I know you will go far, mun. Further'n me, anyhow." Seka stopped talking. Yacoumbe could hear a faint rattle in Seka's breathing. They called it the death rattle. It would seem that Yacoumbe's earlier conclusion was correct. Seka would not see the coast of France. He probably wouldn't last another twenty-four hours, let alone several weeks at sea. Seka's chest was filling with fluid, he was drowning in his lungs. Yacoumbe could think of worse ways to die, to quietly drift off.

Each breath became more laboured, the space between that and the next one further apart. All that second night, Yacoumbe stayed awake, sitting with Seka. Sometimes, Seka's hand would rise slowly, and Yacoumbe would take it in his.

The hours ticked by like years. Yacoumbe's world had shrunk to the spaces in between Seka's breaths. He subconsciously was matching his breathing to the dying man's. The nearest men moved closer, realising that one of them was about to pass. A few asked if they could do anything, but Yacoumbe answered negatively. All there was to do now was offer comfort and wait for the inevitable.

Despite everything, Seka clung to life for two more days. In a rare moment of lucidity, he roused and whispered, "Da mun is dead, on'y the spirit remains."

Seka descended into a twilight world–half-alive, half-dead. Yacoumbe could feel Death's wings beating just out of sight, ready to claim him.

On the morning of the third day, Seka's life left him in a long, deep exhalation. The crew members dragged him out, feet first, simply tossing his body overboard. After he heard the splash, Yacoumbe caught a fleeting glimpse of a shadow out of the corner of his eye. Turning his head to the small porthole that afforded him a narrow view of the world, he fancied that Seka's spirit was returning to his beloved Africa.

Chapter 31

"Does 'e *have* to come with us?"

Thomas glanced over his shoulder at Obidiah Slope, who was following them at a discreet distance. Thomas had managed to dispense with his walking stick, leaning on Daisy's arm. He still suffered from severe headaches accompanied by dizziness, but they were both lessening. Neale had already departed for England, leaving the Crabbes and Slope to follow once Thomas felt fit enough to embark on a sea voyage.

"Slope is 'ere to look arter us, like 'e looked arter me afore. Without 'im I would be dead, m'love."

Daisy's mouth turned down. She couldn't argue with Thomas, but as far as she was concerned that was Slope's only redeeming feature. She hadn't told Thomas about the uncomfortable scene with Slope–they'd all been so preoccupied with getting Thomas well.

They strolled along the quayside at Le Havre, dodging barrels of fish, stray dogs, and lines being thrown to waiting stevedores where women were chattering in rapid French, waiting to greet their men about to disembark a ship. It was hot, the sun beating down upon their shoulders, and Thomas looked into the distance, noticing a gathering. Daisy saw his look, and they began to walk slowly towards what appeared to be an auction.

As they approached, Thomas felt Daisy's hand tighten on his arm. He glanced down at her in concern.

"Thomas, it be a slave market."

"What?"

"Look, it be a slave market." Daisy pointed to a crowd gathered around a wooden platform bordered by a link chain. Inside the chain was a fat, ugly white man holding a coiled whip and a tall, handsome black man. The white man was fully clothed, sporting a tricorn hat, the man of colour wore only a ragged pair of breeches, his only other adornment a metal ring around his neck, a chain from which joined manacles at his wrists and feet.

The fat auctioneer yelled out the bids, which were going up in increments of guineas from what Thomas could make out. Poor sod; the slave was probably off one of the ships moored at the end of the quay. The smell of human misery had reached his nostrils as he and Daisy walked along the harbourside.

Thomas looked over at the indentured man, then he froze.

"Mother of God," he breathed, looking more closely at him.

"What is it?" demanded Daisy, following his squint.

"Sam."

"Who?"

"Sam, I told you about 'im, we were together on the

Donegal. He were the one who 'elped me in the galley, then escaped with a bunch of marrons."

At the exact moment he informed Daisy who he was, Sam looked up straight at Thomas. Even at a considerable distance, Thomas saw his friend's expression change from dull resignation to recognition.

Daisy saw the look the men exchanged. "What yew goin' to do?" she asked *sotto voce* of Thomas, although there was no need due to the yells of the auctioneer, the shouts of the crowd and the general mêlée of the harbour.

Thomas chewed his lip for a moment. There was only one thing in all conscience he could do. He fumbled for his coin wallet and checked the contents.

"I never tort I'd be seein' you again, mun."

Sam and Thomas were sat under the shade of an awning at the back of one of the quieter ale houses dotting the quayside. Daisy had gone off to look for some suitable clothing for Sam, shadowed by Slope.

After making his distasteful purchase and demanding that Sam's irons be struck off, Thomas had removed his coat, draped it around Sam's shoulders (although it barely covered his broad back), and leaning on his arm, walked him away from the jeering crowd. For a few coins, the alehouse landlord let them drink at his establishment, but only if the 'homme noir' sat outside; he wouldn't countenance having a Negro inside, it was bad for business.

"What happened to ya ship, mate? Yew looked all set, yew an' the rest of the maroons."

"Dem men know nuffin' about ships, mun. Dey ran da ship aground an' we were picked up by slave ship jest like that." Sam snapped his fingers. "I back to square one."

He'd spent several months in Halifax, before being shipped to Boston, where he'd served in the household of a tea merchant for several years. Said merchant was declared bankrupt due to questionable business practices and a gambling habit, so he had all his assets sold, including his indentured staff. Sam then found himself crammed into a dirty, dark hold and shipped to France by the creditors to be sold to the highest bidder.

"So, I be here now wid my friend Tom." Sam leant forward and slapped Thomas on the forearm. "So, now yew own a slave, mun. What yew gonna do wid me, heh?"

Thomas hadn't even thought about *that*. All he'd wanted to do was to get Sam away from the auction and to a safe place. Now, to his horror, he realised he owned a six-foot-three West African, called Yacoumbe.

"Ye'll be a free man, Yacoumbe, I promise ye. I'll get the papers drawn up as soon as I can, my friend." He cleared his throat, took a sip of ale, then cleared his throat again. He felt the weight of Yacoumbe's regard like brands on his skin. Then a thought occurred to him. Putting his tankard down, he slowly smiled, a gleam showing in his grey eyes.

Yacoumbe smiled in response to his friend's expression and arched a dark eyebrow as Thomas looked up into his face.

"Yacoumbe, how would you like to work for the King of England?"

THE END

References

Joseph Arnold Journal, 8 march-17 December 1815 C 720/4. Available at: https://acms.sl.nsw.gov.

au/_transcript/2012/D15299/a4146.pdf (Accessed: 15 September 2021).

Sherburne, A., Zeinert, K. and Fleishman, S. (1993) *The memoirs of Andrew Sherburne, Patriot and privateer of the American Revolution*. Hamden, CT: Linnet Books.

Rated Navy ships in the 17th to 19th centuries, Royal Museums Greenwich. Available at: https://www. rmg.co.uk/stories/topics/rated-navy-ships-17th-19th-centuries (Accessed: 15 September 2021).

Dalton, K. (no date) *Hammocks, bedding, and where they slept, British Tars, 1740-1790*. Available at: https://www.britishtars.com/2018/01/hammocks- bedding-and-where-they-slept.html (Accessed: 16 September 2021).

Roosevelt, T. (2001) *The Naval War of 1812*. New York: Modern Library.

Macdonald, J.W. (2014) *Feeding Nelson's Navy the true story of food at sea in the Georgian era*. London: Frontline Books.

Greville, C. and Reeve, H. (no date) *The greville memoirs: A journal of the reigns of king George IV and king William IV* (3 vols).

George IV (2023) *Wikipedia*. Available at: https:// en.wikipedia.org/wiki/George_IV (Accessed: 13 October 2022).

Wikipedia Contributors 2018a, Charlotte of Mecklenburg-Strelitz, Wikipedia, Wikimedia Foundation. Accessed 11 November 2022.

The Stagecoach (2019) *Historic UK*. Available at: https://www.historic-uk.com/CultureUK/The- Stagecoach/ (Accessed: 23 December 2022).

Creevey, T. and Gore, J. (1948) *Creevey: From the Creevey Papers (1903) ed.* London: J. Murray. Public interview with the Duke of Wellington where he was quoted as having said about the Battle of Waterloo, "It has been a damned nice thing–the nearest run thing you ever saw in your life. … By God! I don't think it would have been done if I had not been there."

 Carr, J. (1807) *The stranger in France or a Tour from Devonshire to Paris ... by Sir John Carr. 2nd Edition.* London: J. Johnson.

Chew III, W.L. (2015) 'John Quincy Adams: American eyewitness of the Hundred Days', *Napoleonica La Revue*, 24(3), p. 61. doi:10.3917/ napo.024.0061.

Acknowledgements

My thanks go to the late Ned Kelly, notorious Australian bush ranger who was hanged in Melbourne Gaol. I used his last words for Joseph, Daisy's brother.

A special mention goes to Brian Tyler and his soundtrack to Assassin's Creed IV which gave me inspiration as I was tapping away on my laptop–great music, thanks.

Thanks to my friend Kym, who educated me on the origins of S.H.I.T.

Thanks to my friend Guy, for beta reading the original manuscript.

Another special mention goes to the character of Shegoe. (Not to be confused with the cartoon!). Allegedly there was a master spy around the time of the Napoleonic wars named Shegoe, but no one saw them, or knew what they looked like, so of *course* I had to make the double-agent a woman. And she was just such a fun character to write, I couldn't resist. I indulged in a little joke giving her the first name of Harriet (anyone familiar with the children's book by Louise Fitzhugh, *Harriet the Spy*?)–and also a reference to Wellington's longterm mistress, Harriette Wilson.

About the Author

E Atkinson is the author of the Grace Beale Trilogy, published by Free Spirit Publishers. Short stories have appeared in Grande Dame Literary Journal, Clayjar Review, Idle Ink, Poets Choice, Heart of Flesh and Black Ink Fiction.

Crabbe and the King's Gambit is the prequel to the Grace Beale novels as we follow the young Thomas Crabbe on the high seas in His Majesty's Navy.

 She lives on her farm in rural Australia with her husband, cat, two alpacas and various chickens (not necessarily in that order).

You can find her on Instagram @crabbeshome, Facebook, LinkedIn and her website at www.eatkinson1.com.

Other titles by E Atkinson